Trouble
in a
Small Town

by

M. J. Wilson

Trouble in a Small Town

Cover Art by *Kristian Norris*

The Wild Rose Press, Inc.
PO Box 708
Adams Basin, NY 14410-0708
Visit us at www.thewildrosepress.com

Publishing History
First Crimson Rose Edition, 2016
Print ISBN 978-1-5092-0888-3
Digital ISBN 978-1-5092-0889-0

Published in the United States of America

She squinted into the darkness and took a step forward. Are those Louboutin shoes? Surely, someone didn't throw them out. Maybe things are looking up. She walked toward the dumpster, the rats forgotten. Her laser focus didn't budge from the black toeless pumps with the red soles. *Wonder what size those are?* She strode around the front of the dumpster and halted. A scream wanted to burst from her throat, but couldn't. Her stomach plunged into her feet.

The shoes were next to the feet of a female who lay unmoving on the ground. *Are you okay?* No words materialized from Mallory's mouth. Her tongue was dry like cotton. She closed her mouth, tried to swallow, and work up some spit. "Are you okay?" Mallory asked in a quiet and raspy voice. She looked back and forth, hoping to see someone to help in the alley. Logically, she understood this person definitely wasn't okay, but her brain was having trouble processing.

"Hey." She stepped forward and tapped the arm with her shoe. It shifted with the pressure, but the person gave no other response. "Oh God…oh God. Someone help me." Her voice remained a whisper. "Please don't be dead. Please be okay." She stretched out her arm, staying as far away as possible, to remove the large piece of cardboard covering the upper half of the body. The trembling of her hand kept her from gripping the edge. She took a shaky breath and slid off the cardboard. A shrill scream tore from her body but melted into the thumping bass from the band inside.

Mallory peered down into empty blue eyes staring at nothingness in the sky. The lifeless body's mouth was slightly open with dried saliva crusted in the corner.

Praise For M.J. Wilson

"I look forward to reading more from this author."

~Margaret

~*~

"I could easily relate to the characters."

~Heidi

~*~

"This is a great story! I couldn't believe how much I laughed."

~Dianne

Chapter One

Mallory Larsen plopped on her queen-size bed. She scanned her gaze around the room her parents enshrined after she left for college. Guess they thought she would move back in after graduation, instead of taking on the big bad world. Little did she dream a few years later that would be exactly what happened. How do parents always know? She blew out her breath. Posters of Sugar Ray and Five For Fighting stared back. She traveled a mental time warp back to her high school years and growing up in a town with a population of around six hundred fifty. Years she didn't need to relive at twenty-six.

With its nineteenth-century flavor, Elsah was like stepping back in time. A quiet village located on the Illinois side of the Mississippi River between Alton and Grafton. Concealed by a thick, wooded ravine and nestled amongst the magnificent bluffs. A safe place to grow up, but she'd wanted city life.

"How did I get back here?" Mallory fell back onto her bed, draping an arm across her eyes. "I walked in on my fiancé banging another woman in our bed two weeks before we were supposed to get married—that's how."

"Did you say something?" Charlotte Larsen opened the bedroom door.

"No, Mom. I was just reflecting out loud." She sat

up and brushed back her long blonde hair currently making her look like Cousin Itt. Charlotte defined the quintessential American mother. Her dishwater blonde, shoulder-length hair was cut in the same vintage pageboy hairstyle since Mallory's childhood. She dressed in a feminine fashion with a paper-cut-sharp front crease pressed into all her slacks, and heaven forbid, she be caught without her pearl earrings. Not a style Mallory would use as inspiration in her occupation as a fashion merchandiser, but Charlotte embodied the classic mom.

"Oh, okay then. We are having fried chicken livers and onions for dinner, if you'd like to come down."

Mallory rolled her eyes so far back she could have earned a role in *The Exorcist*. "You know I'm a vegetarian, Mom."

"I just don't understand why. You need your protein."

"I get my protein."

She drummed her fingers on the door. "I don't know how you can without meat."

"Peanuts, yogurt, beans, spinach, soy, eggs…do you want me to continue?" Mallory sighed, falling back onto her bed.

"Well, you don't have to be snippy."

Regurgitating the same conversation innumerous times brought out her testy side. "Mom, I'm not trying to be snippy. I just don't eat meat."

"Chicken livers really aren't meat, so those should be okay."

She sat up and spread her arms wide and high. "I won't eat the meat of the chicken, what makes you think I'd eat its internal organs?"

Charlotte scrunched her eyes and nose. "Don't say it like that—that makes it sound gross."

"Exactly!"

"Fine. Don't eat it then…you're on your own for dinner." Charlotte crossed her arms in front of her chest.

"That's fine, Mom." She took a cleansing breath. "I'm going out with some of the girls tonight," she said, redirecting the conversation away from food.

"Who are you going with?" Charlotte raised her eyebrows.

"Ella, Hazel, and Poppy," she said.

"They're kind of rowdy. Are you sure it's safe for you girls to be going out?"

"We're adults. I think we'll be okay," Mallory said, feeling twelve years old, and being in her childhood bedroom didn't help. The only thing missing was the confirmation teddy bear she used to sleep with. She glanced over her should at the kid-sized rocking chair in the corner. She sighed. *Nope, there it is.*

"Well, be careful not to get one of those S-A-Ds."

Mallory frowned at her mom. "S-A-D? You don't want me to get sad?"

"No, silly." Charlotte's speech faded into a closed mouth chuckle. She waved a hand in front of her face. "Not sad. S-A-D…you know, sexually acquired diseases. I watched a program on cable about them…and trust me, you don't want one of those."

Her tone dripped sincerity. Mallory couldn't help but laugh, and it felt good. "You mean S-T-D. Sexually Transmitted Disease," she said, still chuckling.

"Yes, that's what I said. Don't bring one of those home."

Mallory struggled not to laugh at her mom, but as soon as the door closed she laughed until she cried. Her mom's naïveté about certain things shocked her. How her mother maintained such innocence in this day and age of information technology boggled her mind. But, she loved her mom's earnestness. She drove her crazy, but her heart was in the right place. Not to mention, her arms were open wide when Mallory ran home after her fiancé cheated.

****

Mallory stepped into the den to pick up her purse.

"Where are you going?" Jim Larsen asked.

"Shanghai Gardens—grabbing some vegetable *lo mein*."

"Hey, get me some pork fried rice." He placed the side of his hand to his mouth and whispered.

"Aren't you having chicken livers?" His skewed-up mouth said everything. "I thought you liked them. You ate them when I was a kid."

"Or so it appeared," he said, grinning.

"What will you do with them?"

Jim smirked at Zehn stretched out on the couch.

Zehn's a German Shepherd Mallory rescued when he was about one, and at three apparently had no recollection of being half starved when she took him in. She looked at Zehn who groaned, rolled onto his back with all fours sticking in the air, and curled his tail upright between his hind legs. "Dad. You can't give him fried livers." She shook her finger.

"He'll love them."

"I'm sure he will, but…never mind." Mallory jutted her hands on her hips. "When he has room-clearing gas and diarrhea at four in the morning, he'll be sent to your room."

Jim chuckled.

Zehn rolled his head to the side, his eyes wide open, seemingly knowing he was the topic of conversation.

"Here, take this." Jim handed her a twenty, as he glanced over the top of his wire-rimmed bifocals. He sank back into his recliner.

Her dad was a stark contradiction to Charlotte, wearing his tie-dyed graphic T-shirt, khaki work pants, cut off at the knee, black over the calf dress socks, and feet shoved into house shoes with the back walked down. "Dad, I think I can buy you a four dollar order of fried rice."

"If a dad wants to give his daughter money, then that's exactly what he does. Just consider it a bribe to keep your mouth shut on me not liking your mother's chicken livers."

Such a Dad move and it touched her heart. Mallory took the twenty and grinned. "I won't be long." She grasped the doorknob.

"Mallory. Is that you?" Charlotte yelled from the kitchen.

"Yeah, Mom."

"Where are you going?"

"Cheap Chinese." Her hand rested on the doorknob.

Her mom stayed silent for a long moment.

"Do you think she heard us?"

A tinge of panic colored Jim's voice. Mallory held up her hand to reassure him then started to open the door again.

"Watch out for that MSM. I watched a program on

television the other day, and they said it could cause brain damage and learning disabilities," Charlotte yelled, still in the kitchen.

Mallory rolled her gaze heavenward.

"MSM?" Wrinkles creased Jim's forehead. "Isn't that an anti-inflammatory?"

Mallory gave a slight nod of her head. "You are correct, sir. She means MSG." She chuckled. "You have got to stop letting her watch so much television."

"Mallory," Charlotte hollered.

"Yeah, Mom." Mallory pinched the bridge of her nose. If her mom got on a roll, Chinese could be a ways off.

"Did you hear me about the MSM?"

"Sure did. I'll make sure they don't put any of that on my food."

"Good. Be careful."

"I will, Mom." She directed her attention back to her dad. "Dad, I'm making a run for it before she comes up with something else."

"Egg rolls."

"I'll get you one."

"Two."

"I'll get you two." Mallory blew her dad a kiss then shut the door.

A loud wham startled her as she walked down the sidewalk toward her car. For a moment she considered taking cover, until she spotted the handsome man across the street, kicking the heck out of a trashcan. He caught her gaze before she could look away. The intensity he watched her with froze her where she stood. She wondered if he was processing what to say after being caught acting a fool, or maybe he broke loose from a prison van and saw the first fresh meat in ten years. *Where did I put that pepper spray?*

"Tripped me." He offered as an explanation.

Glad he cleared that up. "Maybe you should treat it nicer, and it will treat you nicer." He smiled, and Mallory took note of the gentle curve of his lips. Not the smile of a mad man, so she didn't go for her pepper spray. She scanned her gaze head to toe. His stunning olive complexion and deep dark brown eyes were so prominent she could admire them from where she stood. *Uh-oh, he's coming this way.* Her mind said stranger-danger, but her libido said danger could be fun when it looks like that. *Am I sweating?*

He walked across the street and extended his hand. "Wade Porter."

"Mallory Larsen." She shook the offered hand, praying her palm wasn't damp. His size surprised her, and she almost took a step back. At five-seven herself, he had to be at least a head taller, but his height wasn't what made her feel tiny, that sensation was caused by his broad shoulders.

"Sorry you had to witness that."

"I'm sure it deserved a good whack. That can looks like a trouble maker to me." She couldn't suppress a grin when his neck and face reddened.

"Rotten day, then I got out of my car and turned, tripping over that miserable thing. I guess I took out all my frustration on it." He shrugged.

"Do you feel better?"

"Actually…yes."

"Well then, if you achieved a Zen place, it was worth the outburst, don't you think?"

He tilted his head to the side. His eyes, the shade of

black walnut shells after a fall harvest, held her gaze..

She tensed and a quiver formed low in her gut. This time, she did take a step back.

"Are you new here?" He glanced over her shoulder at the house behind her.

"Staying with my parents for a little while." She pointed back at the brick-and-stone raised ranch house where the ivy had claimed the lower half of the structure. "I haven't seen you before either."

"I inherited that house from my great-aunt. I've only been in about a month."

Mallory nodded as she rocked back on her heels. Out of conversational niceties, she readied herself to make an escape, but he just stood there studying her and she couldn't convince her feet to budge. Small talk had never been her specialty, neither had ending small talk, and she wished he'd walk away.

He didn't.

Silence hung heavy in the air.

Mallory inhaled and stepped back, angling herself toward her car. "Nice to meet you."

"Yeah. You, too. Guess I'll be seeing more of you."

His voice sounded raspy, and she couldn't help but glance over her shoulder. He hadn't moved. His hands were shoved in his pockets, while his gaze traveled from her flip-flops to her ball cap. When she saw his gaze reach her face, she smiled, unable to control a flush under his scrutiny. "Is that so?"

The right side of his mouth stretched up into a half-smile. "Sure. We live across the street from one another. Bound to cross paths." He winked.

Her stomach tingled. "Then I'll see you later."

The other half of his mouth joined in his smile.

"Oh, and keep your eye on that." She pointed toward his trashcan. "Still looks like trouble to me."

A heartfelt laugh erupted from deep within him.

She liked the warm sound. Unable to stop smiling, she escaped to the green subcompact vehicle before total mortification over her behavior set in.

The car roared to life, and she dropped her forehead to the steering wheel. *What am I doing? Shameless flirting with a total stranger, that's what I was doing.* This behavior was so unlike her. Normally, she controlled and thought through every word out of her mouth. She liked her life structured, until Kyle turned it upside down, and made her a babbling idiot who felt completely out of sync. She needed things predictable because predictable meant safe. Wade succeeded in unnerving her, and she'd rattled on like a schoolgirl with a crush. "Oh God." She moved her gaze to her engagement ring still on her finger. "I'm one messed-up chick." *Get a grip, girl.*

The tap on the window jolted her out of her stupor, and she jerked upright, heart pounding.

Wade bent forward and peered in the window, his thick, wavy, cocoa-brown hair fell forward over one eye.

Watching him brush it back mesmerized. She depressed the power button, and the whirl of the window lowering was deafening.

"You okay?"

Sweat broke out under her armpits, and she fought the urge to fan her top. "Um. Sure…why?"

"You've been sitting here for a while and, with the way you were slumped over the steering wheel, I was starting to worry."

Let me die now. "Nope. I'm all good." She grinned, her lip quivering "Just thinking."

"Must have been about something pretty important."

Blood rushed into her ears, and heat filled her cheeks. "Thinking about going to confession."

"You Catholic?"

"Nope."

He narrowed his gaze and locked on her eyes.

She kicked the air-conditioning on high, adjusting the vent toward her face.

He glanced at her ring and back to her face, his lips twisted to the side causing his cheek to crease.

Her ears started ringing. *Breathe.* She was going to hyperventilate. *This guy's intense.* Her senses rushed back, and she shifted into drive. "Thanks for checking on me."

"No problem." Wade fist bumped the door, stood up, and backed away.

She slammed the gas pedal to the floor, escaping the mortification coursing through her, refusing to look in her rearview mirror. *Great, now the new neighbor thinks I'm a promiscuous fool.* Why did he have to be so good looking? If he had just been ugly, then my inner flirt would have stay buried like where it had been since the day she met Kyle.

****

"Who was that?"

Matt might have been younger, but he was an easy two inches taller than Wade. Obvious sibling genetics bled through in both their facial features, from the strong jaw line, to the same olive skin tone, and dark brown hair. However, Matt's sapphire blue eyes provided diversity. "Hey, Matt. When did you get home?"

They converged on the kitchen at the same time, pausing at the doorway. Wade made a sweeping gesture with his hand, and Matt led the way into their favorite domain in the house. Matt searched drawers, while Wade stepped to his side, and opened a cabinet, only to stare blindly at its contents.

"A while ago. Class got out early. Personally, I think the professor had a date."

"Ah. The life of a graduate student." Wade closed the cabinet.

Matt shrugged. "So, who was the babe?"

"Mallory. Her parents live across the street, and she's staying with them for a while."

"Remind me to thank Auntie when I get to heaven for leaving her house to the Porter brothers." He picked up an apple off the counter and bit into it.

"Don't get too interested. I think she's taken." Wade patted the side of Matt's arm as he passed by. He yanked open the refrigerator.

"Married?" he asked, still chewing the apple and sending juicy particles into the air.

"Looked liked a wedding band on her finger. At the very least an engagement ring." He removed a beer, and then bumped the door closed with his hip.

"Damn. The hot ones are always taken." Matt snapped his fingers. He finished his last bite of apple and did a free throw of the core into the garbage can across the room. "Ahh. Three points."

"Great skill for a soon-to-be licensed social worker to have."

Matt narrowed his eyes. "Don't be a hater. What has your drawers in a wad?"

Wade twisted the top off his beer and took a long swig. "What do you mean?"

"You're tense. The lady piss you off?"

"No. She was cordial and somewhat awkward." Wade sat at the table and picked at the label on his beer.

Matt smirked and raised his eyebrows. "Does my brother have a crush on the married neighbor?"

Wade's gaze snapped to Matt's. His brother's innate ability to get Wade's goat so effortlessly annoyed him. Must be some weird power passed to all younger brothers. "Knock it off. We spoke for all of five minutes. I introduced myself…being polite."

"I see. So, you've met her parents?"

"No." His body tensed as he shifted his position in the chair.

"How about Ms. Emery next door? Who makes excellent brownies, by the way."

"No." His nose wrinkled.

"The Yarbroughs on the corner." Matt crossed his arms, leaning against the counter.

Obviously, his brother was waiting for Wade's reaction. He slammed his beer on the table. "No. I haven't met them yet. We haven't lived here long. How would I have met all these people?"

"The Yarbroughs make their own special moonshine…FYI," he whispered, a hand to the side of his mouth.

"You've seriously met all these people?" His vocal inflection revealed his astonishment.

"Of course, but I haven't met Mrs. Mallory—"

"Larsen." Wade supplied.

"Mrs. Mallory Larsen."

"Look, the only reason I approached her was because she caught me beating the crap out of our trashcans." Wade swallowed the last of his beer and tossed the bottle in the recycling bin.

Matt's eyebrows lifted as the corners of his mouth turned down. "Really? I need to make you my next case study."

"Fat chance, little brother." Wade strode from the kitchen, his brother's chuckle ringing in his ears.

Chapter Two

"Number twenty-four, your order is ready," a voice said over the loudspeaker.

The lighting cast shadows in the hole-in-the-wall restaurant located in a strip mall the next town over. One dropped in for the food and not the dining experience.

Mallory dropped her phone in her purse and stood to retrieve her order.

"Mallory Larsen…or should I say Mallory Malloney?"

The voice sent shivers up her spine. She turned and faced an unwanted blast from her past, Ralph Shimkus. He stalked her through the last couple of years of high school. His obsession started with love notes slipped into her locker. On to rumors they were going steady, and then planned to marry after graduation. He waited for her after classes and followed her home at the end of the school day. Her only reprieve happened at lunch when they had opposing breaks. She reported the situation to the school counselor, and their expert advice included being patient with him. They were sure he was going through a phase and would grow out of it. Be nice to him. She tried… really, she tried to be pleasant and yet firmly discourage his attachment, but he never took the hint.

Finally, toward the end of her senior year, she

dated a varsity baseball player, and Ralph lost all self-control. He fabricated a story saying she was pregnant with his child. Classmates whispered behind her back. Her boyfriend dumped her for the head cheerleader, not wanting to get mixed up in her personal issues.

The school called in her family to discuss how to best handle the situation, and they grilled her with humiliating questions. She wanted to run far away and never come back to this town, where everyone was privy to everyone else's business and no one was shy about discussing it. She swore she wasn't pregnant, but convincing her family required a blood test at the doctor's office. All of the stress affected her final exams and made her last months of high school torture. She didn't eat, and her weight plummeted. She became a recluse and only left her house to attend school. The anxiety destroyed her physical and emotional well-being.

The delicate thread of sanity Mallory walked snapped in the middle of a school pep rally. Ralph approached her holding a sign with, "Will You Marry Me?" written in large block letters. Total mortification surged through her and propelled her emotions over the precarious edge. She verbally ripped him to shreds. Utter silence fell upon the auditorium when she'd finished her rant and left Ralph humiliated. She remembered the hate in his eyes when he vowed to get even, right before he fled the building and didn't return for the final days of school. Her words were cutting and cruel, but she'd endured his antics for two years and her well-being suffered—she cracked. Being nice failed to resonate with Ralph and she needed it to end. Mallory hadn't seen him since…until now.

"Ralph." Her mouth depleted of moisture, but she managed to force out a raspy whisper. She offered a silent prayer he would let bygones be bygones and possessed enough maturity to be cordial.

"What are you doing here?"

"Getting food?" Her scrunched eyes implied *duh*. "What most people do when they are standing in a restaurant."

He watched her without saying a word.

Mallory adjusted her ball cap, and then slid her ponytail through her fist, twirling the end around her palm. "I'm going out with friends to Grayson's Club tonight." Why she needed to fill the dead air, she wasn't sure. Walking away should've topped her choice list.

"Trying to find a fiancé replacement?" The toothpick he chewed on disappeared into his thick mustache with every gnaw.

Mallory's eyes widened and then relaxed. Of course he knew, one of the luxuries of living in this area.

"That's right I heard your fiancé dumped you, and you ran home." He sneered, moving close.

So much for cordial. "Nice to see you, too, Ralph." His facial hair made him look like Yosemite Sam. "Good to see you finally hit puberty." She pointed at his face. "If you'll excuse me."

He stepped in front of her.

She fought the urge to say, "What's up, Doc?"

"Guess he wised up and cut his losses."

And the toothpick disappeared again. A ferret could get lost in that thing. She jutted out her chin. Come hell or high water, she would take the high road, but she wouldn't allow him to bully her either. "Since you know it all, guess there's nothing to talk about." She sidestepped him.

He grabbed her by the upper arm. "When you live in a small town, your business is everyone's business. You should keep that in mind. I'm aware of all the ongoings around here." His cold gaze bore into hers.

Sweat trickled down her back. "Well, bully for you. Now if you'll excuse me, my food is waiting." She stepped forward but he didn't let go.

He glared. His nostrils flared with each breath.

She thought she detected a hint of bourbon on his breath. The high road was getting mighty hard to stay on. "Ralph, you either let me go right this minute, or I will scream at the top of my lungs. Your call." Being in a public place made her a little braver than if they would've been alone.

He held on for another second and then stepped back. He bared his teeth, and his eyebrows tangled together in the middle.

She could sense his gaze on her as she took long decisive strides up to the counter to pick up her food, for which she no longer had an appetite. As she left the restaurant she raised her chin high. The trembling of her hands made grabbing the keys from her purse difficult. "Welcome home, Mallory." She managed to snag her keys and hit the door unlock button. "Your life just keeps getting better."

****

The pulsating bass vibrated through Mallory's grip on the door handle and absorbed into her body. She opened it and stepped into a world of darkness broken by bright flashes of light, music, talking, and laughter. The odor of multiple bodies, alcohol, and fried foods overloaded her senses. She paused, allowing her eyes to adjust to the dim light, and then scanned the vast room for a familiar face. She caught a glimpse of Ella's mass of auburn curls bouncing to the beat of the music and headed toward the elevated corner table. "Hey, ladies." She strode up to them arms wide.

"Mallory." They shrieked in unison, jumping off their stools and embracing her.

"We're so glad you're home," Poppy said.

"Yeah. Even if it took that butt wad Kyle Malloney to get you here," Ella said.

Mallory flinched at the mention of his name.

Hazel grabbed Mallory's hand and made her spin. "Speaking of the man, who should not be mentioned. You are putting him in his place with that outfit. Oh, girl...you look hot."

Mallory did another spin to show off her short faux-leather shorts, a silky cowl neck white sleeveless top, and a short tweed jacket with leather lapels.

"And look at those shoes. Ooh-wee...those are amazing," Hazel said with a smile.

"If I don't kill myself in these shoes." Mallory tipped her foot to the side, admiring her impulse purchase of four-inch gladiator wedges with six buckles from the toe to the upper ankle. Never go shopping after an ugly breakup. She bought stuff she'd ordinarily never consider wearing—letting all her bits and pieces, that weren't enough for the man who vowed to love her for better or for worse, hang out for someone else to appreciate.

"Someone get this girl a whip." Poppy made a cracking motion with her hand.

Mallory flushed, even though the music drowned

out Poppy's voice. "Oh my God. I don't look like a dominatrix…do I?" Her eyes widened as she glanced down at her outfit. So much time had passed since she'd been out dancing she no longer knew how to dress for a club. She tried for the urban boho-chic style, but now feared she looked like Madonna in her *Justify My Love* stage. She tugged at the hem of her shorts.

Poppy grasped her hand. "Stop it. You look amazing. If you haven't noticed, you have captivated several onlookers. Chic slut is working."

Mallory's jaw dropped.

"Kidding….really, I'm kidding. You're a knockout. Now sit and let's get you liquored up so we can go dance. And not talk about he who cannot keep his pants zipped."

Larkin spun, swaying her arms above her head, and stomped, contributing to the vibration from the massive pounding of dancing feet. She whirled and her ponytail whopped Hazel.

Mallory mouthed *I'm sorry* and pointed to their table as Hazel rubbed her face.

Hazel nodded, tapping Ella and Poppy as they danced past.

The ladies laughed and continued to bounce and sway, as they sat at their table.

A waitress placed four shots in front of them.

Poppy raised an eyebrow. "We didn't order these?" She pursed her lips.

"They did." The waitress pointed to the table a couple ones down. She sprinkled sugar soaked in rum on top of the lemons and lit them on fire.

All four ladies lifted their drinks in salute to the six guys for their purchase, blew out the flame, licked the sugar, downed the shot, and sucked the lemon.

Mallory peeled back her lips from her teeth and shook her head. "Holy crap. What was that?"

"Flaming Lemon Drop," the waitress announced, smiling as she placed the glasses back on her tray and walked away.

One of the guys approached from the drink-buying table. "Any of you ladies like to dance?"

All three ladies' gazes snapped to Mallory.

She held up her hands. "Not me. I'm not sure I can stand yet after that shot." In all truth, she wasn't ready to dance with any guy right now. She just wanted to keep a nice buzz, hang out with her friends, and not think about being cheated on.

"Well, I'll go." Ella jumped off her stool en route to the dance floor.

The ladies watched her go.

Then Poppy's eyes widened, and her jaw dropped. She bumped Hazel with her elbow.

"Hey, Mal, let's go dance."

Hazel stepped in front of Mallory, locking her in place with her piercing steel-gray gaze, known to bring many to their knees. The stark contrast from her caramel complexion and coal black hair tended to mesmerize anyone in her path.

"Come on." She tugged her toward the crowded floor.

"What's going on? You two look like you've seen a—" Mallory turned to see Skylar walking right toward them.

At close to six feet, her stature made the woman hard to miss. She'd be the perfect candidate to play a Greek goddess. Her gold-colored hair hung in waves past her long slender neck. The way she carried her body commanded attention.

A pain of inferiority stabbed Mallory right in her self-esteem.

Skylar's gaze landed on Mallory, and Skylar froze.

Mallory couldn't swallow around the lump in her throat. The vodka burned as it raced back up her esophagus. The only thing to make this moment worse would've been if Kyle had accompanied her. Why hadn't Skylar stayed in the city with Kyle? Instead, she showed up at the same bar and filled Mallory with the heavy heart sensation she hoped to avoid by coming out with her friends.

The glare coming from Hazel and Poppy must have registered, because Skylar turned and walked in the other direction.

"At least the fiancé-stealing maid of honor from hell knows not to approach us." Poppy slammed her open palm on the table.

"Let's go dance," Hazel said again. "She's not worth worrying about."

Mallory took a deep breath and faced her friends. "I'm okay... really. Besides, you can't steal someone who doesn't want to be stolen. Better I found out before we married." She put on her best brave face and smiled. "We all grew up in this tiny town, and I'm bound to cross her path when..." She sighed.

"When she's not in the big city doing the horizontal hokey pokey with your fiancé?" Hazel's necklaces jangled in rhythm with her side-to-side head jut.

"Hazel!" Poppy gave her the death stare.

"What? It's the truth, and Mallory dodged a bullet,

if you ask me," Hazel said.

"We didn't, and no more alcohol for you. Now let's go dance." Poppy scooched off her stool.

"You guys go dance. I'm grabbing a beer." Mallory disappeared into the crowd before they could argue.

****

"I can't believe I let you drag me here." Indecipherable lyrics assaulted his ears. His temple pulsated with the driving beat of the drum.

"What?"

Wade shook his head and leaned next to Matt's ear. "I can't believe I let you drag me here."

"Come on, bro. We live in Elsah now. Time to check out the sights, and I see some nice sights here. Let's go make nice." Matt gave Wade a cocky wink before scanning the room.

"I thought, let's go grab a drink, meant at a quiet bar where the decibel scale was under a hundred and fifty, and we could hold a conversation."

"Who needs conversation? When our bodies can do all the talking." Matt accented his statement with a body wave.

"I'll tell you what. You go let your body chatter away, and I'll be at the bar." Wade's throat was raw from making himself heard. He nudged Matt toward the dance floor and then found a vacant stool. He turned his attention to the overhead screen to see what team was ahead on the baseball game.

"Excuse me."

A female wedged herself between him and the three-hundred-pound woman on the other side. He ignored the bump.

"I'll have whatever light beer you have on tap."

He overheard her order.

The bartender tilted the glass, filled it, and slid the glass her way. "Thank you." She handed the bartender a five and waved off change. "Sorry again," she said to Wade. Then slammed up against his side again.

He took a cleansing breath to control his annoyance. Instead, he focused on the game. Her hand clamped on his arm as she shoved away from him.

The large lady on the other side found something hysterical and her body seesawed, taking out everything in its path, including the female struggling to escape the beating.

"Oh crap," she said, right before hitting him hard enough to knock him off his stool. "Damn shoes." Her shriek cut through the noise, as she tumbled forward.

Instinct took over, and he opened his arms to catch her before she fell to the floor. He yanked her out from between the two stools and held on as she got her feet under her. "Are you okay?" he asked.

"Yes…I think so, except for allowing impulse to rule my emotions when I bought these blasted shoes." She shifted back and tilted up her head to meet his gaze. "I really am sorry…I felt like I got stuck in the agitation cycle of a washing machine…Hey, I know you." A slight slur rounded out her syllables.

He gave her a thorough once-over. The high, lustrous blonde ponytail accented her prominent cheekbones. It swayed with every word she spoke, brushing her mid-back. Her smile uncovered deep dimples, and her full, pink cupid-bow kissable lips mesmerized him for a moment. Shaking off his stare, he let his gaze travel over her long lanky bare legs, beginning at her hip down to the four-leaf clover tattoo on her right ankle. *I don't recognize those legs. I wouldn't forget this woman...who does she think I am...whoever it is, I will become.*

"You pummeled that poor innocent trashcan today."

He whipped his gaze to her almond-shaped hazel eyes. He focused on the dark green rim of her eyes and took in the gold flecks surrounding the pupil. "Oh my God. Mallory?"

"You remember. Wade, correct?"

"You look...look..." Once more, he swept his gaze over her length. "Tall."

Her warm laugh cut through all the noise in the bar. "It's these death-wish shoes I'm wearing. Makes me about five eleven." She twisted to the side and struck a pose.

Her cheeks were rosy, he wasn't sure if blush or alcohol caused it, but assumed the latter. He guessed inebriation loosened her tongue, because earlier today, she'd been awkward. Cute, but had a definite shyness about her.

Last time he saw her she wore a pair of cargo pants, loose-fitting T-shirt, flip-flops, and a ball cap. A natural beauty and he'd been drawn to her, but he wouldn't have associated this vixen in front of him with that woman. Now, she looked like a woman with something to prove. He liked both versions. "You've been here a while."

"What?"

He leaned in close to her ear, and his stomach kicked. "I said you've been here a while..." He inhaled. "And you smell like lemons."

She tossed back her head and laughed. "Flaming Lemon Drop. Stay away from that one." She leaned in again.

Her breath on his neck was almost his undoing.

"How did you know I've been here for some time?"

A half grin appeared on his face. "Your rosy cheeks, and you don't seem to be feeling much pain."

Her fists settled on her hips. "I'm entitled. I'm drowning my sorrows." She waved her hand. "But that's my last one before I switch to water," she said, pointing to her beer still barricaded from her grasp by the swaying woman.

The band started a slower song. "How about a dance before you sober up enough to say no?" He gave his best enticing grin. Then wondered what he was doing by asking a taken woman to dance. At this moment, he couldn't make himself care. He'd berate himself later. Right now he wanted to feel her in his arms.

She glanced at her beer.

"It'll be there when we are done."

Smiling, she nodded.

Wade tugged her onto the floor and slipped his hand behind her back, snugging her tight. He took her other hand and turned it so the back rested on his chest. The electricity radiated between their bodies, and he held his breath for a moment, trying to keep his stomach down. "What sorrows are you drowning?" he asked, more to distract from the inappropriate emotions coursing through his veins.

"Don't ask," she said. "Please don't ask."

The pain in her voice stopped his line of

questioning, and he gathered her closer, resting cheek to cheek. She smelled of strawberry shortcake, his new favorite dessert. He rubbed his cheek on hers and closed his eyes. Her body relaxed into his as they swayed to the music. All too soon the song ended, and the spell was broken by three females charging their way.

"Who's this tall drink of water?"

A female with hypnotic steel-gray eyes rested a hand on his shoulder. A petite female with long curly auburn hair that continued to bounce even after she stopped and a glass blue eyed female with an asymmetrical bob materialized on his other side with no obvious concept of personal space. For the first time in his life, he understood objectified.

"Hey, bro. You've been holding out on me." Matt squeezed between the petite curly haired and the blue-eyed ladies, wrapping his arms around their waists.

Apparently no one was feeling much pain tonight. His alone time with Mallory had ended. Probably for the best. And yet, a pang of disappointment still kicked in his gut.

"Introduce me."

"That's Mallory," he said, lifting his hand her direction. "And as for these ladies"—he swept his arm in an arc—"I haven't had the pleasure."

The ladies giggled.

"That's Hazel, Ella, and Poppy. Ladies, this is Wade, and..." Mallory paused.

"Sorry," Wade said. "This here is Matt. My brother and roommate."

With a flurry of movement, they all exchanged handshakes.

"Mallory. From the street?" Matt asked Wade.

Mallory raised her eyebrows.

Wade cleared his throat. "He means earlier today."

Mallory nodded and relaxed her posture.

"Wow. You look different. You're hot," Matt said. "I could tell you were attractive from the front window, but damn, girl. You've got gams." He moved his gaze up and down.

Wade's face burned hot. There was nothing his brother wouldn't say.

The smile on Mallory's face said, yes I'm still tipsy and the inappropriate comment is currently considered flattering.

Matt leveled his stare on Poppy. "What do you say? Want to show these folks how it's done."

Without breaking eye contact, Poppy shimmied against Matt, hooking her arm through his. "See you, ladies. Nice to meet you, Wade."

Wade took Mallory's hand and held it. He gave a gentle squeeze. "Thanks for the dance." He rubbed his thumb over her ring, and their gazes held. He sighed and walked away before he did anything stupid he couldn't take back.

Chapter Three

"Girl, he's yummy. Where did you find him?" Hazel climbed up on her bar stool.

"I didn't find him. We met earlier today." Mallory pushed aside her beer and wrapped her lips around the straw protruding from her water. She held up her index finger, to signal just a minute, as she took a long sip.

Hazel drummed her fingers on the table.

Mallory swallowed. "He lives across the street from my parents."

"Jim and Charlotte need to have me over for dinner."

"Fried chicken livers, that's what's for dinner." Mallory gagged.

"Mmm-mmm. I love me some fried chicken livers, and I already know what's for dessert."

"Come on, Hazel. Get your hormones in check." Mallory tossed her napkin at her friend's head of lush ebony hair.

Hazel batted it away. "Jealous much?"

The moisture in her mouth evaporated and her stomach twisted. "I barely know him. Why would I be jealous?" She glued her gaze to the beer she slid in front of her.

"Because you want to hog him all for yourself," Ella said.

"Hey, two against one that's not fair. Besides, I'm

not hogging him." What was she doing? Having his arms wrapped around her on the dance floor made her feel like she belonged in his embrace. Her gut tingled remembering his cheek caressing hers. She lightly brushed her fingers against the side of her face. "I just met him."

"Could've fooled me. The way you two were doing the bump and grind on the dance floor." Smiling, Ella nudged Mallory's shoulder.

"Hey, don't encourage her. If she doesn't want him…" Hazel stopped.

Tears sparkled in the corner of Mallory's eyes. "I'm sorry." She fanned her hand in front of her face.

"I was only kidding. Don't cry. I won't try and steal him." Hazel placed her hand on top of Mallory's.

Mallory laughed through her tears. *I'm an idiot.* She used her ring fingers to wipe the raccoon eyes she was sure her non-waterproof mascara had created.

Hazel pressed her lips together, forming a grim line. She pulled a tissue from her purse and wedged it into Mallory's fist.

"You know it's not that. It's just—" She blew her nose. "One guy is nice to me, and my ex is a jerk off, and I'm an emotional mess."

"Honey, we know you've had a sucky month, and Skylar showing up here hasn't helped. Our plan was to get your mind off of the crap, and we make it worse," Ella said.

"No, guys. You've been great, and I've had so much fun tonight. I just can't help but feel like I wasn't enough for Kyle. Sometimes I wonder if I'm even desirable to men." She sniffed. "Will I ever be good enough?" She moved her gaze to her ring.

"Wade sure acted as though he liked what he saw." Hazel rubbed Mallory's arm.

Mallory grinned. Tears still dampened her lashes. "He is cute, isn't he?"

"Not cute, hunky, and his coal-black eyes left an impression on my soul." Hazel fanned herself with a menu. "And he likes you."

Mallory waved off the comment. "No, he doesn't. He was being polite since we're neighbors."

"Well, I saw fireworks." Ella arched a sly brow.

"Stop." Mallory sighed. "Even if he had a tiny bit of interest, he doesn't anymore."

"What do you think changed between the floor and this stool here?" Ella asked. "Because out there, he was definitely interested.

"He noticed my ring." Mallory cast her gaze downward and spun the ring on her finger.

Ella and Hazel peered at her hand. "Why on earth are you wearing that thing!" Hazel snapped.

Mallory shrugged. *Because I thought it made me whole.*

"Honey." Ella squeezed her hand. "It's time. You know that."

"It's time, my ass." Hazel smacked her palm on the table. "We're stopping at the first pawn shop as soon as we leave."

Ella narrowed her eyes at Hazel and gave a subtle headshake.

Mallory's heart raced in her chest. She couldn't breathe. "I guess I got used to it. I've worn this ring for so long, taking it off makes me feel like I've failed."

"What do you mean? You didn't fail. Kyle cheated on you with your maid of honor before your wedding.

You know his infidelity wasn't your fault…don't you?" Ella's brows formed a deep V.

She ripped at the corner of her napkin. "I know it up here." She tapped the side of her head. "But in here…" She placed her hand on her heart. "I'm not so sure."

"You need to take off that ring. It's toxic, and a reminder of too many bad memories." Hazel grasped Mallory's hand, sliding her thumb across the ring.

"I've tried, but…" Mallory fell silent, biting her lower lip.

"You pushed back the wedding date several times. Maybe self-consciously you recognized something wasn't right. I'm not sure you even loved him." Ella gave her a hug. "The time has come. You have to let go of the past in order to move forward with a future."

She'd forgotten how to breathe. Mallory wanted, needed air. *Calm down, breathe in*, she inhaled through her nose, *breathe out.* She slowly exhaled. An involuntary action, now a voluntary struggle. She repeated the process a few more times and the tingling subsided. "I'm afraid." Another breath helped steady the tremble in her voice. "We were together for five years. I felt safe knowing someone was there. Even if the passion wasn't, I had this security blanket. I don't know how to be alone." The tears slipped from the corner of her eyes. "Even now, what do I do but run home to Mommy and Daddy. I'm a coward." She hiccupped, and tears rolled down her cheeks.

"Don't ever talk like that." Hazel held Mallory's gaze. "You're strong, and you don't need any man to prop you up."

The three embraced.

"You're the best friends a girl could have."

"We love you." Ella kissed her cheek.

Hazel shoved napkins into Mallory's hand.

She blotted her eyes and blew her nose.

"The alcohol has made me weepy. I'm stepping outside and getting some air." She gave them one last squeeze and walked away, needing a private minute to compose herself.

Mallory spun the ring on her finger and removed it. Was she invisible now? The warm night air hit her as she stepped out the back door and into the alley. Her hand rested over the empty hole in her gut. She put the ring back onto her finger. "Visible once again."

Her friends were correct—Kyle had been safe, and she liked that security. Truth be told, she didn't love him the way a woman should love the person she was about to spend the rest of her life with. When they traveled for business, neither called. Worse, she didn't miss him. Her heart didn't jump in her chest when she saw him. They didn't even hold hands, but like an old shoe, they were comfortable together and seldom argued. Their relationship held no passion. But, she'd rather push forward with the wedding than confront her true feelings. Mallory stared at her ring and again slipped it off her finger. This time, she shoved it into the small pocket on her jacket.

She inhaled the night air and gagged, overtaken by the garbage decomposition process getting a head start before being hauled to the dump. She stepped away from the dumpsters. The traffic hummed in the distance as it passed by in front of the club. The moon shone like a beacon in the sky keeping the darkness at bay. "Beauty still exists in this world...even in a foul-smelling filthy alley."

A scratching sound behind her made her stiffen. *Don't turn around. Don't turn around. Don't turn around.* The sound came again. *I don't want to know.* Please go away. The sensation of a thousand spiders ran up her back. Scratch, clank. "I hate rats. Please don't be some toxic rat monster." She forced herself to pivot toward the sound, three rats munched on something, but her blood-curdling scream sent them scurrying for cover. Mallory flattened her hand against her chest as she took a slow, deep breath.

She squinted into the darkness and took a step forward. Are those Louboutin shoes? Surely, someone didn't throw them out. Maybe things are looking up. She walked toward the dumpster, the rats forgotten. Her laser focus didn't budge from the black toeless pumps with the red soles. *Wonder what size those are?* She strode around the front of the dumpster and halted. A scream wanted to burst from her throat, but couldn't. Her stomach plunged into her feet.

The shoes were next to the feet of a female who lay unmoving on the ground. *Are you okay?* No words materialized from Mallory's mouth. Her tongue was dry like cotton. She closed her mouth, tried to swallow, and work up some spit. "Are you okay?" Mallory asked in a quiet and raspy voice. She looked back and forth, hoping to see someone to help in the alley. Logically, she understood this person definitely wasn't okay, but her brain was having trouble processing.

"Hey." She stepped forward and tapped the arm with her shoe. It shifted with the pressure, but the person gave no other response. "Oh God…oh God. Someone help me." Her voice remained a whisper.

"Please don't be dead. Please be okay." She stretched out her arm, staying as far away as possible, to remove the large piece of cardboard covering the upper half of the body. The trembling of her hand kept her from gripping the edge. She took a shaky breath and slid off the cardboard. A shrill scream tore from her body but melted into the thumping bass from the band inside.

Mallory peered down into empty blue eyes staring at nothingness in the sky. The lifeless body's mouth was slightly open with dried saliva crusted in the corner. The fitted, sea-green, sleeveless linen mini-dress twisted at an odd angle across the body, and a crimson color stained the front of the once-pristine outfit.

Mallory's insides plunged and then raced back up her esophagus. *Oh no.* She scurried backward until she hit the building and then purged everything from her gut. Water, alcohol, remains of *lo mein*. The rough texture of the bricks cut into her hand, her breath came in pants, and gradually the nausea subsided. She straightened and forced herself to walk back to the body, intending to check for a pulse. Instead she stood over her and stared. She couldn't make herself do it. *It's stupid anyway.*

Multiple wounds on the woman's chest and stomach didn't leave much doubt. The lady was dead. *I need to call the police.* She patted her pocket, but she'd left her phone in the car. She hadn't wanted to lose it dancing. She ran both hands over her hair, tugging on the end of her ponytail, unable to tear away her gaze from the lifeless body. "Oh God. Skylar...what happened?"

A high-pitched wail made Mallory's knees buckle.

She pivoted toward the alley opening.

A disheveled female with frizzy uncombed hair gaped at her.

Mallory couldn't miss her tight dirty jeans covering her twiggy legs and a ripped baggy T-shirt.

The woman's hands clenched.

She looked to be running in place. "Do you have a phone?" Mallory's voice barely audible, and the question didn't carry to the female's ears.

The girl turned and ran shrieking from the alley.

Think, Mallory, think. She backed from the body until she slammed against the door she'd exited. Shoving her way through the crowd, she reached the bar.

The bartender was serving a customer at other end.

So Mallory stepped around and grabbed the cordless phone from its hook. She couldn't hear over the band and turned, walking stiff gaited to the bathroom where the sound diminished as the door closed. After three false starts, she dialed 9-1-1.

"911, what is your emergency?"

Mallory's mouth moved, but no sound occurred.

"911, what is your emergency?"

She produced a low faint voice. "There's a body—"

"I'm sorry. You need to speak up, please. If you can."

"There's a body in the alley behind Grayson's Club off of Henley Road." The words flooded out of her mouth, unintelligible to the human ear.

"What is your name?"

Mallory disconnected the call. She faced the mirror, her hands rested on the sink, and blinked.

"Hey, are you in line?" A female with blue stripes in shoulder-length platinum blonde hair asked.

Blink.

"You okay?"

Blink.

"Bitch." The stall door slammed.

Blink.

Numerous people circulated through the restroom, most ignoring Mallory.

"She must be high as a kite." Two young females, who didn't look old enough to be out of high school, giggled as they walked out of the restroom.

A gray-haired female strolled through the door and emptied the trashcans. She caught Mallory's gaze in the mirror and stopped. "Honey. Do you need me to get you some help?"

A warm hand contacted Mallory's forearm. *Blink. Blink.* She allowed her gaze to drift in the mirror to the kind-eyed woman. Mallory released the sink and stepped back. She shook her head then walked out of the bathroom. As she passed the bar, she dropped the phone on the counter, and it clattered to the floor. She continued toward the alley door.

Faintly, she heard her friends call her name, but she couldn't answer them. She stepped out into the unwelcoming alley where death awaited. No longer noticing the heat or rank odor. Red and blue light reflected in her eyes.

"There she is! There she is!"

Mallory wondered there who was, and she looked behind herself. Muffled voices floated in the air. Cold, so cold, goose bumps pricked her exposed skin.

"That's her. That's who stabbed the woman." The

female pointed at Mallory.

Guns yanked from holsters and aimed at her. "Hands where I can see them." Gruff male voices screamed.

She didn't understand. Her heart pulsated in her chest. The haze of confusion hung heavy in her mind.

"Turn and interlace your fingers behind your head." Two men charged, guns held at chest level. They wrenched her arms behind her.

Cold metal banged her wrist bones. *Blink. What's happening? Where are they taking me?* They led her past Skylar, and she glanced away, only to spot Ralph Shimkus standing with the skanky female from earlier. His arms were crossed, and a smirk plastered on his face. Confusion still clouded her thinking. One deputy opened the squad car's back door. Pressure on the top of her head forced her into the car. *What's happening? Where are they taking me?*

****

Chasing after the stunned Mallory, Wade burst out the door with Ella, Hazel, Poppy, and Matt in tow.

"She acted like she didn't even know us," Hazel said, scanning the frenzied scene in the alley.

"I know. I saw her come out this door like she was in a trance. She's scaring me," Ella rubbed her throat with her right hand.

Wade looked down the alley in time to see Mallory being put into a squad car in cuffs. "What the hell?"

A male in navy chinos, a button-down shirt, and tie blocked the entourage's stampede. Light reflected off the badge clasped to his belt.

"Get out of the way, Ralph." Poppy tried to bulldoze past.

"That's Detective Shimkus to you." Ralph sneered.

Poppy's jaw dropped. "You're kidding?"

He narrowed his eyes. "Even though I wasn't good enough to hang out with you and your socialites in high school, I still became a well-respected authority figure in society." Ralph crossed his arms. "I didn't need you and your snobby friends to make something of myself."

"What are you talking about? What does high school have to do with any of this? But for the record, *you* were the ass in high school. We never bothered you or were mean to you. You were a hateful kid always looking to cause trouble. We just stayed out of your way." Poppy jabbed her finger at his chest.

Ralph's mouth clamped so tight together his lips weren't visible.

Great. They know each other. Guess speaking reason won't work. Wade lifted his gaze to the car Mallory sat in. *This is bad.*

She waved him off. "Quite frankly, I couldn't care less. I only want to get to my friend to see if she's all right."

"Well, you can't." He puffed out his chest. "Your sweet and gentle friend is being arrested."

"What!" Voiced in unison from the group.

Ralph laughed. "That's correct. Now you need to leave before I have to arrest you, too. You are interfering with a crime scene."

"Crime scene?" Hazel glanced around the alley with a blank look on her face.

Wade scanned the area and spotted the body being photographed by a deputy. The coppery scent assaulted his senses. Denial lodged in his throat. A pain seized his chest, and he forced a slow breath into his deprived lungs.

"Oh my God. Is that Skylar?" Poppy covered her mouth with her hand.

"You need to leave." Ralph glared, pointing his finger toward the club's door. "Now."

"Why are you arresting Mallory?" Wade asked.

Ralph looked up at Wade who towered over him and snorted. "Why do you think?"

Wade held Ralph in a fierce stare-down. "Are you accusing her of murder?"

"Have an eyewitness."

"Who?" A queasy sensation settled in Wade's gut.

"Can't release that."

Wade spotted a scrawny female next to another deputy. Small sores covered her gaunt, grayish-colored face. Her facial bones protruded, stretching the elastic capacity of her skin. Dark discolored teeth peeped out between cracked lips. Her eyelids hung, giving her a half-mast appearance. He guessed her age to be twenty years younger than she looked. "Her?" His shrill voice drew stares. "That's your witness?"

"That's right. I saw that ice queen stab that woman." The twiggy woman's high-pitched voice penetrated the commotion in the alley. She pointed at Wade while bouncing in place. "There's a reward or something…right?" she asked the deputy standing beside her, as she continued to fidget.

"Did you really? Did you see a weapon of any sort?" Pressure built inside Wade. Was this really happening? He shook his head. The police actually arrested Mallory based on a crack head's statement.

The woman's mouth closed. "I saw her standing over her." She scratched at the sores on her face. Blood trickled down her cheek. "I mean you catch a murderer cuz of me. Gotta be some monies for that…huh?" She glanced at the deputy.

"I thought you said you witnessed her being stabbed?" Wade took a deep breath. Losing his temper wouldn't serve anyone favorably.

"I did." Spit flew out of her mouth.

"You just said you saw her standing over the body. Did you see a knife in her hand?"

"Well, that's kind of obvious." She shifted her weight. "The chick gots knife holes all over her. What you think she used, Mr. Smarty Pants?"

Her wide eyes dilated to the size of saucers. "Did you see a knife?" Wade's voice sounded terse.

"Enough," Ralph said, ushering the group toward the door. "Stop harassing my witness and leave."

"You call her a witness?" Poppy asked. "She doesn't know her ass from a hole in the ground. She's tweaking."

"Last chance." Ralph gritted his teeth and pointed again. "Leave, or be arrested."

Hazel opened the door. "Come on, guys. Ralphie here is letting his personal feelings get in the way of actual police work. Let's get on down to the station."

"You have no business at the station. You can't see Mallory, so go home."

They walked inside without acknowledging Ralph's comment.

****

Wade drove Ella and Hazel in Ella's beetle bug. He slammed his knee into the dash as he shifted. "Do you have something against full-size cars?"

"Stop your jawing and keep up with Matt and

Poppy. He just swung a right at the light." Ella pointed.

"Yeah. Well, he's in my truck. A real vehicle. Not this scooter on wheels." He scowled as he adjusted his long leg to downshift for the turn.

"If you don't like driving it, you could have let one of us drive," Ella said, with a bit of a slur.

"Is that so?" He flicked his gaze to the rearview mirror and then to the passenger seat. "And which of you inebriated ladies was willing to risk your neck and everyone else's by driving?"

Ella stuck out her lower lip.

"Apparently being sober makes you a real grouch." Hazel twisted her mouth into a snarl and gazed out the side window.

"Sobriety also gets you where you're going in one piece, so sit back and hush up so I can…" The gears ground as he rounded another corner. "Get us there."

"Be careful." Ella crossed her arms in front of her chest.

Wade's eye twitched, but he remained silent. One more turn and he whipped the car into the parking space next to his truck. The County Sheriff Department was located in the middle of Jerseyville, a town surrounded by farmland. He grabbed each side of the doorframe and pried himself out of the vehicle, swearing he heard the suction pop. His leg gave way and he smacked his hand on the hood of the car to steady himself.

"Old football injury acting up?" Matt asked.

Wade glared. "Next time you drive the bug, and I'll drive my own truck." He uprighted himself.

"Hey, you offered." Matt laughed.

"My mistake. Come on, let's get in there and see what we can find out." Wade opened the door, allowing the ladies to enter the sheriff's department first, hoping no one asked them to submit to a breathalyzer. They crowded into a small foyer.

A deputy sat at a counter behind bulletproof glass.

Wade tapped on it, as he scanned the rest of the office.

The pudgy, balding deputy looked up from his crossword puzzle.

"A Mallory Lawson was brought in, and we'd like to see her."

Deputy Pudgy shook his head, his jowls flapped side-to-side. "Can't see a prisoner. Come back during visiting hours."

He gave a brusque headshake. "I don't believe you would classify her as a prisoner. She hasn't done anything wrong."

"If she ain't done nothing wrong, why is she here?" The deputy leaned back, cackling.

"Look, I didn't hear any rights being read. Can you confirm if she's being arrested? If not, we'd like to take her home." Wade held the man's stare.

Deputy Pudgy roared with laughter. "Okay. Since you want to take her home. Let me go get her for you." He slapped a hand on the desk.

Wade clenched his jaw. "Either do your job, or go get me your lieutenant so he can do it for you. Oh, never mind I'll just call the mayor. My aunt was a very good friend of his family. Golly, I sure hate to wake him at this hour, but since there's no choice." He took out his phone.

Deputy Pudgy's face turned bright red. He snapped his pencil. "Let me see what I can find out. Take a seat."

"You're so kind." Wade glanced at the name Portly embroidered on his shirt and swallowed a laugh. "Deputy Portly." He turned back to the group and rolled his eyes.

"Auntie didn't know the mayor," Matt said in a low voice.

Wade shrugged. "Maybe she did." He sat on a nearby plastic chair and waited...and waited...and waited.

Forty-five minutes later, the deputy appeared back at the window, wiping mustard off his chin.

Poppy surged to her feet. "Well?"

"Hmm? Oh, your friend. She's in interview. Might be a while, she's refusing to talk." He returned to his crossword puzzle.

"You're interviewing her without an attorney present?" Ella leapt up and stood next to Poppy.

Deputy Portly didn't look away from his puzzle.

She looked over her shoulder. "Can they do that?"

Poppy turned toward the group. "What are we supposed to do?"

Matt bumped Wade with his elbow. "Yeah, Wade. Whatcha gonna do?"

Wade's narrowed eyes connected with Matt's. He chewed on the corner of his lip as seconds passed. "Mmm." He tapped his heel. "Damn. Damn. Damn." He ran his hands through his hair. "I don't even know her well."

"But you're here anyway." Matt stared at his brother.

"Fine," Wade said, through clenched teeth. He stood and walked over to the window, tapped the glass with his knuckles.

Deputy Portly looked up, frowning. "Either leave or sit down."

"I'm Mallory Lawson's attorney. I need to speak with my client."

The deputy's jaw descended and slowly closed. "Nice try, punk. Now have a seat."

"Is he for real?" Poppy asked.

"Yeah. He's for real," Matt said.

Wade ignored the conversation behind him, focusing on the deputy. "Are you refusing to allow my client to speak with me? She's entitled to representation. I want to see her."

He tapped his pencil, eyeing Wade up and down.

"He could have led with the attorney bit," Poppy said.

"He doesn't practice anymore," Matt said in a hushed voice.

"Now." A cool edge colored Wade's voice, and he stiffened his spine.

"Just a minute." Deputy Portly picked up a phone and spoke.

Wade turned and glanced at the group. "You guys might as well head home. I'll find out what's going on."

"I don't want to leave her here." Poppy wrapped her arms around her middle.

"I won't leave without seeing her. I promise. Matt can take you home—in Ella's car." Serves him right.

Matt glared but remained silent.

"I need my car," Ella said.

"We'll get it back to you tomorrow." Wade pointed between himself and Matt.

She surveyed him and let out a sigh. "You'll look after her?"

"Yes. There's no point in you sitting here the rest of the night. They won't let you see her."

"Fine." Ella blew out her breath. "Tell her to call me as soon as she can."

"I will." Wade nodded. "But I'm guessing it will be a while."

The door buzzed and clicked.

Wade strode through, overtaken by the stale, dank smell. He followed Deputy Portly, who was as wide as he was tall, down a long concrete hallway to an interrogation room on the right.

The deputy rapped on the door.

The detective from the alley opened it. A toothpick hung loose between his lips. Acne scars pitted his cheeks. A mustache swayed over his upper lip, giving him a walrus appearance. Premature gray dusted his side-parted brown hair, which didn't quite touch his collar. He stepped out, still blocking Wade from entering.

"Attorney, my ass. You were in the alley." The detective crossed his arms.

"Doesn't make me any less an attorney, Detective..."

"Shimkus."

A detective with a machismo complex, just great. "Detective Shimkus. Now I'd like to speak with my client."

"She's being questioned."

"Without her legal representation being present? I believe that's a pretty big no-no." Wade looked down to stare into the detective's eyes, challenging him.

Detective Shimkus shifted the toothpick to the other side of his mouth. "Well, your client hasn't said a word. You might want to encourage her to talk. She's making this worse on herself by dragging out the confession."

"Confession? To what, reporting a murder?" Wade squared off with the detective's shoulders and stepped closer, forcing the detective to strain his neck and look up.

He spit his toothpick onto the ground. "Yeah right...more like to murder."

Wade glared. "I don't think so. I need to speak with her."

"May I remind you, we have a witness?" Detective Shimkus stroked his mustache downward with his thumb and forefinger.

"Your crack ho'? Please. Open the door." Wade advanced.

Detective Shimkus eyed him up and down one more time and thrust open the door.

Another female detective sat across from Mallory.

Mallory's skin looked pale, almost gray. A thousand-yard stare claimed her eyes. Wade approached and pulled a chair up next to her and sat.

She didn't even acknowledge him. Her trembling hands rested in her lap.

"Mallory?" Wade touched her shoulder. No response. "Mallory."

"See, I told you the bitch isn't talking." Detective Shimkus shoved another toothpick into his mouth.

Wade narrowed his eyes. He looked closer at Mallory to see her pupils were dilated. "You idiot."

"Hey. Watch your mouth."

The squeak from his molars grinding forced him to relax his jaw. He spoke in a low, growling tone. "She's in shock, you moron."

"Oh sure she is." Detective Shimkus leaned against the wall. "Poor cold-blooded murderer is in shock." He laughed.

Squinting, the female detective studied Mallory.

Wade took his jacket off and put it around her. He scooted closer, rubbing his hands up and down her arms. "Can someone get her a cup of coffee, please?"

"She's a prisoner, not a patron." Detective Shimkus bumped the wall with his elbow.

Wade shifted to face the detective. "Have you formally arrested her?"

The detective remained silent.

"Then get her some coffee, and let me see if she'll snap out of it. Or I'm calling an ambulance and have her taken to the hospital for evaluation."

The female detective stood. "I'll get some."

Wade nodded thanks.

Detective Shimkus hovered in the room.

He lifted his left eyebrow a fraction. "Do you mind? I would like to talk to her alone. I have that right."

He snorted. "I'll be right outside."

"Terrific. I feel so much better."

Detective Shimkus scowled and left as the other detective arrived with a paper cup of coffee. She set it on the table and exited the room.

Wade returned to rubbing Mallory's arms and then slid his hands down to grasp hers. They were ice cold. He encased them in his own. "Mallory. I know you've been through a trauma, but I need you to come back to me. We must talk." He rubbed her hands and brought them to his mouth, blowing onto them.

She blinked.

"Mallory. I know we don't know each other well, but I'm here to help you. I need you to fight through what you're feeling, you're safe now. Your friends are worried about you."

****

Trapped inside her own head, Mallory couldn't escape. People directed her from place to place, but she had no voice. Stuck in a sensation similar to coming out of anesthesia and being aware of things going on around you but not being able to completely wake up. She knew she'd been put in a room with Ralph, who continued to yell. Telling her to confess...*confess to what? I'm so confused.* Nothing made sense. *Why am I in this room? Wait, someone else entered. He's arguing. I know him...my neighbor? My neighbor is here? I can feel his hands, and he's talking to me. Blink. Come back to me he says...but I'm here. I'm here. Can you hear me? His hands hold mine. His warmth seeps into me. His presence makes me feel safer.* A deep breath expelled from her core.

"That's it, Mallory...breathe. Come back."

Another deep breath. *Blink.* "I'm here." Barely a whisper.

"Mallory." He laid his hand on her cheek. "Hey there."

She turned to face him. "What happened?"

"Drink this." He moved the coffee toward her.

Mallory clutched the warm cup between her trembling hands. She sat silent, crushing it between her palms. "I don't feel well."

"You experienced quite a shock. I think your body went into self-preservation mode."

"Where am I?" She gazed around at the stark room.
"You don't know?"

"No. I. Um…it's fuzzy." She glanced again at the table and chairs inside a small space with green walls. "Jail?"

"Think back. What's the last thing you remember?"

"Um…" Squinting, she rubbed her forehead with her middle finger. "We danced." She faced him.

"Yes." His lip curled up in the corner. "What else?"

She took a sip of coffee and her lips peeled off her teeth as the bitter liquid descended into her stomach, warming everything in its path. Mallory focused on the far wall, as though staring would force the memories forward.

"Just let it come to you. Stop trying so hard."

She blew out her breath, and a wave of nausea flooded her. "Oh God…oh no…" Her eyes sprung open. Terror took hold again.

Wade's warm hand rested on her arm.

Mallory focused on the reassuring touch dragging her back from the brink.

"You're safe, Mallory."

She believed him. He made her feel safe. "Skylar." The name was spoken in a shaky whisper. "She's dead. Oh God. She's dead." As she cradled her face in her hands the memories flooded her.

"Do you know what happened?"

"No. I…uh…remember being overwhelmed talking to Ella and Hazel about…" She tilted her head to look Wade in the eye. "Stuff. And I needed to breathe, so I stepped out into the alley for a moment of quiet." She took another sip of the bitter liquid. "And she was there. On the ground covered by a piece of cardboard." An involuntary shiver ran through her body.

"What happened next?"

"I pulled off the cardboard. I wanted to see if she needed help. I recognized her. It was Skylar." She sighed. "Her eyes were blank—just staring up at nothing. I knew...I knew she was—" A sob caught in her throat.

"Did you see what happened?"

Her throat tightened, and she shook her head.

"You knew her?" He drummed his fingers on the table.

She nodded.

"Was she a friend?"

A half-crazed laugh escaped her. "That's a whole other story."

"Want to elaborate?" Wade raked his hands through his hair.

"Not really."

He sighed and turned his chair to face her. "Look, Mallory. I'm here to help you if I can, but you have to tell me what's going on. Poppy recognized her in the alley also, so I have to assume some relationship exists."

"Poppy? Is Poppy here?" She whipped her head toward the door.

"No. I sent everyone home. They couldn't get in here to see you anyway."

Her mental processing speed slowed, and she struggled for words. Finally, she looked back to Wade. "How did you get in here then?"

He blew out his breath. "I'm an attorney."

"You never mentioned that." She locked gazes with him. A flicker of distrust tickled her gut. Why hadn't he shared that? What else isn't he telling her?

"In what? The less than twenty-four hours I've known you."

Her shoulders drooped. "Point taken." She picked at the paper rim on her cup. "You're an attorney?"

"I don't practice anymore. I'm actually a private investigator now."

"Why the change?"

"Mallory, I don't want to be rude, but this is not the time for chit-chat. I'm trying to get the storm trooper out there to release you, and I need you to give me information so I can make that happen."

She sighed. Preparing for a huge dose of humiliation. *Maybe I should move my chair in front of the door to keep him from bolting when he finds out my pathetic story.* "Her name was Skylar. She was going to be my—"

Ralph burst through the door.

They both looked up.

"Enough already. She's answering my questions now. You've had enough time."

"No—" Wade started to protest.

Mallory touched his knee. "It's okay. I'm all right to answer his questions."

The female detective sat across from Wade.

"So you want to tell me how you lured Skylar outside?" Ralph yanked out his chair and stared down his narrow nose at Mallory.

"Come on. What kind of questioning is that?" Wade blurted.

"One that will save me a lot of time and trouble getting a confession." He glared at Mallory as he dropped into the chair.

She folded her hands and leaned forward. The coolness of the table caused goose bumps to prick her arms. "Would you like to know what happened, Ralph, or would you like to vent all your dislike of me to everyone here and make this nothing but personal?"

"It's Detective Shimkus to you. And I'm questioning a murderer, which I do take very personally. Understand that, lady." He jabbed his finger toward Mallory.

"Well, that's fascinating since there's not a murderer here." Mallory leaned back and glared.

Ralph scoffed.

"Look, Ralph." Mallory decided to try reason.

He grunted.

"Fine. Look, Detective Shimkus. I walked outside to get some air." Mallory clicked her fingernails against the table. "I saw a pair of designer shoes. I approached, wondering who would toss such an extravagant pair of shoes."

Wade chuckled.

Mallory shot him a stern glance.

Wade cleared his throat. "Sorry. Please go on." He gave a clipped wave, bringing his index finger to rest on his chin.

"The shoes were still half on Skylar's feet, and she'd been stabbed." A coldness pooled in Mallory's chest. *Skylar, are you okay?* Those glazed motionless eyes. Her pulse echoed in her ears. Diffuse blood splattering the delicate fabric. The memories were catapulting her back to those gruesome moments.

Wade touched her shoulder.

The warm hand jolted her back to the present. "I freaked out a bit after that, and everything got hazy. A girl appeared at the front of the alley, and I asked her for a phone, but she ran off, screaming."

"Some witness," Wade said, under his breath.

Narrowing his gaze, Ralph let out a low grumble.

"Anyway…I went inside to call 911, and the events get jumbled after that. Like remembering the parts of a movie you haven't seen in fifteen years. The next thing I know I'm here." She opened her hands.

"We have a witness who saw you stab the victim, Mallory," Ralph said.

"Huh? That's not possible." Mallory scrunched her forehead.

"I'm afraid so."

Who? She glanced at Wade.

"Crack ho'," Wade said.

The gaunt female in dirty ripped jeans. Her jaw dropped. "You're kidding me?" She glared at Ralph.

"Knock it off, Mallory. We all know you killed her."

Mallory's hands fisted as she raised a defiant chin. "No. I didn't."

"What motive would she possibly have for killing this person?" Wade challenged as he leaned forward.

Ralph sneered. His gaze bore into Mallory's.

She swallowed hard, knowing what followed.

"Oh, I don't know. Maybe the fact Skylar slept with Mallory's fiancé right before the wedding. How's that for motive?" Ralph's gaze traveled to Wade.

Tears welled up in her eyes, but they weren't tears of sadness. Her posture turned rigid, and her stomach burned with fury. They might not have any reason to hold her right now, but any second she planned to give them one.

****

The information stunned Wade into silence. In actuality, how well did he know this Mallory? He'd seen a lot of crazies in his days as an attorney, and they presented in all shapes and sizes. Detective Shimkus just provided two of the most common reasons for murder. Jealousy and revenge. Someone might as well have socked him in the gut. He shook his head, struggling to refocus. Surely, she didn't do this, or maybe…

He needed to regroup. To accomplish that, he had to get her out of here and stop this line of questioning. By the look in Mallory's wild eyes, she was about to give them a reason to arrest her.

"You arse!" She surged to her feet, her chair screeching across the floor, and leaned on the table.

Detective Shimkus' gaze moved back to her. He reclined.

"You got me. Man, you're some detective with those skills." She bolted upright and paced.

Wade knew he should stop her, but he wanted to hear what she planned to say. And he had to admit she'd turned from an opossum when he first walked in into a tiger ready to take down its prey. He found the transformation sort-of sexy…what kind of attorney was he?

"That's right, Ralph. I killed her. Stabbed her dead."

Okay, not what he thought she'd say. He should stop this. "Um, Mallory—"

"Yep, I drug her outside by her hair." Mallory yanked her own ponytail. "In my four-inch wedge heels and my extremely tight short-shorts."

Oh. Wade relaxed and decided to enjoy the show.

"She fought me—that she did, but my massive size was no match for her Amazon body." She turned to pace the other way. "I threw her on the ground." She flung her hands to the side and opened her fingers mimicking releasing something large. "Then I yanked out my hunting knife I usually keep for my weekend deer hunting trips." She turned to face the detectives and glared. "We all know how much vegetarians love to hunt." Jerking her chin upward, she resumed her pacing. "I yanked it out of the two-by-four inch pocket in my jacket." She patted her pocket. "And I stabbed her. Yep, you got me, dead to rights, Ralphie boy. I hope this amazing investigative work gets you a promotion."

Wade found containing his laughter difficult and kept his chin tucked to his chest. The detective's face turned so red Wade expected him to stroke out.

Mallory stopped pacing.

He let out a breath, thinking she'd finished her rant, but…

"You know what's the most amazing, Ralph, is how I did all this without one person seeing me drag her so violently outside. And then stabbed her without getting any blood on my hands or clothing, and look"—she held up the back of her hand—"I didn't even break a nail or chip my French manicure." She plopped into her chair and crossed her arms, her breathing raspy.

Guess she's done. He liked seeing the spunky, somewhat quirky, woman he met earlier had returned, even if this wasn't a joking matter. Wade cleared his throat, more to control his urge to laugh. "Detective Shimkus, do you even have a murder weapon?"

Ralph, still shades of red, narrowed his eyes at Wade. "As a matter of fact, we do. One of the deputies found it under the dumpster."

"Fingerprints?" Hopefully not hers.

"Wiped clean." Detective Shimkus glared at Mallory.

She shook her head, but said, "Yep. Me, too. Wiped it on my stockings…oh wait. I'm not wearing any." Mallory gave a noncommittal shrug.

"Mallory." Wade lifted a staying hand. "My turn to talk—okay?"

She looked at him out of the corner of her eye and stuck out her bottom lip.

"Detective. She's right, and you know it. She might not have argued her case in the most professional way, but we all know what she's talking about."

Mallory blew at a piece of hair that escaped her ponytail.

"No one saw her even argue with the victim. She simply stumbled upon the body and did the right thing by calling 911, which I'm more than sure you have the recording of."

Detective Shimkus drummed his fingers on the table.

He made a hand gesture toward Mallory. He really should have been a model on the Price is Right. "Her outfit is meticulous. It's obvious she hasn't struggled with anyone. If she had stabbed someone, she would have blood splatter somewhere, but there's nothing."

"We have a witness." He persisted.

Detective Shimkus' voice had lost some steam, and Wade knew he was gaining the upper hand. "You have an addict looking for a reward so she can score. If you want to take your witness in front of a judge, then fine. Keep Mallory in jail, and let's do it your way."

"Hey, wait…" Mallory shifted in her chair and stared.

Wade touched her arm to silence her.

She returned to pouting.

"You ready to stake your reputation on the arrest of a woman whose family is thought highly of in this tight-knit community? You have absolutely no evidence she did anything wrong, and you can't charge her for reporting a crime." Wade locked gazes with Detective Shimkus who looked ready to tear him a new one.

The detective didn't speak.

But if looks could kill Wade was mincemeat. "You've got nothing, and you can't hold her. So, if no further questions are forthcoming, we're leaving." Wade grasped Mallory firmly by the elbow until she took his lead and stood. He guided her toward the door, praying his bluff worked. The detective might call him out, which meant Mallory could be spending the night in lock-up. Wade blew out his breath as they walked through the interrogation room door.

"This isn't over yet," Shimkus said, before they were fifty feet away. "You'll be back in here before you know it, Mallory. I'm watching you."

"Oh, I feel so much better," Mallory said over her shoulder.

Wade had a death grip on her elbow. "Just keep walking, and no talking."

"Don't leave town."

Mallory spun, breaking Wade's hold. She snapped her fingers. "Gosh-darnit, there goes that trip I was planning to Cambodia."

Wade yanked her forward, almost knocking her to the ground, but quickly steadied her. "Couldn't do it, could you?"

"Nope."

In the parking lot, Wade opened the door of his truck and helped her inside. He walked around and climbed in. "You two know each other?" He started his truck.

Arms crossed over her chest, Mallory harrumphed. "High school. He made my life miserable, and he blames me."

"Want to elaborate?"

"Not really." Mallory tugged at the hem of her shorts.

Wade drug away his gaze from the motion in time to see the red light. He jammed on the brakes and the seatbelts locked.

"Geez. Drive much?" Mallory jerked on the belt to release it.

Wade gave her a brief glance. "Your fault."

"My fault?"

Her shrill voice could've called dogs from three counties over.

"How's you being a bad driver my fault?" She smacked her hand on her chest.

Wade glanced at her legs, and he moved his gaze up to her face.

Her neck and cheeks pinkened. Again, she pulled at her shorts. "They didn't look this short on the mannequin," she mumbled.

"They're nice, really…just distracting." The light changed, and he stepped on the gas pedal. "You recovered well from your shock."

"Being really pissed off can do that for a gal." She smiled.

"You got on a roll in there. I have to admit I worried when you started your rant." So much so, he started planning how to smuggle in a metal file…maybe hidden in a cake. "You have a hard time pulling back, don't you?"

"So I've been told before." She squirmed in her seat. "Kind of my biggest flaw…diarrhea of the mouth." A snort escaped.

Wade laughed. "So really. What's with you and the detective?"

Mallory sighed. "It was so long ago." She adjusted the air vents so they wouldn't blow in her face. "He kind of stalked me my last two years of high school."

"For real?" He wasn't sure where the high-pitch voice asking the question materialized from? He cleared his throat, trying again. "For real?" A little deeper than normal, but better than the voice that haunted him through puberty.

She shrugged. "If you consider breaking into my locker to leave me love notes. Telling the school I'm pregnant, and we're getting married. And following me all over the place, stalking…then yes."

"You're kidding me?"

"I wish, and he blames me for rejecting him. Granted the straw that broke the camel's back happened in front of the entire school. I laid into him and embarrassed him."

He listened as she told him the entire story. He

slackened his jaw. "Unbelievable, and this is the person protecting and serving the community?"

"I had hoped he'd changed, but he's just an older version of that high school kid. He would love to have a reason to make me miserable."

Wade parked in his driveway. "Come in for a cup of coffee?"

****

Mallory stared out the window at her parents' house. All the lights were still off. "It's four-thirty in the morning. I don't think caffeine will keep me awake, so sure." Her feet landed on the angled driveway, and she wobbled. "I hope you don't mind, these are coming off as soon as we cross your threshold."

"That's fine. Although, they're spectacular. Kind of gives you that dominatrix look."

"Great. Just great." She pinched the bridge of her nose. "Hey, is that Ella's car? Oh my gosh—did Ella and your brother hook up?" she asked in a loud whisper.

Wade choked as he opened his front door. "No. The tipsy threesome needed a designated driver. Besides, I think Matt is a bit googly-eyed over Poppy."

Mallory grinned. "Smart man. Poppy's a wonderful, not to mention absolutely stunning raven-haired beauty. Her dad is Italian, and I think she got his genes. But her pale blue eyes come from her Swedish mom." Poppy stood a couple inches shy of Mallory's height. Mallory had always been jealous at how Poppy could pull off the asymmetrical bob. An edgy style and Mallory craved the chance to be edgier, which explained the poor choice of shoes. Instead she had long straight fine hair with no volume. Pretty enough, smooth and shiny, but she'd always wanted to be a risk taker with her looks. If she cut it short, with her lack of voluptuous tatas, she'd look like a boy.

"I'm partial to blondes myself," Wade said, as Mallory walked past him.

She whipped her head around to look at him and tripped, falling to her knees.

Wade couldn't hide his laughter. He grasped her hand and tugged Mallory to her feet.

"You like to mess with people."

"A little, but doesn't make it any less true." He nudged her forward.

Mallory wasn't sure, but she thought the neighbor was flirting. Less than an hour ago, she'd been at the sheriff's department accused of murder, and now he's flirting? Surely not. She looked around his living room. Very nice, in a two-men-live-here way. The walls a pleasant tan color. Deep rich brown leather sofa and a matching love seat. A glass-topped coffee table with *Esquire, Bloomberg Weekly*, and the most recent *Sports Illustrated* swimsuit edition spread across the top. She could see the kitchen through the pass-through. She strolled through the swinging door and stepped aside so Wade could get by. The kitchen walls were a neutral almond color, but the sage, copper, and earthy yellow tile brightened the room. The mosaic backsplash colors were similar to the floor.

Wade took down a bag of coffee and set it on the island. The pots hung above, reflecting the light and creating a mirror ball effect. Stainless steel appliances were tucked in, breaking up the lines of the L-shaped granite counters.

Mallory sat at the rectangular dark hickory colored

table.

Wade put the filter in his coffee pot and added water. The pot hissed and spit as it warmed up.

She liked the easy way he moved. Self-assured and comfortable in his own skin. Someone whose presence was noticed when he walked into a room.

"Cream? Sugar?"

Mallory stared at his backside and wondered what natural wonders his shirt hid. Did he have a smooth chest, or did his shirt hide a teasing of hair just screaming to have someone rake her fingers through it. She sighed.

"Uh…Mallory." He glanced over his shoulder.

His chuckle forced her attention to the present and then to the crooked smile on his face. Heat flooded her cheeks. "I'm sorry, what? My brain is so tired, I guess I dazed off for a moment."

"I guess you did."

She could see his shoulders lightly shaking as he turned to grab a couple of mugs from the cabinet and poured coffee in them. Rubbing her hands over her face, she tried to wipe away her embarrassment.

"I asked cream or sugar?"

"Oh, both please."

He set her coffee and a plate of rich gooey-looking chocolate brownies in the middle of the table.

She snatched one. "Mmm. I just had a small stroke." Her eyes rolled back in her head. "You've met Ms. Emery?"

"My brother has. I'm just reaping the rewards of his charm."

"The day I moved home, she brought me vanilla cream-filled cupcakes. Almost made being cheated on worthwhile." She paused to savor the memory, praying no drool escaped.

Waded touched the white mark on her ring finger. "When did you take off your ring?"

Mallory swallowed. "You noticed it, huh?"

"When you were driving away this afternoon…or is it yesterday afternoon?" He waved a dismissive hand. "Are you still getting married?"

She let out a humph. "Not exactly."

"Exactly what then? I mean if you love him couples have worked through infidelity."

"You sure have gotten a dose of Mallory's personal life in the last twenty-four hours." She stirred cream and sugar into her coffee, tapped the spoon on the side, and placed it on a napkin.

"You want to tell me the whole story?" He situated his cup on a napkin.

She slumped her head forward onto her waiting folded arms. The table muffled her, "No."

"You don't have to. I mean…I already picked up on the fact a girl you knew, or had been friends with, slept with your fiancé. Not much of a friend."

Without lifting her head from her arms she rolled it to the side, so she could study him. He seemed trustworthy. Over just a few hours, he'd been there for her in a way Kyle hadn't for their entire relationship. "It's worse." She groaned and sat up. "How much do you want to know?"

"As much as you want to share." He took a sip of coffee.

"This will require chocolate." And an injection of self-esteem.

Wade slid the plate toward her.

She pursed her lips sizing up which brownie was the largest. Happy with her selection, she placed the brownie on a napkin.

He shifted back the plate and her hand whipped out, stopping the movement. His brows rose.

She smirked and grabbed another one. "This is at least a two-brownie story."

"You already ate one."

How dare he keep track. She felt the tick start under her right eye. She'd had a rotten day and if chocolate made her feel better, then that's her prerogative. Mallory's unrelenting glare must have clued him in to his gargantuan mistake.

"By all means then." He removed his hands from the plate. Then he pointed to the plate, obviously asking permission to enjoy his own baked goods.

Mallory grinned and nodded. Good, she had him scared now.

He took a brownie and bit into it. "Wow. These are good. I'll have to introduce myself."

Mallory swallowed the bite she'd taken. "Skylar and I used to be close. She was the fifth musketeer in our girls' group in high school. We all stayed in contact through college and visited whenever we could, but we were going down our own paths. Our studies and preparation for our future careers took us different directions. Skylar studied Political Science, Poppy was in Accounting, and I studied Fashion Merchandising, so things changed for all of us."

"You work in merchandising?" His brownie stopped halfway to his mouth.

"Hey, don't act so surprised. Walking around glammed up all the time would be like taking work home. All ladies like a comfy pair of sweats. I'm kind of like the hairdresser with dark roots and a terrible cut that does hair really well."

"I didn't say you weren't glam. I mean look at those shoes." Wade glanced at the floor.

She let her gaze drift to the shoes lying askew in front of her chair. Her bare cherry blossom pink polished toes kicked at them. "That's not fashion, it's a torture device. Anyway, I'm good at reading fashion trends."

"You were saying?" He leaned his forearms on the tabletop.

"Huh? Oh, yeah. I met Kyle at Northern Illinois University"—she glanced at Wade—"my fiancé, the end of my freshman year, and by the end of my sophomore year, we were dating." She took another bite of her brownie and a sugar shiver vibrated through her. The ooey-gooey goodness teetered on the edge of causing a seizure. "After we graduated, moving in together was the next logical step. I was twenty-two when we got engaged."

"How old are you?"

"Twenty-six."

He cradled his mug between both hands. "Long engagement." He raised his left brow.

"I kept putting it off. Three times." She held up her last three fingers, the final bite of a brownie clutched between her index and thumb. "This time I planned to go through with it, or so I thought." She started on the second brownie. "Skylar and I grew close. She drove into the city frequently with her work, so meeting Kyle once the wedding grew close was only natural. She insisted on coming over to help me with the wedding details when she was in town, and we'd all hang out." She tore at the napkin. "To make a long story short. I guess Kyle and Skylar grew together." She shrugged.

"Sounds simple for someone who still wore their engagement ring yesterday morning." He shot her a serious look.

Mallory took a second to refocus. Wade's gaze held an intensity capable of making all her dirty secrets spill forth. She dry swallowed. "I thought he made me everything I was supposed to be." How humiliating.

"Why did he need to make you anything? What's wrong with who you are?"

He touched her hand briefly, leaving a feather soft imprint. "You haven't met my family."

"Not yet, but if they are anything like you, then I'd like to." He smiled and got up, their mugs in hand.

"Sure you say that now, but they're crazy. I mean truly crazy...but wonderful too." She warmed at the thought of her family.

He poured more coffee.

His shirt stretched taut across his trapezius as he leaned over to put back the pot. *Focus, Mallory.* "He was safe...or so I thought. Then two weeks before our scheduled wedding, I arrived home a day early from a buying trip. Guess who was warming my spot in our bed?" Queasiness replaced the prior pleasantness her introspection regarding her family had occupied.

"I'm sorry, Mallory."

She waved her hand. "Don't be. I hurt, but more from all my self-esteem issues of never feeling like enough. You know, why settle for me when someone better will come along?" She stirred another spoon of sugar into her refill. "In an odd way, I felt relieved. I had my reason to get out of the wedding for good, and I was at peace with that choice. I didn't love him. I cared for him, but never shared that toe-curling love. He was safe and predictable...well, most of the time." She gave a short laugh.

"Letting go of the familiar can be hard." The chair creaked as Wade leaned back.

"True, but I realize now I found the familiar boring. In a way, Skylar did me a favor." She blew steam from her coffee and took a drink. "Did I mention she was my maid of honor?"

Wade laughed. "I'm sorry, I didn't mean to. It's just...it's just so..."

Mallory held up her hand. "*Telenovela*?"

"Yeah, I guess." He ran a hand down his face. "Do you miss him?"

Wade's fixed gaze told her more than mere curiosity motivated his question. Her cheeks warmed, and she broke the stare. "Sadly no. What does that say about me? I'm willing to marry for all the wrong reasons. Pathetic."

"You didn't, though, and you're anything but pathetic."

"Thanks." She sighed. "I guess you can see why this makes me the perfect suspect in her murder."

For a moment, Wade didn't say anything. "Things are not always what they seem, are they?" He wiped the brownie crumbs from the table. "Can I ask you one last thing about this?"

"You got me out of jail—shoot."

"Why did you keep wearing the ring if the relationship was over?" He locked his penetrating gaze on hers.

She sucked in a breath. "Wow. You don't pull punches, do you?"

He smiled and waited.

She relaxed a bit. "Truth is, I don't know why. Maybe I felt I was less of a failure as long as I wore it. Maybe after almost four years of wearing the ring, I felt naked without it. Or, maybe I would turn back into that crazy girl who belonged to the nutty family across the street if I took it off." She swirled her coffee.

Wade gently laid his fingertips against the skin on her hand. "Mallory, you're enough just as you are, and you don't need someone in your life who doesn't recognize how special you are."

They stared at each other for what felt like an eternity. She shifted in her seat. "Again, you haven't met my family. Trust me—special will take on a whole other meaning." She chuckled. "I have a question for you."

"Shoot. I'm an open book."

"Why did you quit practicing the law?"

The color drained from his face. He recovered. "That's a long story for another day."

"Why not now, open book?"

He snorted. "Because it's too early for the liquor required to get me through that story."

"Rain check?" she asked, with a sideways glance.

Wade nodded. "Rain check."

Mallory grabbed her shoes and stood. "I guess I should get home—before my parents are up, and I get the fifth degree about being out all night."

Wade walked her to the door and followed her out onto the porch.

They stood facing each other. "Wade, thanks for

everything you did for me this morning."

He tucked an escaped hair from her ponytail behind her ear. His thumb traveled down her jaw.

Her stomach plunged to her toes, and a heat flash surged through her in contradiction with the cool morning air. *Oh my. He's going to kiss me. What if I don't know how to kiss anyone but Kyle? What if he thinks I kiss like a dead fish? What…what if he doesn't want to kiss me?* A yip pierced the air.

Wade dropped his hand to his side, and their attention diverted across the street.

Zehn curled into a "C" position in the front yard.

Mallory shook her head. Time to give Wade a taste of the crazy family.

"Come on you stupid mutt. You've had me up every hour on the hour. Surely you've got no crap left." Jim's voice carried. He stood on the front porch with a sleeping mask pushed up on his forehead, making his still-thick graying hair stand straight up. He had obviously grabbed her mom's knee-length orange, pink, green, and yellow fuzzy floral robe. Mallory spotted his mismatched knee-highs from where she stood—one in purple, the other in yellow. He finished the ensemble with a pair of brown wingtip dress shoes. "And that's my dad." Mallory half sighed and half chuckled.

"Huh. Nice gams." Wade gave a low wolf-whistle.

"I'll let him know." She started forward, reaching the first step before Zehn let loose a wild bark. She'd been spotted. Zehn drug his butt the length of the yard until he contacted the sidewalk. Then he sprung to all fours and bolted across the street.

"Hey. Hey! Zehn, you get back…" Her dad's gaze met hers.

Mallory lifted her hand in a still wave. "Hey, Dad," she said so only Wade could hear. "And no, I'm not sleeping with the neighbor." She sighed as Zehn bound onto the porch. "Hey, baby." She stooped and scratched under his chin. "Did you miss me?"

Zehn licked the side of her face.

"Who's this?" Wade stroked Zehn's back.

"Zehn. Zehn meet Wade." He focused on Mallory.

She held her hand in the shake position. Zehn lifted his paw.

Wade took it. "You're kidding, right?" He furrowed his forehead.

"Does it look like it?" She giggled. "He's a smart boy."

"Very." He rubbed Zehn's ears. "Zehn is an interesting name. How did you come up with it?"

"Just made sense. The path I always jogged before going to work ended on a cul-de-sac on Tenth Street. An old abandoned Victorian house stood on the corner, and over several days, I saw this scroungy dog flee underneath the porch whenever I neared. After about four days of this, I had to know if the pup was okay and returned armed with biscuits. He bolted, and I sat on the ground in front of the porch and waited. Finally, he peeked out his head, and I tossed a treat. After retreating in fear, he eventually crawled back out to see what I'd thrown. A few more and about an hour later, he crawled out to check me. Didn't let me touch him at first, but the food had him curious. I gave him my last one and got to my feet with the plan to come back over several days with food until he trusted me." She stroked Zehn's head. "Didn't take long. On my way home, I heard footsteps behind me. He was hot on my tail." She smoothed the hair in her ponytail. "I'm sorry, what was the question?"

Wade laughed. "The name, but I think I got it."

"Really?"

"Yeah had Intro to German in high school. The only thing I remember is how to count to twenty."

"You are correct. Zehn is ten in German, and he's a German Shepherd. I mean there really wasn't any choice." She bumped him with the side of her arm.

"Oh my God!" Wade gagged, and they both covered their nose and mouth.

"Gross. I think I got the stench in my mouth." Mallory wiped her tongue on her jacket.

"It smells like a sewer exploded. What is that?"

Mallory looked down at Zehn who made a low growl and skewed up his face into a dopey "what" look. "Chicken liver." She fanned the air under her nose with her hands.

"Nasty. Wait, what?" Wade still breathed into the crook of his elbow and took a step back.

"Never mind. I have to go scold my dad now. Thanks for all you did today." She walked down the porch steps, Zehn in tow.

Mallory strode up to her dad who waited on the porch. "Chicken livers, huh?"

"The dog can lick his own butt, but he can't handle a few livers? Doesn't make sense."

"I warned you."

"I didn't believe you. I do now." Jim laughed. "Didn't come home last night?"

"Doesn't look like it, does it?" She glanced down at her outfit and shook her hand holding the shoes.

Hurt crossed her dad's face.

"Sorry, Dad. I didn't mean to snap. Look, I'm really tired. Let me get four or five hours sleep, and I will tell you all about my eventful evening."

Jim threw up his hands and stepped back. "Hey…ho. I get you're all grown up, but certain things we don't need to share."

"Honestly, Dad, my being out all night isn't what you think. But I'm so tired I couldn't begin to tell you right now what happened." She patted his arm. "Oh, and give Zehn a couple tablespoons of bismuth. That should help."

He followed her into the house. "Great, so he can have diarrhea and crap pink. Sounds perfect." He scowled at Zehn who wagged his tail.

"Actually it'll be dark blackish." She waved off further explanation. "Trust me, Dad. The meds will help. Just grab the syringe I keep in the dog cabinet and squirt the medicine in his mouth."

"Sure, no problem. Squirting bismuth in a dog's mouth, piece of cake."

She glanced back to see him roll his eyes. "Hey, you created the problem, you fix it," she said, continuing up the stairs yearning for her bed.

Chapter Four

Warm moist air blew across her face. She sunned herself on a sailboat floating in the Caribbean, watching dolphins jump out of the water in front of her. She tilted her face upward, absorbing the rays, as she stared at the brilliant, cloudless, blue sky. The wind carried the fragrance of…she sniffed. Bubble gum? And…she sniffed again. Tuna?

Mallory's eyes fluttered open, coming face-to-face with Zehn resting on her spare pillow less than six inches from her head. His legs splayed in the air, and head turned to the left, snoring softly. Mallory rolled to the other side and grabbed the clock. Twelve sixteen brightly displayed in red. She dropped her forearm over her eyes, allowing all of the evening's events to return. She groaned.

Zehn awoke and flipped over, resting his chin on her belly.

"Hey, big guy." Mallory scratched his head. "That's the best good morning…good afternoon, I've had in a while." Another ten minutes ticked by until she found enough energy to drag herself to the bathroom. She rinsed, spit, and ran her fingers through her hair. Time to face the parents.

Her parents sat at the table, eating sandwiches.

Mallory took a deep breath and shuffled into the room. "What's for breakfast?" She swore a crew of miniature people performed the wave in her gut. Having her parents angry with her she could take, but disappointed ripped out her heart.

Both stopped chewing and stared.

Jim swallowed and took a drink of milk. "Glad you could join us."

Mallory stuck her head in the fridge and shifted a few containers around. "How's Zehn doing?"

"Bismuth seems to have worked. He's bound up like a plugged drain." Jim took another bite.

"Although he took four tries, half a bottle of bismuth, and a clean shirt to get the task done." Charlotte got up to put her dish in the sink.

Mallory closed the fridge, holding a container of vanilla Greek yogurt in hand.

Both parents watched her every motion.

"What?" She opened the drawer for a spoon.

Charlotte returned to her barely cold chair. "Nothing." Jim and Charlotte said in unison and made a failed attempt to turn their attention elsewhere. Jim opened up a sale ad from the paper, and Charlotte started guzzling her milk.

Mallory swallowed a spoonful of yogurt and leaned her back against the counter so she faced both parents. *Thump...thump...thump.* Her heart clobbered her ribcage. A slow deep breath. "I got arrested last night for murder." Well, that came out easier than planned. She shoveled another spoonful of yogurt into her mouth.

Charlotte spit milk out all over Jim and his sale ad.

"Geez, Charlotte," he grumbled, using his napkin to wipe his face and blot the table.

Charlotte gaped wide-eyed as she wiped her mouth

on her sleeve. "That's not funny, Mallory."

"Not kidding." Mallory took the aspirin bottle from the cabinet and shook three into her open palm. She swallowed them dry, walked across the room, and sat at the table.

"Young lady, you need to explain yourself and do it quick before my heart palpitations send me to the hospital." Jim pressed his hand to his chest.

"What kind of joke is this? Is it April first, Jim? It's not April yet, is it?" Tight lines were prominent on Charlotte's forehead.

"No, still March twenty-ninth…all day, darlin'."

Mallory sighed and set her empty container of yogurt on the table. The weight of the spoon caused it to fall over and the *tink* of the metal hitting the table made them all jump. *Where do I begin?* "I went out with the girls last night—"

"We know you went out with your friends last night." Charlotte's voice hit a shrill note. "I thought you might come home with an S-A-D, not a mug shot!"

"S-T-D, Mom."

"S-T what?"

"Sexual Transmitted Disease." Jim scratched the back of his head. Probably wondering why he'd joined in this part of the conversation.

"That's what I said…you did get one." Charlotte pointed at Mallory.

"You said S-A-D, it's S-T-D, Mom." Mallory's head hit the table. "Never mind, it doesn't matter."

"Well, someone dying most certainly matters," Charlotte said.

"What?" Mallory's head jerked upright, her forehead scrunched. "No one died from an S-T-D."

"People die from S-T-Ds all the time." Jim nodded.

Mallory shook her head and grasped the bridge of her nose. "Okay. Let's try this again. No one died from an S-T-D last night."

"But you said…" Charlotte began, looking between them, brows wrinkled.

Mallory cut her off with a raised hand. "If I'm gonna get through this story, I need you two to be quiet. I've had a trying evening, and this morning my head feels like a fat porcupine is running wild inside."

"If you hadn't spent the night with that man, you wouldn't be worried about an S-T-D." Jim peered down his nose.

Mallory sat dumbfounded. Her mouth agape.

"What man gave you an S-A-D?"

Mallory slammed her open palm on the table. "Will you two stop with the S-T-D talk? I don't have an S-T-D. Now please! I need you to listen."

Charlotte didn't blink for at least a minute. "Don't get so upset. We can get you some ointment or antibiotics or something."

This time, Mallory's forehead hit the table hard enough to give a slight bounce. "Ow," she said in a feeble voice. She rolled her head side-to-side. After a moment, she heaved it upright and brushed her hair from her face. "This is important, and I need you to listen. Do not contribute to the conversation…at least not until the end, and I'll answer your questions…reasonable ones at least. Okay? Nod if you can do that."

Jim's mouth opened.

Mallory clamped her fingers to her thumb, signaling *shut it.*

Jim did and then nodded.

She glanced at her mom who made the "turn the lock and toss the key" symbol on her mouth. "Good. Thank you." She recounted the details of the previous evening and when she finished, both parents were speechless for the first time in her life. At least for ten seconds of said life.

"So you don't have an S-A-D?" Charlotte asked.

Hysterical laughter overtook Mallory, and she couldn't stop. Tears poured from her eyes. Jim squinted as he made eye contact with Charlotte who rubbed her index finger across her chin while pursing her lips. They both ended their unspoken conversation and glanced back to her. "You know. You two are the best parents ever." She wiped at the corners of her eyes.

"Do you need an attorney?" Jim asked.

She could tell he grasped the seriousness of her situation. "I don't know. Maybe, but I'll wait and see what the authorities' next move is," Mallory said.

"This can't be happening." Charlotte's voice found her again. "You're too pretty to go to jail…and…and you'll end up being Big Bertha's bitch."

Mallory's jaw slackened, and she looked to her dad who shrugged.

"They delouse you and make you wear an orange jumpsuit." Her hand covered her throat. "Oh, honey. You look terrible in orange." She cradled her face in her hands.

Mallory made a mental note to throw out the orange T-shirt she bought last week. "Is that really her biggest concern out of everything I've said?" she asked her dad.

Jim shrugged. "She's been like this ever since we

got cable. I don't know what's wrong with the six channels we used to get. I got football and the news. What else did I need?"

"Mom, I don't think they delouse you unless you actually have lice." Mallory froze. "What am I saying? Look what you've done to me, Mom. I'm talking about delousing." She shook her head. "You have got to stop with all the late-night crime shows. They're affecting your reality."

"You won't be saying that when I prepare you for the pokey."

Charlotte looked so serious Mallory lost it again. "Mom. Stop. Please. This conversation is getting absurd, and my head hurts to laugh."

"You won't be laughing when Big Bertha chooses your pretty blonde head for her—"

"Charlotte!" Jim cut her off.

Mallory doubled over, gasping for breath between her fits of laughter.

"What? She needs to be prepared," Charlotte said.

"She's not going to jail, honey. She didn't kill anyone." Jim swept his open palm in Mallory's direction.

Mallory stood and took a bottle of water from the refrigerator. She twisted open the top, giving herself time to let her giggles subside. "Aw, Mom. You truly are one of a kind. I wasn't sure I would laugh after last night, but sure enough."

Charlotte's mouth flattened into a firm line. "How did you make bail?"

"Huh? Oh, I totally lost my place with all the Big Bertha talk." Mallory waved her hand. "I don't think I was officially arrested. More along the lines of questioned and released."

"Why didn't you start with that?" Jim crossed both arms over his chest. "You said arrested."

"Well, they put me in handcuffs and hauled me down to the sheriff's department in the backseat of a police car."

"Thugs pee in the backseat of cop cars. You might still need delousing!" Charlotte tore at the corner of her napkin.

"Gross, Mom."

"That sounds like arrested to me," Jim said.

"They didn't fingerprint me or take my "mug shot" as Mom said. They questioned me." She didn't want to get into the shock part. Her mom already teetered on the edge. "Anyway, Wade and Matt, the two guys who moved in across the street…" She pointed over her shoulder. "They were at the bar, and Wade is…or was an attorney. He got me released."

"So, you have an attorney?" Jim rubbed his temple.

"Not really, he doesn't practice any longer. But he knew they didn't have any evidence to hold me and made Shimkus release me."

"Shimkus? Ralph Shimkus? The boy who got you pregnant in high school?" Charlotte's eyes bulged.

The drink of water Mallory took stopped in mid descent and rocketed right up into her nose. Coughing racked her body. She pounded on her chest.

Jim jumped up and patted her back.

"I'm okay," she said in a hoarse whisper.

Jim returned to his seat.

"Mom, he didn't get me pregnant. Sex is required for that…or have you learned differently on cable?"

Charlotte pursed her lips. "I'm well aware of the

process. I made you after all. I just meant he's the ornery boy from high school who made your senior year so difficult."

"Yes, that's him. Apparently, he's a detective now."

"You've got to be kidding me." Jim vaulted from his seat. "Don't they have to pass some psychological testing or something? That boy was one slice short of a loaf." He collapsed onto his chair.

"I wondered the same thing. I don't feel great about him heading up the investigation. If he can find a way to pin the crime on me, he will." Mallory plopped into her chair.

"How could they think you would be tied up in the murder of anyone?" Jim looked her straight in the eye.

Mallory swallowed and studied the yogurt container on the table. She set it upright, and it fell over again.

"Mallory. What aren't you saying?" Jim took the empty container from her hands.

"Did I forget to mention the person was Skylar?" Mallory tucked her chin so close to her neck the position stifled her voice. The ticking from the clock above the sink filled the room. She glanced from her mom to her dad, who were both unblinking. "Say something…please."

"This is bad." Charlotte ripped up the shreds left of her napkin.

"That's the girl who Kyle—"

"Yes, Dad." Mallory cut off the rest of his sentence.

"Oh dear," he said with a shake of his head.

"Yes, Dad, and this entire small town is aware I've

been cheated on by my maid of honor with my fiancé. So with that said, I'm the perfect suspect." Mallory sighed and tucked her hair behind her ears.

"But you didn't do it?" Charlotte wrung her hands.

Mallory's gaze snapped to her mother's. "Is that a question, Mom?"

Charlotte shook her head. "No. No. No. Of course, you didn't do it. We both know that. Right, Jim?"

He stayed silent, and both heads turned toward him.

"Hmm? What? Oh no, of course we know that, honey. I was just thinking," Jim said.

"About what?" A tinge of uncertainty lined Mallory's stomach. If her parents didn't believe her...

"About just how small of a town this is, and how eighty-five percent of them are no good busy bodies."

"I know, Dad. I considered moving back out to the city until this is resolved, but I'm afraid that might make me look like I'm running."

"No. You need to be here where your friends and family can support you. This will all blow over once they find the real killer anyway. We just have to ride out this mess until then." Jim patted Mallory's hand. "You stay here, and that's final."

"Thanks, guys. I'm glad to have your support. This is such a disaster, and I don't know how I stepped into the middle. All I wanted was a night out to not think about those two, and now this." She buried her face in her hands.

"Honey, why don't you go take Zehn for a walk? It's such a beautiful spring day. A stroll always makes you feel better."

Charlotte's suggestion was on point. Fresh air was

just what Mallory needed. Well, that and a miracle. "I think I will. And thanks for listening, guys."

"We love you, honey, and we won't let that Shimkus boy ruin your reputation again. I'll see to that." Jim slammed a fist on the table.

Mallory's throat tightened, and she could no longer speak. She really did love her nutty family.

Chapter Five

The trees bent ever so slightly in the breeze. Mallory walked to the beat of the music thumping through her ear buds. She entered Mill Park, located at the end of her parents' block. She loved how the walking path skirted the twenty-five acre lake. Kids laughed and screamed as they ran around on the playground. A young girl hung by her knees on a set of bars, and Mallory cringed as she did a cherry drop. Visions of emergency room visits danced in her head. But the girl landed on both feet and jumped for the bar, getting in to position for a repeat performance.

Zehn yanked on the leash and tugged Mallory forward.

"Okay. I get it, no stationary people watching."

Halfway around the lake, Mallory paused and her cell phone vibrated in her pocket. They'd reached an isolated area so she turned Zehn loose to play in the water. She sat on the sandy bank, yanked out her ear buds, and plucked her cell from her pocket. Restricted caller. "Hmm." She considered not answering it, but with everything going on, she was afraid not to. Tapping the green answer button, she then held her phone to her ear. "Hello." Silence. "Hello?" Silence. "I can hear you breathing so either speak, or I hang up." Silence. "Fine—"

"Wait. Don't hang up."

Nausea unrelated to her hangover made the yogurt roll into her throat. Her turn to be silent.

"Mallory? Are you still there?"

"What do you want?" she said, in a hoarse whisper.

"To talk."

"About what?" Her grip should've snapped her phone in two.

"Skylar." He let the word hang.

Mallory shivered despite the warm breeze. The moisture in her mouth dried up.

"Your little town made the national news this morning."

"Fantastic. What, a slow news day for the rest of the world? Just my luck." Mallory chewed on the corner of her lip. "What do you want, Kyle?"

"I told you. To talk."

She stared so hard at a family of Canada Geese gliding through the water her eyes burned. "So talk." Mallory spoke through clenched teeth.

"You don't have to be so cold. We were together for a long time. We were good together." Kyle paused.

Waiting for her to agree she assumed. "Not as good as you and Skylar." Her words sounded bitter.

"Don't, baby—"

"Don't call me baby." She cut him off. "I'm not your baby. Not anymore."

"Mallory. I miss you."

Mallory raked her free hand through her hair. "You miss me? Your new girlfriend was killed last night, and you miss me?" Her voice raised an octave. "What's the matter with you? I didn't know you at all."

"Skylar wasn't my girlfriend. What she and I had together wasn't like what we had…what we have."

"What was it then?" She paused. "Forget it, don't tell me. I don't want to know." Mallory stopped and watched as Zehn swam after a duck.

"You know you still love me."

"Huh? I what?" She sucked in a deep breath. "Kyle, truth be told, I never loved you." Something cut into her left palm, making her look down. Her nails. She opened her palm and stared at the impression left behind.

"You don't mean that, baby."

"I'm—not—your—baby!" Realizing she'd shouted, she glanced around for onlookers. "And I mean every word. Get this through your head, you were safe for me. You were the opposite of everything I had in my life." Her body shook to the point her voice vibrated. "A life I was running from. I hid who I really was…am, and you were my mask. I never loved you. Understand that."

"How can you say that after what you did for us?" Kyle's voice whined into the phone.

Mallory's mind blanked. *What is he talking about? What did I do for us?* She thought back about something she did or said he could have misconstrued, but nothing brought clarity to his statement.

"Baby—sorry. Mallory, for you to take such extreme measures, you have to love me."

He can't think that. Mallory's heart pounded. Her air sucked away from her lungs.

"Skylar wasn't ever a risk to what we had. I'm sorry you didn't fully understand that before…"

"Oh my God!" Her entire body tensed to the point she thought a tendon would snap.

"I'll be by your side through the trial. I'll get you

the best representation my family can buy."

Tear of rage stung her eyes. "You think I killed her!"

Silence. "The news said—"

"What? What did the news say?"

Zehn walked over and leaned into her.

Instinct made her stroke him, not caring about the dampness of his fur.

"That...that you were a person of interest. I thought after everything that happened—"

"Ha! You thought I knocked her off in a fit of jealousy. Over the likes of you?" She stroked Zehn faster. "You're a fool, Kyle. If anything, I would've shook her hand. She did me a favor, opening my eyes to the kind of man you truly are. Skylar saved me from a lifetime of misery and grief."

"But the news said..."

His voice sounded small, unsure. "I don't care what the news said. It's called sensationalism, Kyle. And for you to think I'm capable of something so horrific...well, you never really knew me at all." Her muscles ached. "I got to go. I can't do this." She pulled the phone from her ear.

"Baby. I'm sorr—"

Mallory clicked off the phone. Fury ran through her body. She cocked back her arm to throw it into the lake and stopped. She still had a year left on her contract. Thankful that good sense prevailed. "Ass...ass...ass...ass...ass-wipe." Her outburst drew stares from a couple on the opposite side of the lake. Good acoustics. She wrapped her arms around Zehn, burying her face in his wet furry neck gave her an instant boost.

Zehn rested his paw on her knee.

"You always know what to do to make me feel better." After a moment, her adrenaline high subsided and her heart rate returned to normal, so she released Zehn and stood. She brushed the wet grass from her butt and marched on. When her cell vibrated again, she glanced down at Restricted Caller and slid her finger over the screen, refusing the call.

Her gut churned during the remainder of the stroll. What had the news reported about her involvement? *All I did was call 911.* She gnawed on her thumb's cuticle as she walked down the street to her parents' house. *If the news is calling me a person of interest, that detail will be all over this town by five. How would they have gotten a hold of the information?* She stopped in her tracks. "Shimkus."

Zehn looked up.

"It's okay, Zehn. I'm all right." *That man is out to get me.*

****

Familiar laughter carried from across the street. Mallory veered off the sidewalk and crossed the road, Zehn at her heels. Sun reflected off a mass of long brazen auburn hair spiraling midway down a petite lady's back. Mallory smiled. Ella had more hair than anything else. She stood barely five-foot-two, but she wouldn't tolerate being called five-foot-one and three quarters. The sound of her heart-filled laughter could put down a man twice her size.

Ella waved as Mallory approached.

She always wondered how Ella kept her ivory complexion from burning, but she never sustained even a hint of sunburn on her perfect skin. The only markings derived were a dusting of freckles across her nose, which matched the reddish-brown flecks in her chestnut eyes. "Hey, guys," Mallory said.

"Jailbird." Poppy embraced her. "Matt filled us in on the rest of your excursion after we left."

"I'm out, thanks to Wade. Ralph wanted to lynch me on the spot."

"Ralph has been obsessed with you since high school. To this day, he won't let go of the fact you weren't interested." Ella gave Mallory's hand a squeeze. "He's kind of scary in an I've-lost-my-mind way."

"Wade gave me the down low on the detective fellow. Said he's a real piece of work." Matt slid his computer bag to the ground and repositioned the books he held.

She could hear the calm reassuring tone of Wade's voice replaying in her mind. Having him in the interrogation room with her gave her much-needed courage. "Please thank him for me again. He should've run in terror after meeting the wacky neighbors' daughter, but he just stepped right into the slime pit. He's a good guy."

"I'll tell him everything but the good guy part. I have to live with him and don't want it going to his head." Matt gave a subtle wink.

A soft laugh emitted from Mallory. "Whatcha doing over here?" she asked Ella and Poppy, but she skimmed her gaze between Poppy and Matt.

Poppy's neck turned shades of red. "I brought Ella to pick up her car."

"I told her." Matt pointed to Ella. "I would bring it over once Wade got home from work, but I guess a girl needs her car." He repositioned his books again.

Mallory covered her mouth and leaned next Ella's ear. "But then Poppy wouldn't have had an excuse to stop by."

Ella snorted and nodded.

Poppy glared at them.

Books titled *Critical Analysis for the Social Worker*, *Policies on Social Work*, and *Community Outreach for Wayward Youth* loaded down Matt's arms.

"Riveting stuff." Mallory tapped his books.

"Thesis time. Not a lot of fun, but a necessary evil." Matt rearranged his load. "Well, ladies, as much as I'd love to stay and chat with you beauties, I need to get this stuff inside." He winked in Poppy's direction.

"Let me help you." Poppy didn't wait for a response, snatching the top book and picked up the laptop bag resting at his feet.

Mallory stepped forward. "Oh, I can grab something—"

Poppy splayed her hand over Mallory's face and nudged her back before she could get out her offer. "We've got this," she said, in a saccharine-sweet voice.

The glare she shot Mallory over her shoulder would've stopped a speeding bullet. She blew her a kiss.

"You know she's been dying for some alone time with him," Ella said.

"Figured as much. That's what made it so much fun." Mallory faced Ella and smiled.

"You're rotten."

"Like you weren't doing the same thing."

"Sure was." Ella put her arm through Mallory's as

they walked toward her bug.

Zehn let loose a shrill yip.

"Sorry, big guy, were we ignoring you?" Ella released Mallory to crouch and give him a good belly rub. She stood and leaned against her car door. "How are you really doing after your ordeal?"

Mallory shrugged. "I'm okay right now, but I can't say having Ralph on this doesn't worry me."

"He can't manufacture evidence that doesn't exist. Can he?" Ella's eyes widened.

"No...no...no...he can't do that. He'd lose his job. Right?" Mallory leaned on the car next to Ella.

"Saw the news this morning."

A weighted sensation dropped from Mallory's head into her feet. She summoned the effort to kick at a pebble. "I missed the broadcast, but I gathered from Kyle I'm listed as a person of interest."

Ella whipped around in front of Mallory. "Kyle? You gathered from Kyle? When was this?"

"Oh, about thirty minutes ago. He called me." Mallory studied her feet. "He thought I killed her because of my lustful feelings for him." She rolled the rock under her shoe, leaving a white mark on the sidewalk. "Guess he doesn't realize my only feelings for him now are disgust."

"Unbelievable! His new girlfriend dies, and the first thing he can think to do is call his ex? What a dirt bag." Ella's hair bounced with each word.

"Tell me."

"Disaster averted with him." Ella bumped her with an elbow. "Pawned that ring yet?"

Mallory snickered, but a little pang of failure vibrated through her.

"I better head on home. For some reason, I have a hellish headache. And I never want to see another lemon again in my lifetime." Ella grasped the door handle.

Mallory laughed. "Amen to that."

Ella drove away.

As Mallory watched her leave, she spotted a black Dodge Charger parked at the end of the street. One Mallory noticed before leaving on her walk. The driver chose an inconspicuous spot in the shade of the large oak tree, but all the shininess and polished chrome trim screamed look at me. The hum of an engine resonated in her ears. Wade's truck passed in front of her line of vision, breaking her trance as he turned into his driveway.

She ambled up her parents' sidewalk and sat on the top step of the porch, letting Zehn enjoy his nap in the sunshine. Wade waved and Mallory lifted her arm high returning the gesture, before he disappeared behind his house. The sun soaked into her skin and she leaned back on her elbows, stretching out her legs to rest on the edge of the five remaining steps. *Now this is a cure for a hangover.*

"How are you doing?"

Mallory's elbows slipped from the step, and her head whacked it.

"I'm sorry. Are you okay?" A strong hand encircled her upper arm and hauled her upright.

Her eyes fluttered open. The inside of her head sounded like church bells ringing in a tower. The shadow of a man towered over her, but she wasn't processing recognition.

His head blocked the sun, providing a halo effect.

Is this heaven?

"How many fingers do I have up?"

What?

"Mallory, focus. How many fingers do I have up?"

The ringing subsided. *Wade.* She swatted his hand from in front of her face. "Didn't you just go into your house?" Her senses trickled back.

He stood upright. "About ten minutes ago."

"Geesh. Really? I must have dozed off." She rubbed the back of her head. "Ouch."

"Let me see." Wade maneuvered behind her and ran his fingertips through her hair.

Stroking her scalp. "Mmm." She leaned into him. "I'll give you thirty minutes to stop—ouch!" His magic fingers found the tender spot.

"You were saying?" His hands disengaged from her head.

"Never mind." She smoothed down the back of her hair. "Don't tell my mom. She watched a program on post-concussion syndrome, and she'll be all over me with questions she heard on the show. She'll probably start documenting my every movement and wake me up every couple of hours for the next week."

Wade's forehead scrunched. "Seems extreme for a bump."

She waved a hand. "Not to her. My mom has always been a bit of an extremist."

He stared in silence. "I've got to meet your mom."

"No you don't, she watches way too much cable." An uncontrollable chuckle followed. She sighed and averted her gaze to Zehn, who had no modesty, splaying his hind legs wide.

"Still recovering from last night?"

"Yeah, and that wop on my head did nothing for my headache."

Wade sat. "Let's try this again. How are you doing?"

"I'm fine…all things considered." Mallory picked at a section of peeling paint from the porch steps. "What drags you over here?"

He stretched his legs out, crossing them at the ankle. "Some heavy petting in my living room."

She laughed, turning her head to face him. She put up her hand to block the sun from her eyes. "Poppy?"

"Think they've hit it off. I felt creepy hanging out in the kitchen and there was no way for me to get to my bedroom without crossing their path. And the noises they were making…" He shuddered. "Let's just say I don't need to hear my brother make those sounds." His nose crinkled.

"Banished from his own house in the name of L-O-V-E." Mallory faced forward, chuckling. She returned her gaze to the car, still parked.

"Hope you don't mind the company." He followed her gaze.

"Of course not. You can escape to my porch anytime."

"Sounds promising."

She momentarily shifted her gaze back and half smiled. *He's a good flirt, and I'm enjoying the attention way too much.*

"What's with the unmarked cop car?" Wade nodded in the vehicle's direction.

The muscles in her stomach stiffened. "I thought that's what the car was. It's been parked for a while, and I can't see through the tinted windows. I think someone is inside though. Looked like a shadow moving in there."

"Your detective friend?"

She scowled. Ralph's words of warning echoed in her mind. "You think? Wouldn't that be stalking?" She squinted her eyes and put the side of her hand to her forehead.

"It's a public street." He shrugged.

"I guess but weirds me out." She scooted up a step.

"One way to find out for sure." Wade stood and headed down the walkway.

"Wait up." Mallory jogged to catch up. Halfway to the car, she heard the engine rev and the vehicle took off. They stopped in the middle of the street and watched it drive away.

"Guess they weren't feeling social." Wade shoved his hands into his jeans pockets. "You've got some interesting friends, Mallory."

"Not my friend." She shook her head a little too emphatically, a pinching sensation in the base of her cervical spine made her flinch. "Never was…never will be." She stretched her neck side-to-side hearing the *pop*. They made an about-face and strolled toward her house.

"Hello." A gray-haired lady headed their way. Her hair gathered into a neat tight bun at the nape of her neck. The apron tied around her waist strained against her full apple shape. A plate of something rested in her hands. "Yoo-hoo." She skip-walked toward them.

Mallory blocked the sun with her hand. "Oh, that's Ms. Emery. Wonder if she's here for you or me?"

"Wade, right?" She stuck out her right hand.

"Yes, ma'am." Wade shook the offered hand.

"I'm Linda Emery."

"Nice to meet you. I've enjoyed some of your brownies recently." He placed a hand over his stomach. "Delicious."

Giggles overtook her. "Oh. You're too kind. I'm so glad you enjoyed them."

I tried one, too, but I'll be dipped if I'm paying you a compliment when you won't even acknowledge my presence. Mallory crossed her arms.

"I've been wanting to meet you. I always see your brother. He's such a lovely boy. He helped me fix the lock on my front door, and I wanted to thank him." She raised the plate of muffins. "Almond poppy seed. My specialty." She leaned in toward him. "And they're still warm."

Ms. Emery's whisper was like a national secret. Mallory wondered if she was invisible, and considered grabbing the muffins and running. She'd be using her new super power for greater good…her stomach. *That makes stealing okay, right?*

"It's so nice to have some decent young folk moving into the neighborhood." Her glance brushed Mallory head to toe, and her smile melted into a grimace. "So many unsavory people out there these days." Her attention drifted back to Wade. The smile returned as she met his gaze. "Please enjoy these."

No, I don't want a muffin, but thanks for asking. Mallory rolled her eyes, releasing a small humph.

"I'll make sure Matt gets one." He gave her a wink as though to say, "yeah right, these will make it to the house."

Giggles befell her again. "You're so sweet. Please don't be a stranger. My granddaughter comes over

95

every Sunday for lunch. Maybe you'll join us?"

Ms. Emery clasped her hands in front of her chest.

Mallory's stomach lurched, waiting for his response. *The nerve of this lady, pimping out her granddaughter right in front of me.*

Wade stood with his mouth open, but he produced no sound.

"Her name is Candy and is absolutely lovely. Very single." She rested her hand against the side of her mouth.

Apparently, another top-secret piece of information. *If this keeps up, I'll need security clearance.*

"Hard to find a nice girl these days." She squeezed his hand and gave a momentary snarl toward Mallory.

Mallory's jaw slackened. *The gall.* She was too polite to get sucked into this. She was the peacekeeper amongst her friends. Heck, she was an all-out diplomat. "Wasn't Candy working at the tittie bar on the outskirts of town a few years ago?" Nope, not too polite.

Ms. Emery curled her lip. "She bartended there to work her way through college." She stuck her nose in the air and whipped her focus back to Wade.

Who looked like a deer caught in headlights and on the verge of a hysterical breakdown. Socking him in the gut would fix his smirk.

"Oh, my mistake. I mean if stripping was paying for college..." She shrugged. "I myself took a job as a secretary in the business office of a department store. Guess I missed the memo on strip joints being the way to go." Mallory couldn't stop her bitter words. She leaned back and jutted her head side-to-side like a gangster. *What is the matter with me?*

Wade had his chin tucked.

She could hear him fighting back laughter.

"Anyway. Please keep Sunday in mind. We would love to have you." Sweetness dripped from her words. Ms. Emery took a step back and scowled one more time at Mallory before she turned on her heel and strode back to her house.

"Brrr." She gave an exaggerated shiver. "Did the temperature drop twenty degrees, or is it just me?"

Wade laughed. "Guess she saw the news."

"What happened to innocent until proven guilty? She used to like me. I'm really likeable." She crossed her arms and stuck out her bottom lip. "I lent her flour one day so she wouldn't have to run to the store. Granted it was my mom's flour, but I gave it to her. Probably made those stinkin' muffins with it." She considered spitting on them, but the fault wasn't with the yummy smelling muffins, and she really wanted one. "I mean, come on. I'm a nice person."

"It's okay." Wade stroked her upper arm with his hand. "She'll get over this and borrow flour again."

"Like hell she will. I'm not loaning her jack ever again." Jutting out her chin, she blew out her breath. "I'm not one to hold a grudge, being the kind person I am. I just don't like her anymore. *Humph.*"

"Come on." Wade tugged her forward.

She jammed her fists on her hips. "I mean she brought me cupcakes when I moved home. Remember, I told you about that?"

He pulled again. "I remember."

They strolled back to the front yard, and Zehn had yet to wake up from his nap.

"He's quite the watch dog."

"Depends on what he's watching. Squirrels, rabbits, the ever-entertaining grasshopper—he's all over it." They laughed.

Wade stepped in front of her. "I was wondering…I mean I know we just met…you've got a lot going on right now." He shifted his gaze over her shoulder.

"Is this going somewhere?" Her eye twitched in the corner. She fought the urge to press her fingertips to stop the sensation.

He paused, fidgeting with the foil over the muffins. "Would you like to have dinner with me sometime?" His neck reddened.

Oh boy. Why am I staring? Speak. Say something. She opened her mouth…nothing. Terrific, panic rendered her mute. Butterflies soared in her stomach. For five years, she'd been in a monogamous relationship with Kyle. Well, monogamous on her part. The prolonged silence turned uncomfortable. Her flight response surged in.

"That doesn't look promising." He shifted his feet. Disappointment washed over his face.

She forced herself to speak. "Um—It's not you."

"Please don't say 'it's me'." He slumped his shoulders.

She chewed her lower lip, wincing as her teeth pinched skin hard. "I haven't dated in forever. I don't think I know how to anymore."

"Just like riding a bike." Hope glittered in his eyes.

Her heart rate had to be pushing a hundred. She wanted to go, but… "So much is going on in my life right now. Everything is messed up. I don't think I'd be a good date." She glanced down at her feet. "Maybe you'd be better off with Candy." She said "Candy" with a nasal tone.

"Does sound like she has great…assets."

His tone was teasing, but Mallory punched him in the arm anyway.

"Ow. What did you do that for? You suggested it." He rubbed his arm and then stopped to use the knuckle of his first finger to lift her chin, forcing eye contact.

Sparks sizzled as their gazes connected. Looking into his dark brown eyes robbed her of words. Longing rushed through her like a tidal wave.

The backs of his fingers brushed up her cheek, and his thumb traced along her bottom lip. Wade's head tilted.

Pound…pound…pound, her pulse went wild. *Run.* Her legs wouldn't budge. Instead, her lips parted ever so slightly. She raised a hand to his chest and slid it around the back of his neck. The foot gap between them narrowed to an inch. She could feel his warm breath caress her face. He smelled of sandalwood and musk…and almond poppy seed.

A shrill scream pierced the air. "Let me go. Put me down right this minute."

Mallory jerked back. The moment shattered. Her gaze still held Wade's. She bit her lower lip, waiting for her adrenaline and hormones to return to normal.

Wade sighed and cursed under his breath. He broke their eye contact and glanced over to his front yard where Matt had Poppy around the waist, feet flailing in the air.

Mallory was relieved and disappointed, all balled up in one. She took a large step backward.

Matt set Poppy on her feet, she spotted Mallory and waved. Then she grabbed Matt's hand and tugged him toward Mallory and Wade.

"Muffins!" Matt said. "Ms. Emery?"

"Yep. Apparently you've been quite helpful." Wade lifted the corner of the foil, revealing the muffins.

Mallory went up on her tippy toes to get another peek. She really wanted a muffin.

"Her latch wasn't catching on her door. I only had to adjust the hinges, but if she thinks that's worth muffins, then who am I to refuse?" Matt grabbed for them.

Wade jerked the plate back.

"Hey."

"I've got them. If I give them to you, they won't make it through the front door," Wade said.

"What's your point?" Matt fingered the wrapping.

Wade smacked his hand. "I want one. That's my point."

Matt glowered at Wade. "I fixed the door."

"And she gave *me* the muffins."

"All right, boys." Poppy slipped her arm through Matt's. "Enough about food. So, let's talk about food." She grinned. "I thought it might be fun if we all went to dinner and then the outdoor concert at Riverfront Park next week. They have a new amphitheater that sounds amazing. The string instrument group who plays current music is performing. Very cool."

Mallory had a momentary panic attack. "You mean, Ella and Hazel, too." The realization lifted a boulder off her chest and she could breathe again.

"No. I mean us four." She spun her finger around, pointing at all parties currently standing there.

The boulder crashed down on her chest. *How will I get out of this?* She frowned at Poppy, who smirked in return. She looked to Wade for help, but his focus was on the muffin wedged in his mouth. She raised her eyebrows and jutted her head toward Matt and Poppy. Doesn't Wade understand sign language for *fix this*?

He dry-swallowed his bite. "Sounds super to me. Mallory?"

She almost threw up. She opened her mouth and squeaked.

"What was that?" Wade leaned in closer.

"She'd love to," Poppy said, and then nudged her.

They took Mallory's silence as acquiescence. *Great. Just great.* She tucked a stray hair behind her ear.

"Great, it's settled then." Poppy gave a single nod.

"Great," Wade said, jumping on the *great* train.

He waggled his eyebrows making eye contact with Mallory, who still felt ill.

"When did you get home, bro?"

"About thirty minutes ago." Wade took another bite of the muffin.

"Thirty?" Matt looked at Poppy, eyes wide.

She shrugged.

"But you came straight over here?" Matt's voice cracked.

Wade swallowed and took another bite. "Nope." He cocked an eyebrow.

"I didn't hear you." Matt shifted.

"Guess not." Wade winked at Poppy.

Poppy's dark skin turned crimson.

Now who's in the uncomfortable position? Mallory smirked, enjoying the show.

Matt cleared his throat, but he didn't ask any further questions.

Probably didn't want to know the answers.

"I'd better get going." Poppy studied her feet.

"I'll walk you to your car." Matt grabbed her hand and they scurried toward her vehicle.

"Hey, Matt. If you don't mind disinfecting the couch before Sunday's basketball game that would be great." Wade pressed his tongue into the side of his cheek.

Poppy and Matt halted but didn't look back. They shared a glance with each other, their shoulders slumped, and then they staggered forward again.

Mallory grabbed Wade's upper arm. Tears poured from her eyes. She couldn't rein in her laughter. "I can't believe you did that." She choked out, in between gasping for air.

"Couldn't stop myself." He shrugged, giving a little chuckle.

"Embarrassing Poppy isn't easy, and you did it." She clapped her hands together. "Oh my. I'm a terrible friend."

"Matt was my target. She was just collateral damage."

"Doesn't matter." She waved her hand in front of her face. "I still really enjoyed watching her squirm." With the tip of her ring finger, she wiped away the tears.

Wade crossed his arms and caught Mallory's gaze. "Guess we're going on a date." His broad grin spread ear-to-ear.

Mallory's remaining giggles ceased. "Hmm— what's that?"

"Date. I'm escorting you to a concert. Might be a ways off but you're getting back on that bicycle."

Mallory stood slack-jawed, all ability to form a sentence lost.

Wade used his knuckle to bump her chin upward, closing her mouth. "Don't get flustered, Mallory. I don't bite…unless you ask me real nice." His voice became husky.

Her jaw began its downward descent and his knuckle caught her chin again. This time, he leaned in.

*Brum…brum…brum…*her heart drummed. *No. Yes. Stop. Go. He's going to kiss me. Close your eyes. Relax. Shove him away. Turn your head. Close your eyes.* Thoughts careened through her brain, and she'd gone on to the next one before her body could react to the first. Instead, she stood statuesque.

But then he repositioned his head ever so slight and his lips brushed her cheek.

She blinked. *Hey wait, you missed.* She blew out the breath she didn't realize she'd been holding. "Thanks."

Wade gave a belly laugh. "You're welcome?"

Oh no. She cradled her face. *I said thanks. Please tell me I didn't say thanks.* She shook her head. "I don't know what's the matter with me. I'm such a dope." Tilting her head, she peeked through her hair. "I'm so sorry." She held her head upright and squared her shoulders. She'd take her humiliation like an adult. Clenching her hands next to her thighs, she closed her eyes. "Okay. Laugh at me. I can take it."

A warm puff of air brushed her lips the second before his soft lips touched hers. Simple and perfect. He rested his forehead against hers, and her eyes fluttered open, peering into his beautiful dark eyes. She sucked in her lower lip, trying to hide her smile.

"I'm not laughing." Wade rubbed his thumb along her lower lip.

"That you're not, but the evening is young."

"I figured if the cheek got me a thanks, I wondered what the lips would bring."

Mallory stepped back. "You're sneaky, you know."

"Just an opportunist."

"And you didn't even drop one muffin. You're amazing."

"Thanks."

She laughed. Spine-tinglingly magical. *So, this is what flirting is supposed to feel like. Nice.*

"I'd love to stay and play"—he winked—"but I've got to do research for a client." His smile faded.

"I can't say I've been too productive myself. Even though I'm on hiatus, I'm still doing what I can for Gracie's House of Style. I'm not traveling right now, but if I can handle work online, I will."

"Until next time then." Wade started across the street.

"Hey, wait." Mallory ran after him. Not-so-innocent intent danced in his eyes as she neared. His gaze drifted to her lips. Nope, not back for round two. Instead, she grabbed a muffin from the plate. "I so earned this," she said, as she ran back to her house.

Zehn leaped up and barked at her heels as he followed her inside.

Now I have two weeks to figure a way out of this date.

Chapter Six

"Poppy and Matt seem to be hot and heavy," Hazel said as she and Mallory walked out of the Galleria Mall, exhausted from their day of marathon shopping.

"It's crazy. In only a week they've become inseparable." Mallory grabbed Hazel's arm. "Do you know yesterday I saw her standing in Wade's front yard talking to Matt and she just got into her car and left?" She put her hands on her hips and grinded to a halt. "Didn't even come over and say hello." They started walking again, moving out of the way of a minivan looking for a space.

"She's got herself a man now. What does she need with you?" Hazel snorted as she sucked in air, breathing through her laughter.

"I forgot what it's like to feel that way about someone. You know when everything is new and exciting. You can't get enough time together." Mallory paused to search out Hazel's dark blue SUV.

"Yeah. You're an old lady." Hazel clicked her key fob's panic alarm button. "Where did we park?"

"I didn't think we were down this far." Mallory rearranged the bags she carried to one hand. She screened her eyes from the sun and searched. "I thought we were straight out from the main door."

"Me, too. Maybe we're over an aisle." They started walking again. "My nana ties a balloon to her antenna to find her car, if that gives you an idea of how old that jalopy she drives is. I found the balloon floating above her car embarrassing, but now I think she's a genius."

They strolled down a third row of cars. "I think I'm a bit jealous of Poppy. She put her heart out there with no fear. I don't think Kyle ever looked at me the way Matt already looks at her." Mallory stuffed her purse in one of the bags and adjusted them. "Man, these are heavy."

"I told you not to buy those boots."

"You'll be so jealous when I'm noticed by all the boys in my four-inch, black, knee-high boots."

"Nah. I'll just be thinking *I'm not picking her skinny ass up off the ground when she wipes out*." They both laughed. "Why didn't you go outside to say hi to Poppy when you saw her?" Hazel glanced at Mallory before her gaze slid past and traveled down the next row of vehicles. She switched her purse to her other shoulder.

"It wasn't a good time." Mallory stopped, set down her bags, and rubbed the marks on her hands. "This is getting absurd." She refused to meet Hazel's gaze, who apparently waited for clarification.

"Mallory."

"Hmm?"

"Mallory. Why wasn't it a good time?" Hazel bumped her. "Look at me, girl."

"It just wasn't, okay." She jerked away her arm from Hazel's bump.

"Mmm-hmm. And by that you mean…"

"God, you're annoying." Fear, desire, uncertainty, infatuation—all emotions playing a cut-throat game of tug a war within Mallory whenever she thought about

Wade. She didn't like internal confusion. "You should interrogate prisoners with those unfeeling steel gray eyes forcing everyone to confess their sins."

Hazel shifted up her head, making her glare even more effective. She crossed her arms and tapped her toe, waiting.

"Fine. Wade was outside with them, and I didn't want to run into him." She flung her arms wide and heaved a sigh. "Happy now?"

"Not quite. Why did that keep you from going out to speak to your dear childhood friend?"

"The better question is why didn't she come over and knock on my door, see if I was home, and say hello?"

"Mallory!"

"Okay, he makes me nervous. Is that what you want to hear?" Mallory snatched up her bags and stormed down the rest of the row.

Hazel jogged to catch up. "Why does he make you nervous?"

Mallory halted. "Poppy set up a double-date thing that's coming up soon, and I don't want to go. I don't know how to get out of it."

"Why do you want to?"

Because I'm terrified. Because I want to go way too much. Because I don't want to get my heart broken. Because... Mallory shrugged.

Hazel nodded. "I get it."

Mallory tilted her head to catch Hazel's gaze. She tried to read the expression on her face and what she saw made her insides constrict. The stare-down ended when a truck honked. Mallory and Hazel jumped, slamming into each other.

The guy behind the wheel waved his hand—universal for "move your butts, I want to park in the space you're blocking."

Hazel snarled one last time at the rude driver before they forged ahead.

"What do you get?" She didn't care to hear Hazel's response, but if she didn't address the issue now, then Hazel would scowl the entire drive home.

"You're scared."

As she sucked in her breath fast, Mallory let out an airy whistle. "I am not."

"Yes, you are, and you know it. You were comfortable with the sheltered relationship you had with Kyle. You were set in a routine, and your life was boring." Hazel stopped and glanced at Mallory.

She turned down the corner of her mouth. "No, Hazel, I don't have feelings."

"Bad choice of words. Your life with Kyle was boring, and that made you feel safe."

Mallory sighed, she wasn't wrong, but admitting that fact would be hard. The truth was, she'd failed, which bothered her more than she let on.

"You're not a failure, Mallory."

Mallory halted and whirled toward Hazel. "Did I speak out loud?" *I'm losing my mind.*

Hazel laughed. "No, girl. You didn't speak at all, but I hit the nail on the head, didn't I?"

Mallory blinked, still processing.

"I've known you since we were ten years old. I'm aware how you think. You always take the blame for everything, saying whatever happened must be something you did or said wrong. Just like with Kyle. You said you weren't a hundred percent in the relationship, and something had been missing for a long time." Hazel gave a vigorous rattle of her shopping bag. "That's why Kyle cheated. You weren't there for him. When in fact, yes the relationship was broken, but you didn't make Kyle cheat. He did that." She managed to jab a finger at Mallory's chest while still clutching her bags and purse. "Instead of calling off the engagement, he cheated, not with some Jane Doe, but with your friend. Your maid of honor. That's messed up."

Talking about the turmoil with Kyle didn't make her sad. Instead, in a strange way, she was relieved when he gave her a reason to walk away. *I'm not normal. I should be broken hearted over this, but I'm not.* She didn't like to talk about it, because the situation embarrassed her. She'd been made a fool. "I know you're right, but what does any of this have to do with me not wanting to date Wade?"

Hazel hesitated at the end of the next row and hit her panic alarm again. "This is ridiculous," she said, frowning. "Surely, no one stole my car." She dropped her keys into her pocket. "With Kyle, you didn't care. Let me ask you this. Did you miss Kyle when you were on a business trip?"

"Sure." Mallory scraped the sole of her shoe on the pavement.

Hazel arched an eyebrow.

Mallory dropped her head forward. "No."

"Did you call him while you were gone?"

Guilt itched along her shoulders. "No."

"Did you kiss him goodbye before you'd leave or tell him how much you loved him when you returned, and mean it with every fiber of your being?"

A sigh escaped her, blowing her hair forward. She

looked up again. "No. Hazel, you're making me feel like a horrible person." Mallory wished for a sinkhole to open and swallow her.

"Did you get those crazy butterflies in your gut when you looked into his eyes?"

"No." She flung her hands wide, swinging her bags. The handle ripped, and she grabbed the top of the bag. "What does any of this have to do with Wade?" Her patience unraveled with the unrelenting third degree. She took a cleansing breath and adjusted the rest of her bags.

Hazel rolled her eyes. "What do you feel when you look in Wade's eyes?"

The question befuddled Mallory. Several seconds passed, and she couldn't get control over the waves of nausea rolling in her gut.

"Well?"

"Shut up." Mallory marched off to the next row, leaving Hazel's laughter in the wind.

Hazel skipped to catch up with Mallory who'd stopped at the end and looked straight ahead at the Dillard's sign.

"Didn't we park in front of Macy's?" Mallory asked.

Both women busted out with hysterical laugher.

****

Mallory removed her packages from the back of Hazel's SUV. "Thanks, babe."

Hazel turned, glancing over the seat. "I had fun. Let's do it again soon…or after my credit card recovers."

The car shook when Mallory slammed the hatchback.

Hazel rolled down her window. "Let me know how the date goes."

Mallory stuck out her tongue. She waved as Hazel drove away. The black Charger entered her line of vision. Why was the car parked at the end of the road again? A shiver cascaded through her. *Gives me the creeps to think he's watching me.*

Ready to escape prying eyes, she hurried to the front door. She repositioned her packages and grasped the door handle. Locked. After setting down all of her bags, she fished the keys from her purse. One of the bags tumbled over and a zebra print bra and panty set spilled out. A bra big enough to hold two bowling balls. Mallory peered down at her chest. "Well crap." She dug in her purse for her cell phone.

No phone and come to think of it, she hadn't seen it since yesterday. Mallory scooped everything back into the bag, and then still on her knees, she jammed the key into the lock. The door gave and she tumbled forward. Fortunately, the ginormous bra padded her fall. She left her loot in the entryway, hustled into the living room, and grabbed the phone.

"Hello." Hazel answered on the second ring.

"Hey, come back."

"You miss me all ready."

"No, but I got a bra here that has enough material I could make my high school prom dress and still have some left over for a lovely shawl."

"You small-chested women are such haters."

"Hey. I'm not small...unless I'm standing next to you, and that's not a fair comparison for ninety-five percent of women."

"Ha. I'm making a U-turn now. I'll be there in

three."

Mallory hung up and headed back outside with Hazel's bag. She'd developed the habit of looking for the unmarked car every time she stepped outside. Relief washed over her to find it departed. She didn't know for sure who sat inside, but something told her the person was watching her. Ralph was watching her.

Hazel whipped her Suburban over to the curb and stopped right in front of Mallory's green subcompact vehicle.

Great, even her car is bigger than mine. She opened the hatchback and tossed in Hazel's bag, swapping for her bag with the killer boots. "I want to know who that getup is for."

"A girl's got to feel pretty under her clothes." Hazel flipped her hair.

Mallory regarded Hazel's reflection in the rearview mirror. She shook her head before slamming the door shut then strolled over and leaned on the window. "Sorry about that."

"No worries. I was only two blocks away."

"Do you see my cell phone in there?"

Hazel whirled her upper body around. "I don't see it. Wait, I'll call your number to be sure."

Mallory waited, glancing around and listening to the ring on Hazel's speaker. "You've reached—"

Hazel disconnected the call. "Nope, not in here."

"Okay. Thanks for checking." Moments passed as Mallory stared at Hazel's shrinking taillights. She chewed on the corner of her lip, struggling to remember when she last had her phone. She walked to her car and searched the center console and seats. *No dice.* She wedged herself into the floor under her steering wheel with her back to the pedals. The power seat mechanism made seeing under the seat difficult. She folded her knees on the driver's seat and rested her hands on the floorboard of the passenger seat. Hopefully no one would walk by. The downward dog-style pose provided quite the view.

The blood rushed into her head as she searched under the seat. *What's that?* A shiny object caught her eye. Stretching her arm as far as it could go, she still couldn't get through the mechanical parts. She boosted herself upright and backed out of the car, wobbling sideways before her equilibrium returned.

She opened the passenger door and slid the seat as far forward as possible. Her cell phone fell from in between the seats. *A-ha. There you are. But, what's that shiny thing?* Leaning the seat forward, she began the same process. Her knees were on the ground and her upper body on the floorboard. She stretched her arm under the seat and fumbled around with her hand, something smushy and sticky attached to her fingertips. "Eww." She yanked back her hand.

A cracked dark-cocoa brown round chocolate, with creamy white filling oozing out, dangled from her fingertips. "When did I eat Junior Mints?" Dumb question since it'd been her snack of choice since she was six. She shook it off in the street and returned to her previous position, fishing around some more.

Something smooth and kind of square… She finger walked until she had a better grip and backed it out. "Oh my. Nice." She eyed the pewter leather Coach credit card case. "Poppy's, maybe?" She shook her head. "This is more Hazel's style." Grabbing the doorframe, she hauled herself to her feet. Mallory put the seat back into its rightful position and slid it back, so she could sit.

Hazel surely would've mentioned missing this. She flipped it over. "What's this?" She scratched at a dried red substance. Tunnel vision whooshed over her. All the moisture in her mouth evaporated, and her tongue felt twice its size. Her pulse slammed against the skin covering her neck. She shook her head, denying what her brain told her.

The trembling in her hands made it almost impossible to unzip the case. After four tries she opened it and removed its contents. Fifty dollars in cash, two credit cards, a bonus card for a grocery store, and a driver's license were inside. The cards toppled to the floorboard. She slumped back her head against her seat and took a deep breath. "Cool it, Mallory." This is probably one of the girls'. She picked up the cards and blinked, focusing her eyes on the quivering pile. The picture before her caused the knot in her stomach to climb. Skylar Renee Masterson.

Mallory struggled to breathe around the lump racing its way to her throat. Skylar stared back, almost accusing. Mallory's body numbed all over, but her brain progressed into rapid-fire mode. *What does this mean? How did this get here? What should I do? Should I call the police? I need to call the police.* She grabbed her cell and woke up the screen. A melody sounded right before her phone shut down. Battery dead.

Her senses returned, albeit slower than she needed them to. "Oh no." Her head whipped up to look down the street. A breath of relief escaped her. The unmarked car hadn't returned. *I need to think this through.* She stuffed the contents back into their compartments and dropped the case into her shopping bag. She got out of her car and shut the door, and then darted to the safety of her house. She vaulted over the first two steps landing on the third.

"Lamb chops for dinner." Charlotte's voice carried from the kitchen.

How did her mom always sense when she was close? "Vegetarian, Mom." Mallory refused to stop and converse, when she couldn't disguise the shaking in her voice. Her mom would be all over her with the third degree.

"You need protein." The water shut off.

Mallory tensed. *She's coming. Move feet, carry me out of sight, and fast.*

"Had an egg salad sandwich for lunch." Which might migrate up into her mouth from her digesting gut. Mallory cleared the top step and slammed her bedroom door behind her. She plopped down on her bed and dumped out the contents of her shopping bag. She studied the pewter-colored case shining like a beacon in the middle of the other items she bought today. The red smudge glared against the shimmer of the leather. "Oh God." She flipped over her hand and studied her nail. Red showed underneath her index fingernail. The egg salad soared upward, and she bolted into her bathroom and wretched.

The warm water ran over her hand as she scrubbed her finger until it turned red for a different reason. *This isn't good enough.* She turned off the water and dropped to her knees. Pulse still racing, Mallory rummaged in the cabinet, locating a bottle of hydrogen peroxide and poured some over her finger, letting the liquid stream into the sink. The peroxide fizzed as it escaped down the drain. She set down the bottle and screwed on the lid. *Still not okay.*

She opened the closet to the side of the toilet and removed a bottle of alcohol. *Yes. Yes. This will do.* Back at the sink, she repeated the same process, with one change. "For the love of—" The burning from her raw finger caused her eyes to water. She turned the water back on and let the cold rinse away the discomfort.

The shock stopped her rampage. She leaned on her arms resting against the basin. Her head slumped forward. *I didn't do anything wrong. Why is this happening to me? I should turn it into the police, but how do I explain how it got in my car?* She walked into her bedroom and sat on the edge of her bed. Mallory cradled her head in her hands. *I'm innocent.* Her head shook side-to-side. *But this makes me look guilty. God, Ralph would love nothing more than to see me behind bars.* She rotated her head to look at the leather case. *Just looking at it makes me think I'm guilty. I only have one choice.*

The sun set as Mallory casually strolled the park with her accomplice, Zehn. They made their usual loop. Most park goers had cleared out—probably driven out by the mosquitoes. Mallory stopped next to the lake. This section of woods provided screening from the main entrance of the park. She slipped her hand into her back pocket and grabbed the edge of the Ziploc bag, tugging it free. She stared at the pewter-colored contents and her stomach rolled as she thought about what she was about to do. She removed the case from the bag, looking from it to the water.

*Breathe in...breathe out...breathe in...*she kept reminding herself how to perform an involuntary process. *Stop thinking. Just do it.* Calling upon her softball days in college, she used a windmill technique, making a full circle before releasing. The case soared through the air. Her muscles started to relax as the item, possible of landing her in jail, sailed farther away.

"Okay. That's—"

A wild yip sounded behind her and Zehn flew by and bound into the water.

"Zehn, No!" Mallory lunged as he passed and tried to snag his collar. Instead she ended up on her hands and knees in the water. "Crap." She got to her feet. "Zehn, no fetch. Come...Zehn...come now," she whisper-yelled. Then scanned her gaze over the area to see if anyone was nearby. "No, Zehn," she said in a weak, pathetic whine. She watched Zehn clamp down on the credit card case before it could sink.

He made a hairpin turn and swam back.

Her fingers threaded through her hair, and she clenched and yanked as she turned away from the water.

The water lapped at the shoreline as Zehn exited. Zehn's tags clinked on his collar as he shook.

The water spray landed on Mallory's already-damp legs.

Zehn dropped the case at her feet and did his version of downward dog. He barked, which obviously meant "let's go again."

She dropped her hands to her sides as she peered at the excited dog. A half smile made an unwanted appearance. "You're a good dog, Zehn." She scratched his head. "It's not your fault. I know you're just playing a game." *I, on the other hand, am committing a crime by getting rid of evidence.* She began the process of psyching herself up once again. Leaving the case lay, she stepped away and paced the shoreline.

Footsteps? She froze. Blood pumped in her ears. *Do I hear footsteps?* Before she could react, she saw a couple of females jogging on the path leading out of the woods. They gave Mallory the customary nod of acknowledgement as they passed. Mallory's gaze was fixated on the credit card case. *Keep going. Please keep going.*

The girl on the right tilted her head down and to the side. She spun, jogging in place. "Hey, lady. Did you drop your wallet?"

Mallory blinked, as she lost her grasp of the English language. Zehn leaned into her leg. The motion helped snap her out of her stupor. "Oh my. Yes, thank you so much." A forced smile plastered on her face, she stepped forward, bent over, and picked up the bane of her existence.

"No problem." The women turned and took off down the path.

This is why I don't ever speed. I can't get away with anything. "Come on, cut me some slack," she said to the universe. She waited until the joggers disappeared from sight. More determined than ever, she approached the water and snapped on Zehn's leash. Hooking her left arm through the handle of the leash, she wound it around and gripped tight. She then whipped her right arm around and released.

The case rocketed even farther this time, splashing on landing, and the next moments blurred. Her body catapulted forward. She did a belly flop into the sand

and hung on for dear life as Zehn drug her toward the water. "Zehn, no. Zehn, sit. Zehn, down." She tried every command. Unfortunately, Zehn flunked out of dog school when he grabbed the instructor's pant leg and depantsed him in front of the entire class. But what do you expect when sweatpants are your garment of choice?

She spun herself around, got her butt underneath her, and braced her heels in the sand.

Zehn stopped.

And now she sat in the semi-cool water.

He tugged.

"Sorry, babe. No fetch this time." The water absorbed into her clothes.

He barked.

Give me a break Zehn. She patted her pockets. "Want a treat?"

Zehn turned and jumped into her arms.

"Flaky dog. So easily influenced." She bumped him off and stood, making her way to dry land. She fished the damp treats out of her pocket and tossed him one. Mallory turned her attention back to the water in time to see the credit card case get swallowed up by the murkiness. Relief flooded her, but guilt still poked her in the gut. "Come on. Let's go home." The only thing worse than the squish of her tennis shoes was her wet underwear. After a quick glance around, she gave a discreet tug to readjust her clingy drawers. Didn't help.

The streetlights hummed as they warmed up. Mallory's steps faltered. The black car was parked, yet again, at the end of the street. Exhaling, she picked up her pace only to hesitate when she spotted Wade coming toward her.

Chapter Seven

After a long day of surveillance for one of his clients, Wade wanted to get inside, eat his Italian takeout, and go to bed. He squinted his eyes and observed Mallory coming out of the wooded path from the park. He set his food on the porch and waited. *She's been avoiding me and doing a great job.* Even now when he could tell she'd spotted him she looked like she might bolt. A moment of uncertainty passed and he started across the street. "Hey, Mallory." Wade took in her disheveled appearance. "Want to tell me about it?"

She blinked and gave him a grim smile. "Tell you about what?"

"You're soaked from the waist down for starters."

She looked down at the water puddle around her feet. "Um…I…uh…well…Zehn took off after a duck before I could get the leash off my wrist." She blurted without a breath.

Wade studied her. Between working as an attorney and a PI, he had a pretty good sense about reading people. And his instincts told him she was lying. "Want to try again?"

Her lips sucked inward, and she rocked back on her heels. "Not really."

He paused and decided not to press. "All right then. If you change your mind, remember I live right over there." He pointed over his shoulder and winked.

Mallory remained quiet and turned her head away.

"What's that? I think you have gum in your hair?"

Her jaw eased downward. "You're kidding?"

She widened her eyes to the point he worried her eyeballs might pop out.

Mallory fingered through her hair.

He tugged at a section of her hair and leaned in for closer inspection. "Nope," he said, stepping back. "Not gum." He crossed his arms and pressed his lips tight.

"Thank goodness. That's just gross." Her hand rested on her chest.

"Bird poop."

Her mouth gaped. Nothing resonated. She spread her fingers wide and shook her hands with sharp jerks. "Ew!" Mallory added bouncing, and Zehn barked and jumped up on her. "Ewww!"

Wade tried hard not to laugh, but he failed. "It's all right, Zehn. She's having a moment." He stroked Zehn, who now sat by him. They enjoyed the show together.

Mallory had a section of her hair between her index finger and thumb. She spun in a slow circle and struggled to look at the damage. Staggering sideways, she stopped spinning. "Don't just stare at me. Help me! I have crap in my hair."

A belly laugh rolled out of Wade, and he braced his upper body by leaning forward and resting his hands on his knees.

"Stop it!" she whined. "Ewww!"

Wade stood, but his gut ached. "Oh God. Please give me a minute, and I'll try to help." He straightened himself. "Whew. Okay. I'm okay now." Then he looked at Mallory's face. "Nope. Going to need another second." He turned his back, as to not laugh in her face.

"Wade Porter! This is an emergency. Pull yourself together."

He put up his finger to signal one minute. Slowly, he turned back. "Got a tissue or something."

Mallory patted the outside of her pockets. She jammed her hand into her pants pocket and extracted a wet tissue, disintegrating on exit. She stared at the pile of white confetti in her hands and then peered up at Wade with her brow furrowed.

Her expression almost asked "what now?" His laughter erupted again.

"This isn't funny." She stomped her foot. "I have had a lousy day, and bird poo is the icing on the cake."

She appeared to be about to cry. This wasn't something people normally cried over, so she'd probably truly had a rotten day. He channeled his inner gallant knight and pulled himself together. He fished a tissue out of his pants pocket. "Come here." He used his soothing voice.

Mallory shuffled her feet toward him, her gaze casting downward.

He wiped the excrement from her hair. "There you go." The tissue still in his hand, he looked around, walked over to a neighbor's trashcan, and tossed it in.

"Is it really gone?"

"I'd still wash your hair, but yeah, it's gone."

"Thank you." She shifted her weight between her feet. "Sorry for my melt down." She tilted her head and gave a sideways glance.

"Hey, don't be embarrassed. It happens to all of us. Especially with those ornery seagulls. Personally, I think they aim."

Mallory gave a genial smile. An uncomfortable

silence followed. "I better get inside." She walked past him.

She was escaping from him, and his gut twisted. *I don't get why she's avoiding me.* She'd been weird ever since they agreed to the date. Wade watched her backside for a moment. "Mallory, wait."

She stopped and turned, eyebrows raised in question.

"About Sunday's concert."

"What about it?"

"I don't think I can make it." When she didn't speak, he continued. "I have a big case I'm working on, and I'll have to log some hours that day." A look of relief crossed her face, and a pang of disappointment twisted in his chest.

Mallory exhaled. "Okay. Sure, I understand." She shrugged, headed down her previous path, and closed the door without glancing back.

"Damn." Wade retreated to his house with a heavier heart.

****

Phone records covered the kitchen table. A cup of steaming coffee sat to Wade's right.

Matt padded into the kitchen in pajama bottoms, bare feet, and shirtless. "You're at it early." He scratched his back on the doorframe by rubbing side-to-side.

"Couldn't sleep any longer and figured I might as well get some work done." Wade yawned. If he didn't get some rest soon, he'd have to hire someone to think for him.

"Whatcha working on?"

"This employer thinks one of his employees is

running a business on the side." He flipped to the next page and highlighted a number.

"What's the big deal? A lot of people have to work two or even three jobs in this economy."

"True, but not all employees use the employer's resources to conduct said business."

Matt frowned and nodded. "Got it. But that shouldn't be too hard to find, should it?"

"He has five hundred employees and only an anonymous tip this is going on. And whoever made the tip didn't feel the need to provide any other details, such as a name for the person or company, or type of service." Wade looked up, rubbing his eyes. He stretched and then took a large drink of coffee. "So basically, I'm looking for the needle in the proverbial haystack."

Matt took out a skillet and set it on the stove burner. He opened the refrigerator and removed a carton of eggs, cheddar cheese, milk, and butter. He put them down on the counter. "Want some scrambled eggs?"

"Sure. I could eat. I had a toaster pastry earlier, and its fuel is long gone." Wade gathered the papers and stacked them in piles. He transferred them to the far side of the table to make way for Matt.

Matt cracked four eggs into the pan. He whisked as he poured some milk and added salt and pepper. "You want to tell me what is buried in your psyche that's disrupting your sleep?"

"Will I be charged for this session?" Wade stood, walked to the coffee pot, and refilled his mug.

"Hey, send one of those my way. And I'll give you the older brother discount." He sprinkled cheddar cheese over the eggs.

Wade placed a mug next to Matt and sat again. "The session will be short, because it was a simple case of insomnia."

Matt plated the eggs and placed them on the table. "Sure. Happens to all of us."

Wade could hear the sarcasm in his voice.

Before joining Wade, Matt grabbed two forks and his coffee. They both dug in and ate in silence for a moment.

"You and Poppy seem to be going strong."

"Yeah." Matt swallowed. "She's great. The right mix of sweet and spicy, not to mention intelligent, funny, and driven. And as a CPA, she can do my taxes, probably correctly for the first time ever."

"Never thought I'd see the day you would be dating just one girl at a time. Guess little brother is growing up."

"It's the first time someone has caught and kept my attention enough to want to be exclusive." Matt wiped his mouth with his napkin. "She's really looking forward to the concert on Sunday with you and Mallory."

The clank of Wade's fork hitting his plate was deafening. He pounded on his chest to get down his bite of eggs.

"What? What did I say?" Matt's brow lined with mystified crinkles.

Wade ahemed one more time. "I can't attend." He shoveled the last bite of eggs into his mouth.

"Why not?" Matt crossed his arms high on his chest.

Wade pointed to his mouth. "Chewing." He gave

his chompers an over-exaggerated work out.

"I'll wait." Matt raised his eyebrows and drummed his fingers on the table.

His already-soft egg now was pulverized. Wade had to swallow. "Got to work." He stood, picked up both his and Matt's plate, and dumped them in the sink.

"Bull."

Wade turned.

Matt was already on his feet. "What changed?"

"I don't know what you mean."

"Don't play innocent. You were all aboard the Mallory train, and now you've jump off while it's moving."

"Any type of relationship between us won't work."

"I saw you two at Grayson's Club and everything worked just fine." Matt crossed his arms.

Wade exhaled all his breath. "I don't know, man. It's complicated. She's complicated."

"How so?"

"Come on. She's in the middle of a murder investigation."

"That's not her fault. All she did was call for help. That detective guy has it out for her. Poppy told me about what he did to her in high school."

Wade's arms flailed wide and then smacked his thighs. "That's another thing. She has so many issues. I don't know I want to be drug into all of them. Trouble seems to follow her wherever she goes."

"So you bail on her?" Matt pointed an accusing finger. "When she needs people the most."

"I'm not bailing. We aren't an item. Not to mention we pressured her into going to the concert. She looked like she might throw up. I don't need to force someone to go out with me." He raised his chin. "I'm a good-looking guy…a real catch."

"Ha!" His lips pressed inward. "Sorry. I mean you're the man."

"When I told her, I couldn't go—"

"Wait." Matt interrupted. "You already told her you were bailing? Cold, man."

"Look. I like her. I think she's beautiful, hilarious, a real Calamity Jane, and she has no censor when she speaks. So, I'm always surprised by what comes out of her mouth." Thinking back at the things she'd said, he gave a quick laugh. "But so much drama follows her around, and if I hang with her, I have to shoulder all the crap that comes along. With my work schedule, I don't have the time."

"Things aren't that bad. You make her sound like Job from the bible."

"Kind of."

"Come on, Wade. She's a great girl." He grinned. "Poppy says so. Don't you think you're overreacting a bit? I mean her life isn't that drama filled."

Screeching tires and loud voices ended their conversation. They strode to the front window.

Three police cars and the black unmarked car, usually positioned at the end of the street, parked out front. Three uniform deputies and two detectives converged on the Larsen's front porch.

Wade raised his eyebrows and smirked in Matt's direction.

"So, maybe she has a bit of drama." Matt shrugged.

Chapter Eight

"What in the world? Is that thunder?" Mallory shut off her hair dryer. Someone pounded on the front door. *Geez, break it down, why don't they?* She slipped on her flip-flops and headed downstairs to see about the commotion. Her steps slowed as she neared the bottom.

"This is my house, and you will not speak to me like that in my own home."

She overheard her father's affronted speech. Her feet moved again, and she rushed down the remaining steps. Ralph? She approached the front door where Ralph squared off with her father. The female detective from the…the…mishap, if you can call murder, mishap, at the club also stood on the porch. Three other deputies leaned against her vehicle, making it resemble a matchbox car.

"What's going on?" Mallory shifted her gaze from her parents to Ralph.

"I'll teach this young man some manners," Jim said without breaking eye contact. "Pounding on a citizen's door. There's just no cause. If you need something, try a knock that doesn't rattle my windows."

"Threatening a deputy of the law is a good way to get yourself arrested." Ralph stepped forward, getting in Jim's face.

Mallory laid a hand on her dad's shoulder and stepped in front of him. "Don't harass my parents. Your beef is with me, Ralph." Her words were cold and cutting.

Jim leaned over Mallory's shoulder. "Or I'll be on the phone with the mayor so fast you won't make it back to your car before the county council knows about your inappropriate behavior here. Police harassment is a good way to get yourself fired. I don't know who you think you are."

Charlotte stood to the side of the door, wide-eyed and speechless.

"I'm a deputy of the law. That's who I am." A red-faced Ralph jammed his finger at Jim with each word.

"You act like some punk kid."

Ralph tried to charge past Mallory.

Mallory didn't budge. Instead, she laid a hand on her father's chest. "Dad, go inside. They are obviously here to talk to me. It's okay."

"I'm not leaving you out here alone with that cretin."

Sweet how he wanted to protect her, but this was her fight. "Dad. Please. You can watch from the window. But you're making things worse. Let me see what they want, so they can get it and go." She patted his chest. "I'll be fine." She glanced over her shoulder at her mother. "Mom."

Charlotte snapped out of her funk and rested her hand on Jim's arm. "Jim. Come with me."

His posture relaxed, and he took a step back. "I'm watching your every move." He retreated from the door.

Mallory stepped outside, glad Ralph decided not to add fuel to the fire. "All right, Ralph, what do you want?" She crossed her arms to hide her clammy palms.

Internal emotional warfare waged in her gut—flipping between rage for the way he treated her dad, and terror they were here to arrest her.

"How many times do I have to tell you it's Detective Shimkus!" His lips and lower eyelids twitched under the tension.

"Stop acting like some jealous schoolboy and start acting like a professional. Then maybe I'll treat you as such."

"Why, you good for nothing, cheap—"

The female detective stepped forward. "We have a warrant to search your car." She handed a folded paper to Mallory.

She speaks. And her first words pack a wallop. "What's this about?" Mallory opened the warrant and had no idea what she read. Her stomach constricted at the mention of her car. "Detective?" Frowning, she looked up.

"Alvarez."

"Detective Alvarez."

"The situation is just as the document states. It gives us the right to search your car."

"So, either open the door, or I'll break the window." Ralph rocked back and forth like a bull about to charge.

Mallory swore Detective Alvarez rolled her eyes.

"Do you have your keys on you?" Detective Alvarez stepped closer.

Relieved Detective Alvarez took charge, Mallory focused on her. "Um, just a second. They're right inside the door." She opened the front door, snagged them off the stand, and then handed them over. A little deliberate snub to Ralph.

He managed one last glare at Mallory before exiting the porch.

Mallory's stomach dipped and swirled, and she was glad she hadn't eaten breakfast yet. *Did they know about the wallet? If so, how?* Her heartbeat pulsed in her ears. *What if something else is hidden in there I missed? Why is this happening?* She sank to the porch steps, her legs quivering to the point wet noodles would have done a better job of supporting her.

She'd never survive in prison. She needed her flat iron. Mallory gnawed on her cuticles as five officers crawled in and out of her car. An impressive feat such as that should be viewed by the world, but sheer terror kept her from taking the picture and posting it on the web. When she went out with the ladies, she never considered her car, because packing in all four with their belongings gave her an idea of what sardines felt like.

Her mind ran rampant. The search had to be related to Skylar. Someone put the wallet in her car and then turned her in. *Who would hate me so much they'd want to frame me for murder?* Mallory abandoned her cuticle for her lower lip. Not one name popped to mind. She snapped her gaze to a deputy on his belly digging under her seat. Her body posture snapped rigid to the point of being painful, staring intently. *I look terrible in an orange jumpsuit.*

No spit remained in her mouth to help her swallow. *Oh no. No…no…no. He found something. Sweet Jesus, something else is under the seat.* A cold sweat broke out all over her body.

He backed out of the car.

I'm dying. It's a heart attack. I'm having a heart

attack. He's looking at me. His eyes scream "you murdering bitch." Oh crap, now he's pointing my way. Oh, wait. Every muscle in her body turned to jelly.

He tossed a box of Junior Mints on the sidewalk.

Whew. She slumped her head forward, hair falling over her face. Physically and emotionally exhausted. *I wonder if any are left in that box?* She tilted her head to focus on the candy and silently willed the box to come to her hand. Didn't work.

Movement across the street caught her attention. Wade headed her way. "Great. Just great." *He already thinks I'm a loser. This will surely help change his opinion.* She exhaled all her breath and forced herself to stand on her boneless legs. How she managed to put one foot in front of the other amazed her. Finding the strength to nudge the Junior Mints box with her toe, not so much. Darn, empty.

Wade crossed the street before she made it off the curb.

"Hey." Her shoulders slouched.

"What's going on?" Wade gestured toward her vehicle.

Mallory handed him the warrant.

He perused the document then looked up. "You're kidding?"

She nodded her head toward her car. "That look like a joke to you?"

"What are they searching for?"

Her friends always called her a terrible liar, but she managed to look him in the eye. "I have no idea." *Okay, so I'm getting better.* He studied her so long little beads of sweat broke out over her upper lip.

"We're searching the house next."

For once, Ralph saved the day. "I'm sorry?" Mallory asked.

Wade and Mallory turned toward him.

"I said we are searching the house next." Ralph approached.

Will this ever end? And now he plans to decimate her parents' house. Would curling up into the fetal position right here on the sidewalk look odd? "What are you looking for, Ralph—Detective Shimkus?"

"Don't play dumb with me, Mallory. We both know you did it, and I'll find the proof, and you'll spend the rest of your days behind bars." Ralph's voice vibrated through his clenched teeth.

Sound working its way through the wad of hair on his upper lip surprised her. "Why, what on earth are you referring to?" Mallory fluttered her lashes.

Ralph's face turned red enough to explode. "Get out of my way. We're tearing that house apart until I find the evidence I need."

"I don't think so," Wade said, his raised hand stopping Ralph's forward momentum.

Mallory snapped her head to look at Wade. Her jaw lurched downward. How could he stop Ralph?

"Called your attorney, Mallory?" Ralph didn't take his gaze off of Wade.

"Seems like." Relief palatable in her voice. Wade to save the day…again.

"Pretty clear that's something a guilty person would do," Ralph said.

Wade narrowed his eyes. "Or someone who is well aware she's being hung out to dry by someone who has no professional ethics—"

"You're walking a fine line, counselor." Ralph

snarled, displaying his eye teeth, his fists pressed firm into his thighs.

Wade fluttered the document. "And someone who's committing an illegal search by rolling over an innocent due to their lack of knowledge regarding the law."

Ralph stabbed his hand toward the house. "You don't know what you're talking about. We have every right to search that house."

Hmm. How will the standoff play out? Mallory shifted her neck side-to-side, wanting to relax the growing tension in her muscles.

"Your warrant is for Mallory Larsen's car." Wade tapped a finger on the printed page. "Not Jim and Charlotte Larsen's home."

Oh boy. I like where this is going.

"Trying to bluff your way into that house shows your moral compass is so twisted by your personal feelings toward Ms. Larsen that you are willing to commit an illegal act. You're a disgrace to your department." Wade stepped closer to Ralph.

"My job is to put dangerous criminals in jail, and I'll do it by any means necessary." Ralph jammed his finger in Wade's chest.

"You won't do it by an illegal search. You want to search that house, convince a judge to give you a warrant." Wade slammed the warrant against Ralph's chest.

Ralph's mustache twitched. "You're harboring a criminal."

"Does that look like a criminal to you?" Wade pointed to Mallory who once again gnawed on what little was left of her cuticle.

She dislodged her finger from her mouth and gave her best angelic grin.

Ralph quivered. A seething rage boiled from the depth of his eyes.

Detective Alvarez approached. "Come on, sir, they need us at the department." She handed Mallory her car keys.

Ralph locked gazes with Mallory and the evil pulsated through their connection. He held her stare a moment longer and then got into his car.

A shiver surged through her. But her bitterness overruled her fear, and she put her thumb to her ear and pinky to her mouth giving the universal symbol for call me.

"Mallory!"

She jerked her attention to Wade. "What?" She shrugged and looked away. His laughter made her smile.

"You never learn."

"I can't help it. He pisses me off so bad." She stomped her foot.

"I get it. Really, I do. Do you want to reconsider telling me what they were looking for?"

Mallory shuffled to her car without answering. The contents of her glove compartment were dumped onto her floorboard. Black powder smeared her dash and windows. Her back seat was pulled loose and the carpet yanked up. In plain English, they trashed it. Her gut twisted as though someone tied it into a thousand knots. Stress crushed in and her head throbbed with so much pressure she wanted to pop it. Instead, the dam broke, and tears trickled down her cheeks.

Wade stepped up behind her and wrapped his arms

around her, squeezing tight. She welcomed the pressure of his embrace. Mallory slumped her head forward, resting her chin on her chest then clutched the hands intertwined in front of her.

"It'll be okay," he whispered in her ear.

The warmth of his breath caused her heart to flutter, and she sucked in her breath. "I'm not sure my life will ever be okay. I try to be a good person. I always believed if you do the right thing everything would work out. But this…this nightmare I can't wake up from. It just won't end."

Wade spun her to face him and used his thumb to wipe away the last of her tears.

She hid her face, but he put his finger under her chin, making her look him in the eye. "I'm sorry." She waved her hand in front of her face. "I don't cry…at least not in front of people." Mallory sniffed and wiped away her tears.

"Mallory, it's okay to cry. It's the body's way of release, and with all the recent stress you've been under, you're entitled. Please don't feel embarrassed."

The back of his hand brushed down her cheek, and she inclined her head toward his touch. Warmth replaced the dread of moments before. She wanted to be closer and shuffled her feet forward.

He accepted, slipped his hand behind her, and hugged her tight.

Her hand rested on his chest and she felt the *lub-dub…lub-dub* under her palm. The comfortable connection surprised her. She skimmed her gaze from her hand to his eyes, to a flash of movement over his left shoulder.

Ms. Emery's curtain fell across her window.

"Great." The warmth from a moment before was pushed out by tension. Mallory stepped back.

Wade frowned. "I'm sorry?"

"No. But I will be…just wait for it."

His forehead creased under the pressure.

"Yoo-hoo." A high-pitched voice wailed.

"And there it is." Mallory exhaled.

Ms. Emery jog-walked toward them, spastically waving her hand in the air. She really should consider work as an Aircraft Marshaller.

Wade glanced over his shoulder.

"We know she's not coming to see me." The edginess made her want to scream, or hit something—anything to release this agitation blowing up inside. "It's for the best anyway."

Wade narrowed his eyes. His lips pressed into a tight line.

Stupid move, Mallory. She couldn't do anything right. Here, Wade was being nice, and once again Mallory acted like a jerk.

"Wade…oh, Wade, dear." Ms. Emery found a moment to snarl at Mallory before sending a big toothy grin in Wade's direction. "You're still coming to lunch Sunday?"

Mallory wanted to hurl. She turned her attention to her car and started shoving everything back into its place. She could sense his gaze burning into her back, but she refused to turn and show him her devastation.

"Yeah. I'll be there." Wade's voice held little emotion.

Mallory closed her eyes and fought tears for the second time today. She stepped back and slammed her door. The cleaning could wait until later.

"Wonderful. Absolutely wonderful."

The sound of Ms. Emery clapping her hands made Mallory flinch.

"Candy is so looking forward to it."

The cheer in Ms. Emery's voice made Mallory want to break a window. She scurried to her parents' house, trying to silence the conversation she had no desire to hear. She refused to look back.

"Can't wait."

Were the last words of Wade's she caught before running inside and up to her bedroom to cry her heart out. She didn't understand why knowing he'd accepted Ms. Emery's invitation hurt, but having confirmation hurt bad.

Chapter Nine

You've Lost That Lovin' Feelin' blasted from her bedside table. Mallory's hand automatically slammed down on top of her phone. Slowly, she grasped it and inched it toward her without lifting her head from the pillow. She dragged the phone under the covers and held it to her ear. "Yeah," she said through her yawn.

"Rise and shine."

The voice sounded so cheerful she wanted to reach through and choke Ella.

"You have twenty minutes to get your butt over here. I'm making waffles. Zehn's invited."

The disconnected phone hummed in her ear. *Did I dream that?* She opened her eyes. Nope, classic Ella style. She probably anticipated Mallory would be in the dumps after being uninvited to today's concert and, as always, wanted to get her mind off of the situation. She shoved back the covers and rolled to the edge, forcing her feet to the floor, but left her upper body in the prone position.

Zehn sprung to the rescue and licked her in the face.

"Quit." She nudged him. "I'm up…I'm up." Again, she opened her eyes, and then scratched Zehn's ears. "We have plans, Zehn. Hurray us." She succeeded in getting to her feet, put on a pair of khaki shorts, and a tank. Even managed to run a comb through her hair and brush her teeth before bolting out the door to her car, now clean after a much-needed detailing from last week's assault.

****

"You're ten minutes late." Ella yelled, still in her kitchen.

Mallory turned the corner and entered. "You gave me twenty minutes, it's a fifteen-minute drive here. I think you should be thankful I brushed my teeth."

Ella bounced back and forth from the waffle maker to the stove. Her ponytail resembled an overactive Komondor puppy.

"Oh, I am. I actually planned on thirty, but I know you and if I told you thirty, you'd be here in forty."

Mallory's jaw slackened and then slid into a smile. "I'm never late. I'm just living each moment to its fullest."

"You were late to your own birth." Ella shot her a look over her shoulder.

"Not my fault. I still think the doctor counted wrong. No way was I two weeks overdue." Mallory dropped her purse and keys on the floor.

"I'll ask your mom about it next time I'm over." Ella poured the last of the batter into the waffle iron.

"Please don't. She takes longer to tell that story than it took for me to crawl out of her womb."

Ella laughed. "You should be able to crawl at nine and a half pounds." She grabbed the spatula and plated the fried eggs, two pecan waffles each, and a few slices of bacon on her own plate.

Mallory climbed on a barstool in front of the counter as Ella placed a baconless plate in front of her.

Ella took the adjacent seat. She drenched her

waffles in syrup and passed it to Mallory.

"These are my favorite." Mallory snapped the top closed on the bottle. "But, I guess you know that." She glanced sideways at Ella.

Ella shrugged.

Zehn plopped down on Ella's side.

"You know I have a slice of bacon for you, and all your mama gives you is that nasty tofu jerky." She smooched toward him.

"That's not true. Dad gives him fried chicken livers." She slipped her fried egg in between her two waffles and cut into it, sending the bright yellow yolk to mix with the maple syrup.

Ella snarled her lip.

"Yeah, I agree. Tofu doesn't sound so bad now, does it?"

"I wouldn't get all crazy." Ella took a bite of her bacon and slipped Zehn his piece. "Do you want to talk about it?"

"Not really." The large bite in her mouth muffled Mallory's voice.

"Poppy told me all about the concert, and how Wade backed out." She stopped eating and studied Mallory.

Quit your gurgling stomach. I won't let depression-induced nausea ruin my waffles. She shrugged to reinforce how little she cared. Yeah right. "Can't really blame him. I mean my life is in shambles right now. Why would he want to date me?" She took a drink of her orange juice. "Honestly, it's probably my fault. We got roped into going. Not like he even asked me. But, I panicked. I haven't dated in five years…besides Kyle, and I froze." She waved a hand, still clutching her fork.

"You know you want to go, but the thought terrifies you. I think he might have mistaken fear for lack of interest." She started in on her waffles again.

"You two seemed pretty compatible at Grayson's that night, and for not knowing you well. He went out of his way on your behalf."

"It's bizarre, he continues to go out of his way for me. I think he's just a nice guy, because I know he's lost interest."

"How do you know?" Ella let Zehn lick her plate.

Mallory shoved the last three bites in her mouth at once.

"Mal, I'm going to wait, you know."

Mallory held up her finger and chewed, but she'd put so much in she couldn't get her lips to close. Two solid minutes passed before she got the food broken down enough to speak. "He's hovin lunch woth Wonde." Not a word understandable.

"Swallow and try again." Ella slid what was left of her own juice toward Mallory.

She swallowed and washed it down. "He's having lunch with Candy."

"He's what!" Ella's wild ponytail nearly vaulted off her head.

Mallory jumped and knocked over the empty glass.

"She's a stripper. Does he know that?" She drummed her fingernails on the counter.

"I mentioned it, but for some guys, that might be a plus." She shrugged. "I didn't ask his reasoning."

"I'll have a talk with him. This is crazy." Ella hopped off her stool and took both plates, rinsing them in the sink.

"Please don't. He can date whomever he wants.

142

I'm not a good candidate right now. I get that." The emotion was still raw in her chest.

"Bull. None of this is your fault, and he should know that." The dishes clanked together as she rammed them into the dishwasher. "You like the guy. I can tell."

"No. I mean not in that way. Not in any way." Mallory dropped her head into her hands. "That's a lie. I'm crazy attracted to him." She rolled her head and peeked at Ella through her fingers. "I hate he's dating Candy. Why am I so screwed up?"

Ella wiped her hands and approached. "Honey, you're not. You got dealt a lousy hand, but things will turn around for you. Wait and see." She patted Mallory's shoulder. "Enough romance talk. I want to show you something."

Mallory sat up. "What?"

"It's not here. You're driving." Ella grabbed her house keys.

"I am?"

"Yep. Zehn there's a charmer, but I can't have him poking holes in my leather seats."

"Come on, boy." Mallory whistled.

Zehn ran out the door in front of them.

****

"It's only about another two miles." Ella pointed as she gave instructions.

They wound their way around the bluffs heading away from the river. They were near Riverview Lake. She'd come out here to a couple of parties during high school. The black walnut, red oaks, ash, hickory, elm, and maple trees filled the forest. Wildflowers added splashes of pinks, yellows, and purple and outlined the road. A deer trotted across the road in front of them, appearing not to have a care in the world. The curves in the road prevented her from going above twenty miles an hour, so not a huge threat to wildlife.

"Up there. Turn right." Ella pointed.

"Up where? I don't see a road sign...or a road."

"Trust me. And there's not a road sign. I think it must have gotten knocked down, and never replaced. Or maybe stolen...who knows."

Mallory slowed and hesitated at the sight of the unpaved road. *She's got to be kidding.* A dirt lane with a few pieces of scattered gray rock cut through the trees. "Seriously, turn here?"

"Yes, here. Now turn please." Ella's ponytailed head nodded.

Mallory turned and drove about another mile, steering around massive potholes. The sun's rays shimmered off the clear lake materializing in the distance. Behind the cedar and stone two-story house, the water was expansive. The cottage-style created a warm comfortable sensation. *Beautiful here.*

"Turn in there." Ella pointed to the driveway.

"What if someone's home?" *Great, all I need is to be arrested for trespassing. Let's just tack that on to the murder charge.*

"Don't worry. Just pull in."

"Easy for you to say." Mallory parked, and they all three got out.

Ella strode to the front door. "Come on."

Mallory dawdled, taking in the plush green grass, probably cut with a riding mower, since uneven tufts covered the yard. The push mowers gave a uniform appearance. The grounds had once been landscaped, but needed TLC. She guessed there to be at least a couple of acres. She slid her gaze over some of the largest hostas she'd ever seen, planted in the flowerbeds against the house. They were mixed in with the water grass, rudbeckia, sedum, and lungwort. Those summers working at the nursery stuck with her. She even impressed herself on what she remembered. The stone walkway separated another bed filled with variegated weigela, daylilies, primrose, and salvia. She inhaled the sweet smell. Winter creeper ground cover hid the abundance of weeds, but even in its plush ground coverage, the weeds were still winning.

Zehn yipped.

She turned in time to see him plunge into the lake. Blue phlox in full bloom blanketed the steep slope to the water. This place gave the illusion of being secluded, but other homes and roads, albeit not great roads, were close by. A hummingbird zoomed past her head on its way to a butterfly bush. Its aerobatic flight ability amazed her, and she watched it hover as it fed.

"Mallory!" Ella's shrill voice called from inside the house.

She snapped out of her stupor and proceeded up the sidewalk. "Sorry, taking in the view." She strolled through the double door entrance. A lockbox hung on the doorknob. "Where are you?" She moved her gaze around the huge great room. The exposed timbers were breathtaking. A majestic stone fireplace with a bottom ledge centered on the far wall. Her footsteps echoed in the empty structure.

"In the kitchen."

Mallory rolled her eyes. "Where's the kitchen?"

"Marco." Ella's sing-song voice echoed off the walls.

She laughed and yelled "Polo." By the third round, she found Ella gazing out the kitchen window. Cherry cabinets graced the walls and complemented the quartz countertops. The kitchen didn't have an island, but the enormous amount of counter space was drool worthy. "I'm guessing this is one of your listings, but what are we doing here?"

"Isn't this house fantastic?" Ella clasped her hands together, her contained excitement ready to burst through her restraints. "Come with me." She clasped Mallory's hand as she flew past, jerking Mallory in her wake and nearly yanking her neck out of alignment. "Look at this screened-in porch. Imagine having your coffee out here in the morning with the gentle breeze warming your skin." She closed her eyes.

"It's lovely, Ella, but why would I imagine this? I live in the city." Mallory studied Ella's face. The overzealous sprite was up to something.

"Correction, you live with your parents." Ella crossed her arms high on her chest.

"That's only temporary."

"So where's all of your stuff? In your Chicago apartment?"

Mallory scrunched up her face. "Fine, so I moved out of the apartment and put my stuff in storage until I get a new place."

"And this…" Ella spun, arms wide, "is a new place." She pumped her hands in the air.

Mallory's jaw dropped. She scanned the room. "This is a lovely place." Her mouth closed. No, this was crazy. "Not possible, I work four and a half hours from here."

"You work from home most of the time anyway.

You can Skype your meetings and when you have to travel, there's an airport forty-five minutes away."

Mallory narrowed her eyes. "You've been thinking about this for a while?"

"Yes." She grabbed Mallory's hand again and yanked her along.

She showed the spare bedroom, which was a pretty standard design. They dashed up the stairs. "This is my favorite of all." Ella couldn't stand still.

A work loft overlooked the great room and the huge window offered a view of the lake. Where she could see Zehn swimming after some geese. He hastened a reverse and beelined for the shore. Mallory chuckled, watching two geese stand tall while flapping their wings wide. *Must have a nest nearby*. "Better hurry, boy." They were gaining on him.

"One last thing." She reached for Mallory.

Mallory jammed her hands in her pockets. "I already need surgery to repair the damage you've done to my shoulder."

Ella jutted her hands on her hips. "Follow me, delicate princess."

She took her to the master bedroom. A girl's dream come true. The huge walk-in closet would've encased her entire bedroom at the old apartment. "Oh my." She fanned herself.

"Oh, it gets better."

They walked into the master bathroom. Mallory's steps faltered. "Oh-my-goodness."

"I know, right?" Ella bounced in place.

She slid her hand across the cool marble of the double vanity as she glided toward the walk-in shower with glass doors. But, she got distracted and made a sharp veer to the spa tub, big enough to swim in. She climbed in and sat. "I'm in a happy place right now. Start talking." Leaning back in the tub, she visualized the jets massaging away all her stress and her eyes fluttered closed.

"It's been on the market for a year. The man who lived here had a motorcycle accident and lost his leg, so this place is too much for him to care for. Another firm had the listing and inflated the price, so it fell into a bit of disarray. I'm sure you noticed the lack of upkeep on the outside." Ella's heels clicked on the tile floor as she paced, moving her hands with each syllable. "The inside is fantastic. Needs a good scrub down, but it's in working order. He listed with us a couple of weeks ago, and I explained we really needed to reevaluate his asking price. He's come down a lot, and he needs to move this place. But even in this economy, I don't think it will last long at the new asking price. As soon as I saw this house, I thought of you."

Mallory opened her eyes, defenses weakening. "It's beautiful here, but I don't know about moving back."

"Would you rather live in the city filled with people like Kyle?" When Mallory didn't speak, Ella stomped her foot. "Come on, Mallory, you've been gone long enough, and we miss you here. Having the gang back together again would be so fantastic. Come home to us, Mal. It's time." She clasped her hands in front of her chest.

Little by little, the corners of her mouth curved upward. Having people around to support and love her would be nice. Ella said all the right words. She glanced at Ella, and she looked like a kid waiting for Santa

Claus to come. "Let me think about it."

"Hurray!" Ella launched herself into the tub with Mallory and gave her a massive squeeze.

"I didn't say yes." She pointed out while being choked.

"You didn't say no either." Ella released her neck. "Don't take too long. I wasn't kidding about this place not lasting. And don't forget you would have the most fabulous real estate agent to negotiate on your behalf."

"How could I forget that? You tell me all the time."

Ella slugged her before climbing out of the tub. "Not tooting your own horn never got a real-estate agent far." She extended her hand to Mallory, helping her do the same.

As they exited the house, Mallory took one last look, chewing on her lower lip. Her house? An eager beaver must live in her gut, because something was sure pounding its tail in there. Then apprehension over the enormity of this kind of decision forced it out. She turned away. Can't think about this now. "Zehn, leave that goose alone and get over here."

"You're waning. I can tell." Ella poked her. "You missed us. You want to see us more. You really missed us." A goofy dance accompanied her truly awful song.

Mallory bumped her. "You're pretty hard to take. Zehn!" The shaking dog doused them in water, bringing an abrupt end to the conversation. Mallory removed a towel from the back of her car and dried him off as he wiggled around, capturing any opportunity to lick her face. "Get in, you unruly animal."

"Wow, what a great place for a dog." Ella tapped her index finger to her chin.

"Get in the car and lose the high-pressure sales

tactic." She prodded her toward the car.

"Tick-tock." Ella tapped her wrist.

"Get in!" Mallory pointed a stern finger at Ella who put three fingers up in a childhood promise.

"That's great. You weren't a scout." Mallory started the car and could sense the enormity of Ella's smile. Annoying friend. She aimed at, and drove into, a pothole.

Ella's head bumped the window, and she choked as the seatbelt locked up.

"Road needs work." Mallory snorted, sending them both into fits of laughter.

Chapter Ten

A homeowner. Up to now, Mallory rented houses or apartments, but to own her own home? Logistically, she could work it out with her job. Working as an independent contractor for the company gave her freedom to pick her office, and she worked mainly online. Her family and friends lived in Jersey County—that's a plus, now that she figured out how special her parents are.

All the crazy things they did used to embarrass her as a kid, but now she found them funny or endearing. Like most kids, she grew up to look back and appreciate all their oddities. They're what made her the person she is today. *Could I do it? Do I want that responsibility? I have a murder investigation hanging over my head.* Ralph was determined to see her behind bars. Whether she did it or not wouldn't matter to him. He wanted revenge pure and simple. Revenge for something he'd concocted in his own head.

Zehn yanked on his leash.

Mallory had been oblivious to the fact she'd stopped moving. "Sorry, boy, got my head in the clouds."

He tilted his head, upper lip caught on a tooth.

Mallory laughed and ruffled the fur on his head.

The black Dodge Charger had returned to the spot under the oak tree.

Her heart weighed heavy in her chest. Would this ever end? She turned Zehn loose in her parents' front yard and picked up a well-chewed tennis ball then launched it through the air.

Zehn bounded after it and caught it mid-bounce.

There you go, Ralph, hope you're getting some real good footage of this. Headline, "Murder suspect plays fetch with over enthusiastic dog."

She cocked back her arm and swung her arm forward in a circular arc with the intention to release mid-way through the circle.

"Mallory."

That voice filled her veins with ice water. Her throw flew awry, slamming into the clay pot filled with Geraniums. She cringed as the pot shattered on the porch.

Zehn cowered and gave her a look that said *you're fired*.

"Mallory." The voice sounded closer.

Her neck hairs stood on end, the sensation of needles piercing her skin forced a shiver.

"Mallory."

The presence loomed right behind her now. She turned with a slow pivot. Her hand shielded the sun from her eyes, and Kyle took shape. Not one word articulated. Only the overwhelming urge to vomit. She blinked several times as though he was a mirage…or a nightmare. He didn't disappear. "What-are-you-doing-here?" The words were forced through clenched teeth.

"Hello to you, too."

Kyle's teeth would have dentists breaking down his door to get him to sign a contract agreeing to be their cover model for whitening procedures.

"Why are you here?" Mallory's gaze drifted to the unmarked car. Great, that's all she needed—Ralph to see her with Kyle.

"Would you believe I came to see you?" Kyle flashed his dazzling grill.

She recoiled at the way the words slithered out of his mouth.

"No." *Please, Mother Nature, open the heavens and save me with a monsoon. Send Kyle scurrying back into his hole to protect his perfectly groomed hair and clothing.*

His laugh ripped through the air. "Now, Mallory, be nice. We were engaged."

"Before you banged my maid of honor. Or, did you forget that part?"

"We have been over this before. You weren't around enough for me—"

Mallory's narrowed gaze locked with Kyle's.

"Never mind." He waved a hand and grinned.

She needed sunglasses to reduce the gleam from his teeth.

"The authorities released Skylar's body, and her funeral is day after tomorrow."

At least he had the decency to lose the smile. Mallory nodded. She didn't like the girl anymore, but she'd never wish such a heinous end. They'd been friends once, though she couldn't forget their past, nor could she forgive Skylar for her betrayal. "So, again I ask, why are you here?"

"Can we talk?" Kyle stepped closer.

"I have nothing to say to you." Mallory glanced again to the unmarked car. She pressed her palm to the center of her chest. Blood pounded underneath her hand. If it wouldn't draw attention, she'd haul him to the side of the house for this conversation, and out of Ralph's view.

"I'm not leaving until you hear me out." He crossed his arms.

She knew from experience that like a petulant child, he wouldn't give up. She sighed. "Not here. Give me a minute to put Zehn in the house and grab my keys."

"You can ride with me." His posture relaxed.

"You can follow me." *I'm not leaving it open for further discussion.* Being trapped in a car with her ex wasn't a viable option. At least, this way she could make a break for it, if needed.

****

Pungent scents of fish and decaying organic matter wafting from the river assaulted Mallory as she exited her car. She glanced at the towboat pushing several barges up river.

Kyle parked next to her at Mocha Fusion, the local coffeehouse…the sole coffeehouse in town. He held the door for her to enter.

Him playing the chivalrous gentleman plain annoyed her. She ordered a vanilla latte with extra whip cream, the least she deserved if she hoped to stomach this conversation. Kyle offered to pay but she refused. Never would she take anything from that man again.

He grabbed his bold brew coffee and followed her to a table along the wall.

They sat silent, sipping their drinks until Mallory couldn't take it any longer.

"Tell me what you want so we never have to see each other again." The sentence flew out of her mouth in a single breath. The surprise on Kyle's face pleased her. He almost had the nerve to appear hurt.

He took another sip of his coffee, set it down, and stared into the dark liquid.

A millennium seemed to pass before he looked up. The cocky smile on his face made her gut tense.

"I think we should get back together."

Her upper eyelids shot up so fast she thought she'd knocked her eyebrows clean off her forehead. "You what!"

People in the coffee shop stared in their direction.

Her body scorched her from the inside out. She glanced around, her cheeks burned hotter at seeing the crowd's attention on them—on her. She put up her hand and gave a clipped wave. "Sorry, folks, nothing more to see here. Please go back to enjoying your delightful pastries and beverages."

The background chatter started up again as everyone determined they weren't interesting.

Mallory fanned herself, not sure if the heat manifested from rage or embarrassment, but figured more than likely a bit of both. Once composed, she looked at him again.

"That's why I love you. I never know what you're going to say or do next."

She clenched the sides of the table, her knuckles turned white. "Are you kidding me? Are-you-kidding-me?" The corners of her mouth quivered. "You come to my parents' home. Drag me away, for this? What kind of game are you playing?" The words forced through gritted teeth were only a loud whisper.

"Mallory, I'm not kidding. I miss you, and we made…we make a great couple." He laid his hand palm up halfway across the table.

Fuming, she just stared at it.

He slid it back to his coffee cup.

"Bull. We were never good together. I was too blind to see how dysfunctional we were then. I spent so much time conforming to your world, I completely lost myself." She paused to catch her breath. "And what are you thinking, doing this when you've come for your girlfriend's funeral?" The disgust crushed in, and she fought down the emotions driving her to scream at or choke him…or scream while choking him.

"She wasn't my girlfriend." He peered into his coffee. "We were just…compatible."

"Ha." The single word burst out, and she took a quick glance around to ensure she hadn't again drawn attention. Lowering her voice, she said, "Exactly how many companions did you have while we were together?" She leaned back in her chair and crossed her arms, waiting for his answer.

"Come on, Mallory." He twirled his coffee cup and tilted his head to the side.

His notorious aren't-I-so-sweet-and-innocent pose, she was all-too-familiar with—it's probably the one he used to bag her maid of honor.

He moved his gaze to hers.

Her forehead crinkled under the strain, still waiting.

"It wasn't like that—"

"Yeah, that's what I thought." Mallory had suspected there had been others before Skylar, but wanted to confirm it. The chair screeched on the tile as Mallory placed her hands on the table, pushing up to stand.

Kyle grabbed her hand in a firm hold.

"Let go."

"Listen to me."

"I'm done listening to your lies. Now let—" She moved her gaze over his shoulder. This can't be happening. *Come on, universe, give a girl a break.*

Wade and Candy walked down the sidewalk toward Mocha Fusion.

Kyle stroked his thumb across the back of Mallory's hand. "Baby, I—"

He obviously took Mallory's sudden quietness as willingness to listen instead of shock. "Shut up, Kyle." She wanted to duck into the bathroom and hide until Wade left. Kyle had one heck of a grip and wouldn't let go. She yanked again desperate to make a break—too late.

Candy caught her staring and drug Wade in their direction.

His scowl and the way he attempted to redirect Candy to the counter made her think he wasn't enthused either. *And smile.* She told her lips but it felt more like when you were at the orthodontist and they filled the trays with impression material and told you not to gag.

Candy popped her gum. "Mallory. I haven't seen you in so long." She slid her gaze to Kyle.

"We bumped into each other at the grocery store last week." Mallory struggled not to look at Wade.

Candy waved her hand in front of her face. "Oh, that's right, I totally forgot." She flipped her hair to the side and then slid her arm through Wade's, snuggling close. "Anyway, I mean like really sit and talk."

"Why would we?" And why did Wade just stand

there mute? To rub her nose in his new relationship? *Retract the claws. Don't show he's getting to you.*

"I was being nice."

"Why start now?" They'd never been friends, and Mallory wasn't in the mood. Being surrounded by three people she wanted nothing to do with made her surly.

"Who's your man?" Candy winked at Kyle.

Mallory glanced in his direction. If he stared any harder at Candy's chest he'd pop out his eyes. Her surgeon must have believed bigger was better. *I wonder if you threw her in the lake, would she float?* "What man?" She snickered to herself.

Kyle's hand squeezed tighter. "I'm Kyle, Mallory's fiancé."

Mallory yanked, freeing her hand. "Oh, I don't think so." *Why isn't Wade hauling Candy away? Why is he allowing this to go on?* Mallory refused to be the first to run.

"And you are?" Kyle asked, half standing and extending his hand.

She released Wade and accepted Kyle's hand. "I'm Candy, and this is my man, Wade."

Oh gag. Mallory turned her head to hide her snarl.

Kyle kissed Candy's hand and uncontained giggles erupted from Candy. He then extended his hand to Wade.

Wade raised his hands to the position of surrender. "No thanks, I'll pass on the smooch."

Mallory snorted. "Sorry." She thought Wade grinned.

"Oh, Mallory, you have such a charming fiancé."

Not my fiancé. "How's work, Candy?" This time, she shared her snarl with Candy.

158

The plastered smile melted of off Candy's face. "How's the murder investigation?" She shot back.

Touché. Mallory hadn't thought she had a nasty retort in her. And as quick as Candy's smile disappeared, it returned.

"Don't you two want some coffee or something? I mean you are in a coffeehouse." This time Mallory captured Wade's gaze, and she couldn't look away. The nonverbal communication linking them required an "R" rating. Something had sparked between them from the day they met. Mallory didn't understand it, but when she's around Wade, nothing else mattered. He's attractive, sure, but the connection was unlike anything she'd ever shared with anyone. Her breathing turned deep and regular, but her heart raced.

Wade's gaze burned into her, and she imagined an x-ray of her gut would show butterflies on the image. Mallory sucked in hard on her lower lip. She hadn't realized she done it until Wade's gaze left her eyes and slid down to her mouth. She released it, unaware of anyone but them in the establishment. The silence had a blaring effect and then…

"Baby."

Candy's whine was like a bucket of cold water.

"I need a muffin."

The noise rushed back into the room. Mallory looked away.

Candy tugged on Wade.

He exhaled. "Fine." Nicety forgotten, he let her yank him away without a goodbye.

Mallory sighed.

"What was that?" Kyle's narrowed gaze followed Wade and Candy.

"What was what?"

"Whatever that was between you and the guy." Kyle scrutinized her.

He had the nerve to come off as jealous. "I don't know what you're talking about. Look, Kyle I've got to go."

"Mallory wait."

"What now?"

"You've had your freedom, and now it's time for you to come home." He reached for her hand again.

She jerked away before he could grab it. Mallory stood, taking her coffee. "I am home." She walked away.

Chapter Eleven

Tightness formed in Wade's chest as Mallory left. Candy wouldn't let go of his arm, and he only half listened as she rattled on, deciding if she wanted the cinnamon scone…or the blueberry muffin…maybe the lemon loaf cake…or the cinnamon scone…oh wait, I already said that…insert laughter. Wade rolled his eyes in plain sight of the cashier.

Candy giggled. "Guess it's the cinnamon scone then."

Thank goodness. Get her food and get her home. That's all he wanted to do. She'd shown up at his door this morning, begging for a ride home, because she'd ridden with her mother to her grandmother's house, and they'd left abruptly on a family emergency to her Aunt Helen's house. "Could she pretty-please have a ride home" turned into "I'm hungry, let's grab a pastry and coffee."

All this because he'd agreed to have lunch at Ms. Emery's just so she would continue to supply him with her delicious baked goods. Instead, the lunch ended up being "let's marry the granddaughter off to the neighbor meal" and the granddaughter seemed to be on board. Then to top it off, he bumped in to Mallory with her ex-fiancé. He wasn't sure why that bothered him so much. He had no claim on her. They weren't seeing each other. But, every time he was around her, he couldn't think straight. The tension crackled in the air between them and fried his brain. So, instead of ending the awkward encounter, he'd stood like a dope, letting Candy rattle on.

The cashier slid their coffees across the counter and handed Candy her pastry. His arm finally free, he stretched and flexed to get the blood back into his hand. Wade beelined for the exit and opened the door. No Candy. *Where did she go?* He looked back to the register, not there. He swept his gaze around the room, and she'd taken a seat in the far corner.

Candy waved him over.

He exhaled slowly, and he'd swear he carried a seventy-pound bag of flour on his shoulders. This girl was never going home. He approached the table. "I thought you needed to get home."

"I've got time. We need to get to know each other better. Sit." She scooted out a chair with her toe.

"Look, Candy, I've got work to do—"

"You work too hard." She crossed her legs and waved his words away. "I don't want my man running himself into the ground. We should be expending energy in other ways." Candy fluttered her eyelashes.

Telling Candy he wasn't interesting in pursuing a relationship made dread whirl in his stomach. What if she didn't take it well? Would Ms. Emery stop supplying him with baked goods?

She shimmied in her chair.

Thank goodness, the coffee shop support beams were square. "Candy, I don't want to hurt your feelings, but I'm not your *man*. We just met."

A sly smile played on her lips. "Which is why we are getting to know each other better."

Is that a toe sliding up my leg? Wade discreetly shifted away his leg.

"It's just a cup of coffee." Candy slid her finger up and down her mug.

The way she ogled him made him feel like he should have a wad of ones to stuff into her waistband. In the end, he decided conceding might be the fastest way to get this over with and get her home. Lesson learned. He'd find a way to avoid her from here on out or relocate to a new neighborhood…or state…maybe country. He'd always liked Switzerland. Weren't they neutral?

****

Poppy and Matt stood on the front porch when he drove in.

"Hey, guys," Wade said, coming up the steps. "Hanging out here or got plans?" He jangled his keys.

"We're going for a hike at Bluff State Park. Want to come?" Poppy asked.

"No, thanks. I've already had a workout this morning." Getting Candy off his arm and out of his truck.

The green subcompact vehicle parked in front of the Larsen's.

"Hey, there's Mallory—Mallory." Poppy called and waved as Mallory exited her vehicle.

Mallory hesitated.

"Get your skinny butt over here." The tone of Poppy's voice issued an order, not a request.

Mallory's shoulders drooped, but she shuffled across the street. She let her gaze gravitate to Wade's as she climbed the stairs, but snapped to Poppy.

"Guys, I've got work to do, so I'm heading in."

Wade thumbed over his shoulder.

"Don't you move." Poppy froze him with a look.

Wade raised his eyebrows and glanced at Matt who offered a shrug.

Poppy stepped where she could see both Mallory and Wade. "Look, I don't know what's going on between you two. First, there are fireworks, and you're bumping and grinding on a dance floor like a roller coaster ride."

"Poppy!" Mallory's cheeks pinkened.

Poppy held her gaze.

Wade waited to see if Mallory would rise to Poppy's challenge and deny it. *Guess not.*

"Next, you two don't want to be in the same state as the other, and I have no idea why. I do know anytime I'm around you both there's enough sexual tension filling the air I need a cold shower. So, whether you want to admit it or not, there's something palpable between you two."

Wade started to speak, but Poppy put up a finger and held him quiet with a stare. *Wow, she's good. Matt's in trouble.*

"What I do know is, I care a great deal for this man over here." Her voice softened, and a warm smile filled her face as she looked at Matt who returned her smile. "And I won't have you two screwing it up for me. You're my best friend, Mallory, and Wade is Matt's brother, and all this crap going on between you two is making us feel like we can't all be around each other at the same time, and that stinks." She swiveled her head back and forth between them.

Wade hung his head like a kid being scolded and spotted Mallory do the same.

"I won't choose which one of you we can be around when Matt and I are together. You two have to coexist. We each love you and want you in our lives. So both of you in that house right now and figure out a way to handle being near each other, if even just as friends."

"I don't think I can—" Wade started but was cut off by Poppy's gaze that was capable of filleting him.

"You can and you will. If not for yourselves, then you'll do it for us. Inside." Poppy stomped her foot and pointed toward the door.

"I need to head home." Mallory skulked back a step.

"Now!"

Mallory jumped.

Wade held the door open and Mallory scurried through as he followed, both with sulking postures.

"Good. Now I'm going to enjoy my day and go hiking." Poppy brushed her hands in a *glad that's settled* motion.

The couple's departure left a deafening silence between Mallory and Wade. They stood watching each other.

"Want a drink?" Wade asked, uncomfortable with the silence.

"Yes, something in the mind-numbing vintage please."

"Beer?"

"Perfect."

Moments later, Wade returned and handed Mallory a bottle then directed her to his couch. "Your friend has a way with words."

She gave a short laugh. "She's plain bossy with a

little terrifying on top."

"Always like that?"

"What do you think?" Mallory leaned away, staring down her nose.

Wade nodded. Silence overtook them again.

Mallory blurted, "Where's Candy?"

The air turned frigid. "Home." Not feeling the need to elaborate, he took a swig of his early afternoon beer and sat on the couch. The hum of the DVR grated on his nerves. He'd never noticed how loud that thing was. "Where's your fiancé?"

Mallory pursed her lips as she ran her finger through the sweat on her bottle. "You know he's not my fiancé." Her voice chilled the room. She tilted her head, glaring in his direction.

"You seemed pretty friendly with all the hand holding." Why did that bug him so much?

"Surprised you noticed with hoochie mama hanging onto you like a spider monkey." Mallory took a guzzle of her beer.

This wasn't going well. "It's really none of your business."

"Ditto."

"What's your problem?"

"My problem? My problem?" Her voice elevated an octave. "Take a gander in the mirror, Mr. Perfect, because you're the one with the problem."

"That's bull. You're in trouble up to your eyeballs, and you can't even be honest about it." Wade stood, towering over her. "The police are watching and waiting for you to screw up."

Mallory slammed her bottle on his coffee table, sloshing some of the cool liquid onto her hand and the tabletop. She sprung to her feet, advancing on Wade. "How dare you throw that in my face. You know good and well I didn't ask for any of this. I'm a victim too. Ralph is desperate to frame me for Skylar's murder, and I had nothing to do with it."

"Didn't you?" Why couldn't he shut his mouth? He didn't think she murdered Skylar but couldn't stop himself. His taunting was a verbal form of poking at a rattlesnake to see if it would strike.

Mallory wrenched her head back, eyes wide. "With friends like you who needs enemies?"

Okay, that hurt. This time he kept his mouth shut.

"I thought you believed in me, but I can see I was wrong. You're even less of a man than I first thought."

"I got your butt out of jail, didn't I? You're welcome by the way."

"I guess a lot has changed since then."

"Lose the pity party, Mallory. You got yourself into this mess." Why was he being so hateful?

Her eyes appeared watery. Her fists clenched. "You're a class 'A' jerk, Wade Porter. That's right I asked to stumble upon a dead body. One who was supposed to be my maid of honor. My maid of honor that liked doing the horizontal tango with my fiancé. Yeah, I asked for that." She shook with rage as she marched forward nearly nose to chest with him now. "I wanted Ralph to arrest me and accuse me of her murder. I wanted the guy who stalked me in high school to make my life more miserable now than he ever did then. Back when I'd been terrified to walk anywhere alone in school because he was always there, watching me. Just like he's doing now."

She shoved him backward, hitting his sternum with

the heel of her hand. "Not to mention, I wanted to come running home with my tail between my legs and live with my parents, which is made even better in a small town where everyone knows everyone else's business." She shoved him back again. "And hurray for me, I end up with the worst neighbor ever who is so full of judgment he's forgotten how to have any compassion." She gave a last jab, cleared the couch, and backed toward the door.

"Sure, I even asked for someone to plant Skylar's wallet in my car to make it look like I'd done something wrong. Then Ralph shows up with a warrant to search my car. How freaking convenient is that?"

The resonant frequency of her voice was capable of breaking glass. *Huh?* He wasn't sure he heard the last one right.

She yanked opened his door. "Yeah, you're correct, Wade, I asked for my entire life to turn into some black murky cesspool that feels like it's swallowing me whole. I'll be damned if I know how much more I can take. And to people like you, who dump salt in my wounds, whose only intention is to make me feel more alone than I already do. Thanks a lot."

Wade's shock wore off a bit, and he hurried after her. "Mallory, wait." Guilt ate him alive.

She rushed down the sidewalk. Hightailing it for her parents' home. She screeched to a halt and pivoted to face him. "Go find Candy, Wade, you two were meant for each other. Be sure you take plenty of one dollar bills when you escort her to the next outdoor concert." She turned and ran.

Wade sat on his porch and rested his head in his

hands. Why had he picked a fight? He knew why—he thought if he riled her, she'd open up. Which she had, but now she was so furious he didn't know if he could repair the damage.

Chapter Twelve

Mallory stormed through the front door, rushing straight for the stairs.

"Mallory, is that you?" Her father's voice drifted from the den.

She paused. "Yeah, Dad." Her voice came out defeated. She stepped into the den. Her mom sat on the couch, cross-stitching, with Zehn curled up next to her, asleep. Her dad worked on a crossword while reclined in his easy chair.

"Is something wrong?" Jim scribbled on the folded newspaper.

"No. I'm fine." Unless you consider feeling like someone ripped out all my innards and stomped on them was something wrong.

"You don't look fine the way you raced through the door." He set aside his crossword. "Want to talk about it?"

She forced an insincere smile. "I'm just not feeling well. I'm going to go upstairs to lie down."

"Do you need an enema?" Charlotte looked up from her cross-stitch.

Mallory's whipped up her head to lock gazes with her mother. "What?"

"Do you need an enema?"

"No, I don't need an enema. Why would you ask me that?" Mallory kept her mouth agape, perplexed by this line of questioning.

"Because you don't feel well. That's what I used on you as a child. Always did the trick." She focused on her cross-stitch.

"Gross, Mom. Thanks, but no thanks." Mallory stepped back to leave.

"You really should consider it. I watched a program on cable and the spokesperson talked about coffee enemas. The enema can be a powerful detoxifier, people report having more energy and being in a better mood."

"There's nothing wrong with my mood." Could this day get any worse?

"Humph." Charlotte pulled another stitch through the fabric secured in a wooden hoop.

Mallory's eyes widened, the entire conversation took her back. "Really, Mom. I prefer my coffee orally with cream and sugar."

"Consider it. They say enemas can keep your digestive tract clean and promote a healthy gut. Might help with that bloat." Charlotte gave her a sideways glance before highlighting a completed section on her diagram and switching thread colors.

Bloat? Mallory placed her hands over her stomach and looked down. "I'm not bloated."

"Humph."

This time the noise articulated loud enough Zehn woke up and realized his dog mom was home. His tail thumped on the couch.

"This is utter nonsense. I'm done with this conversation, and Mom, you need to start watching the Family channel. And thanks for your help, Dad."

"I know I'm switching to tea." Jim didn't even

glance up from his crossword.

Mallory turned.

Zehn jumped off the couch to catch up.

"Too much even for you, baby." She scratched his head.

"Tremendous health benefits are obtained by filling your rectum with coffee." Charlotte's voice chased Mallory up the stairs.

"Thank goodness I called Ella, and told her to put in an offer on that house on my way home. I love my parents, but visiting would be enough."

Mallory climbed into bed.

Zehn curled up at her feet.

She did a pretty good job of feeling sorry for herself and wanted sleep to stop all the crap running through her mind. She'd rolled over for the umpteenth time, leaving her back to the door. A knock jarred her awake, moments away from deep sleep taking her. She refused to open her eyes. "Go away."

The person knocked again, a little firmer. The hinges on her door creaked.

"I don't want a damn enema!"

"That's good, because we don't know each other all that well." A deep familiar voice said.

Mallory's eyes shot open, and she stared at the wall, unable to turn over. Her breath jammed under the lump in her throat. An unrecognizable groan escaped her. She yanked the covers over her head. *This isn't happening. Surely, he'll go away.*

No such luck. The mattress rolled her toward where Wade sat.

He placed his hand on her shoulder. "Mallory. We need to talk." He tugged on the comforter.

Having him sit on her bed made her edgy. "We talked already. Go away." Her words were muffled by the comforter.

"No, we argued." Wade tugged harder on covers.

Zehn helped by walking on top of the heap that was Mallory to greet Wade.

"Hey there, big guy."

"Ugh." The sound whooshed out as Zehn stepped on her stomach. Wade must have known her grip released, because he gave a good yank and she was exposed to air. "Thanks a lot, Zehn."

He rewarded her with tuna-scented lick.

"Can we talk—please?" Wade brushed her tangled mess of hair from her face.

His touch was warm and soft. Wade's fingertips had a firm texture, not callused just thick, and they lingered on her cheek. "I think we proved earlier we can't. Go home, Wade, I'm not in the mood."

"I'm not leaving." He scooted closer, kicked off his shoes, and spun, positioning himself beside her.

Well, this is unnerving. Still in the prone position, she stared up into Wade's dark brown eyes. She pushed off Zehn, and he crawled back to the foot of the bed. Mallory forced herself to a sitting position and clutched her pillow to her stomach. "Tell my parents to be more selective about whom they let in this house on your way out."

A smirk crossed his face. "Your mom really liked me. I could tell."

"Traitor." She blew at the hair in her face.

Wade leaned back against her headboard. "I'm sorry I picked a fight with you."

"That takes the wind out of my sails. I was revving

up to recite the long list of the ways you wronged me, but now…" She readjusted her hold on her pillow. "I'm sorry, too."

"Can we try this again?" He turned his head to study her.

"Try what again?"

"Being friends."

Her facial expression softened. "I think I'd like that."

"Good. Let's start with you telling me about the wallet in your car."

Mallory's spine stiffened. *Well, that tosses cold water on our warm and fuzzy reunion.* "I don't know what you're talking about." She glanced away.

"Nice try, but your words not mine. You've got to trust someone."

"And it might as well be you?"

"Sure, I mean I'm an upstanding guy." He bumped her, rocking her with the motion. "If I can help you, I will."

Silence followed. *What am I supposed to do?* After Kyle, Mallory found trusting hard. "Trust is a two-way street. If I'm to trust you, you need to trust me."

Wade narrowed his eyes. "What did you have in mind?"

"I want you to share something personal about yourself."

"I love watching old reruns of *Punky Brewster*." He hung his head.

Mallory slugged his upper arm. "Not what I meant. Something you don't like to talk about."

"Well, I'm not proud about that."

"Something that makes your gut twist when you

think about it."

"Why don't you ask me something, and I'll answer?"

"Anything I want?"

"This is your game."

Mallory rubbed her chin with her first two fingers. She adjusted her head tilt so she could lock eye contact. "Why did you stop being an attorney?"

The color drained from Wade's face. He banged his head back against the headboard. "You don't play around."

Mallory planned to hit him with the one story he wouldn't tell. "It's something I've wondered about. If you don't want to share—"

"You're not getting off the hook that easy." He paused. "I was on the fast track to make partner at my firm. I took on a high-profile case involving a city councilman who planned a run for senator." Wade yanked the pillow from Mallory's arms and clutched it. "I need this more than you."

"I have a blankie over on that chair—should you need it." She pointed.

He followed the movement with his gaze. "I'll keep that in mind."

He drifted into a silence, as though collecting his thoughts.

Leaning back his head against the headboard, he closed his eyes.

The pain radiating from him made Mallory's heart hurt. Maybe she shouldn't have pushed. She opened her mouth to tell him he didn't have to divulge his secret when he spoke.

"His wife accused him of domestic violence, and

he was charged. Her injuries were quite severe, ranging from a concussion to a compound fracture of her fibula. She alleged he stood on her leg and snapped it by almost bending her leg in two."

A little vomit surged into Mallory's mouth.

"I convinced a jury she'd set up her husband, because she wanted a huge divorce settlement. That she was having an affair and her sole reason for filing these charges was to ruin her husband's run for senator, because he'd refused to give her the divorce."

"How did they explain the broken leg?"

"He claimed he saw her fall down their basement steps when she tripped over one of their kids' toys."

Mallory's leg ached in sympathy. "Sounds plausible."

He caught her watching him. "My job was to defend this guy, and that's what I did. I planted enough reasonable doubt that he got off. Even subpoenaed the guy she was having the affair with."

"What was the truth? Did he do it, or not?" If Wade clutched the pillow any tighter it would split in two. Mallory feared she'd be sorry she asked.

"A few days after I got him off, he…he…he…" Wade pinched the bridge of his nose. His breathing grew faster.

Mallory could tell whatever it was still tore him apart. She laid her hand on his thigh and squeezed. He put his hand over hers and held on, and unlike when Kyle did it, she found she liked the gesture.

He continued on without letting go. "He shot and killed his wife and two kids before turning the gun on himself."

Mallory gasped and then tried to suck back the

sound. Her gut rolled, but she didn't want to make him feel worse than he already did. She didn't know what to say to take his pain away, but she didn't want to invalidate the things he felt either. He's entitled to his emotions. Flashes of that story being on the news came back to her, but she didn't mention it. "I'm sorry."

He stared deep into her eyes. "Thanks for not saying it wasn't my fault."

She took her other hand and brushed his cheek. "I don't think it was your fault. He made his own choices, but I can understand how something like that would weigh on you. You're a good man, Wade." She wanted to take away the guilt he obviously still carried.

"That wasn't what you were saying earlier, I believe I was the worst neighbor ever."

"You're a good man, but a lousy neighbor." Mallory smiled. He hadn't relaxed his grip on her hand, and she could get used to his touch. "Thanks for trusting me."

"Anyway. I haven't practiced law since. Now, I think it's your turn. I need to talk about something else." He rubbed his eyes.

"I collect toys from happy meals."

He gave a belly laugh.

Mallory took the opportunity to get her hand back.

"Nice try." Wade leaned into her.

"You were right. My life's a mess." She yanked back the pillow and wrapped her arms around it. They passed it back and forth like a truth pillow. "I keep going through all the motions, but in the back of my mind, I'm terrified they'll throw me in jail." She buried her face in the pillow. "I jump when I hear a knock at the door, thinking it'll be Ralph, waiting to slap on the handcuffs."

"I can't understand you." He tugged at the pillow.

She lifted her head. "I couldn't find my cell phone, and I thought my seatbelt hole might have eaten it. So, I dug under my seats and found a credit card holder wedged way up under there."

"Belonged to Skylar?"

Mallory nodded. "It even had a smear of dried blood. I lost it. I know Ralph wants to find something to arrest me on and I panicked."

"What did you do?"

She sucked on her lower lip then buried her face in her pillow. "I threw it in the lake." Her words came out muffled.

"What?" He yanked away the pillow.

"I threw it in the lake! Okay." The back of her head bounced off the headboard. "I freaked out."

"That was evidence, Mallory."

His scolding didn't help her guilt. "I know," she whined. "I panicked." Her voice weak. "Ralph wants to arrest me so badly."

"When did all this happen?"

She told him the story of how she got rid of the wallet.

He laughed until tears fell. "Zehn brought it back to you, for real?"

"Yes."

"Then yanked you into the water?"

She covered her warm cheeks with her hands as she nodded. Memories flashed, and she couldn't control her snicker.

"That's hysterical." He wiped at his eyes. "Is that the day I saw you soaked?"

"The one and only."

"Mallory, that's why I like being around you so much."

She squinted her right eye. "You like being around me?"

He skimmed his gaze across her face. "Yeah, I do. You have a way about you. My day could totally suck, and you just being you do something that makes me laugh." He gave her a gentle smile.

Her cheeks ignited and she looked away. Wade stayed quiet long enough Mallory turned to study him. "What's going on your mind?"

He gave her a quick glance. "You were right."

"Of course I was."

"Do you even know what I'm referring to?"

"Don't care. Completely happy with, I was right."

Wade chuckled. "When you mentioned the convenience of Ralph getting a warrant to search your vehicle. You were right. Too much of a coincidence."

He stared at nothing.

Mallory would swear she could see wheels turning.

"He had to have grounds to get the warrant." Wade rubbed the back of his neck.

"Yeah…and?"

"That means someone knew Skylar's credit card holder was inside your vehicle."

Silence descended over Mallory, and she joined Wade in looking at the nothingness. "You think the person who killed her put it in my car?"

Wade shrugged, turning to face her. "It's the only person who would've benefited from you being caught with it. Who else would have had the opportunity to take it?"

"There's one other possibility." That possibility scared the crap out of Mallory.

Wade narrowed his eyes.

"Ralph could have found it at the scene and planted it there. The guy really has it out for me. Not to mention, I don't think he has one of the most stable minds."

"Tell me something I didn't notice." Wade took her hand, turning the palm side up and tracing his finger along her lifeline.

"You read palms?" she asked to distract herself from her body's volcanic eruption his simple touch created.

"Nah." He turned his head and pinned her with a smile. "I just really like the feel of your skin."

Spontaneous evaporation of all the moisture in her mouth left her with cotton tongue. She swallowed, trying to work up some spit. His dark eyes transfixed her, and she couldn't look away. If his finger on her palm could make her feel like this…she was in trouble.

"I have a proposition." Wade continued to trace her palm with his finger.

Please let it involve sex.

"I want to help you."

Get undressed? She licked her lips.

"If you're okay with this."

Heavens yes. Thank goodness, I didn't wear shape wear. She couldn't stop the prickly tingles coursing through her.

"I would like to investigate Skylar for you." Wade released her hand.

Ice water on her fantasy. *Bummer.* She blinked, not absorbing what he said. "Huh?"

"I don't want to invade your private life, if you don't want me to, but I might be able to help. This is what I do for a living…now."

Mallory's libido crawled back into its hole. "What can you do?"

"I want to look into her background. I'll check her credit card statements, phone records, anything that gives me some clue as to what might have gotten her killed."

"Someone wanted her dead?" A terrible foreboding settled in her bones.

"And I'll dig until I know everything there is to know about Skylar. Maybe a drug deal went wrong. Maybe she blackmailed the wrong person."

"I can't imagine Skylar into drugs."

"You probably couldn't imagine her sleeping with your fiancé either."

She tilted her head side-to-side. "True."

"I'll poke around and see if I can figure out what she was in to. If there's something to find, I will."

"You'd do that for me?" This man managed to awaken a bit of hope she'd long since buried.

Wade nudged up her chin with a gentle bump from his knuckle. "You bet."

Tears filled her eyes, and she glanced away. Kyle wouldn't even hold the elevator for her if he didn't think she hurried enough.

He put his arm around her, allowing her to rest her head on his shoulder.

"I take back the 'worst neighbor ever' comment. You're pretty terrific." What she did next surprised even her. Mallory slid her leg across Wade's thighs and sat on his lap, facing him, instantly swallowed up by

181

shock in his deep brown eyes. She folded her legs underneath her.

His breath caught.

She wiped away her tears, never taking her gaze off of him. She placed one hand on each side of his head, resting them on the headboard, and leaned in, stopping inches from his face. They were silent except for the sounds of their rapid breathing.

He reached for her face.

Not yet. She leaned back. *Don't mess with my game.*

He drew back.

She returned to her prior position. The smell of ale assaulted her olfactory sense. She inhaled deep. Wade smelled like a citrus-sprinkled forest. The pheromones in the room set off a sexual attraction fireworks display.

Wade slid his hand behind her neck and tugged her closer.

Still no. She retreated.

A groan escaped him, and he dropped his hand.

Leaning toward him, she skimmed her nose across his. His lips parted and his warm breath danced on her skin. She leaned to the side, her nose tracing the backside of his cheek. His breath caressed her ear. She repeated the process on the other side.

He clenched and unclenched his hands at her hips. The tension was palatable. He tried to scoot her closer.

Mallory resisted, holding her position nose to nose with him. She brushed her fingers down his cheeks, resting them on his chest.

He slid his hands under her shirt.

His featherlike touch left behind a heated sensation on the contacted skin. Her body quivered. She'd erupt any second. Mallory parted her lips, and her tongue traced her lower lip.

He followed the motion with his gaze, and he bit hard on his back teeth.

She was driving him crazy, and she knew it. She leaned in and let her lips touch his.

He lunged forward, but she retreated yet again. She quirked up her mouth in one corner. Mallory closed her eyes, tilted her head, and glanced away. She looked back and saw his pupils were raging pools of blackness. Lust filled his eyes, and his pulse pounded against her palm. He stared hard at her mouth, and his fingers bit into her back.

Her willpower crumbled, game over. Her fingers weaved into his thick hair. She traced the inside of his lip with her tongue and nipped. A possessive grumble escaped his throat, and she jumped. He overpowered her and crushed her against his chest. Their lips intertwined, his warm sweet tongue found hers. Blood pumped to places in her body she didn't know existed. He'd awaken a desire she found impossible to pull back from.

Wade lifted and twisted her until her back hit the mattress. A schoolgirl giggle escaped. He dropped on top of her, and they became a tangled web of arms and legs. The pressure of his body sent shivers surging through her. A well-placed nip on her neck unglued her. She clawed at his shirt and yanked his mouth back to meet hers.

"Mallory."

The door clicked. Mallory's eyes flew wide open at the same time she launched her hips into the air and catapulted Wade onto the floor. *Not fast enough.*

"Oh my word!" Charlotte slapped her hand over her eyes. "Oh my!" She spun, retreating out the door.

"Mom. Wait. It's okay." Humiliation heated her cheeks.

"You're having sex. That's not okay. You shouldn't have sex until marriage." Charlotte bounced on her heels, ready to bolt.

"I'm not having sex, Mom. You can open your eyes."

"No!"

"Mom, it's okay."

A hesitant Charlotte turned back and parted her fingers to peek through.

Mallory sat alone on her bed, smoothing down her hair.

Charlotte dropped her hand from her eyes. "What happened to Wade?"

"I'm down here." He groaned from the floor on the other side of the bed.

Mallory couldn't stop the sheepish smile plastered on her face. This situation was worse than the time in high school when her mom caught her necking on the couch with her then-boyfriend. After her parents kicked him out, they chastised her and made her read bible verses on premarital sex, followed by the dreaded sex education pregnancy pamphlet.

"Is he okay?" Charlotte rose up on tiptoe, stretching to see over the bed.

"I'm fine."

"What did you want, Mom?"

"I wanted to know if Wade wanted to stay for dinner?"

"That would be lovely. Thank you." His voice

carried over the bed.

Mallory bit back her laughter.

"Twenty minutes then." Charlotte shot her one more disapproving glare. She turned, pulling the door, only to pause and thrust it wide open.

Okay, point made, Mom.

At the sound of her mom's footsteps on the stairs, Mallory let loose and roared with laughter, grasping her stomach, she tumbled onto the bed. She hung her head over the side and peered down at Wade who had yet to stir. "Are you really okay?" She chuckled.

"Do you have an 'S' on your chest or something."

"Pure adrenaline. I was reliving my childhood. You should know by now I don't think when I panic."

"Unbelievable." He sat up, rubbing his head.

"I'm so sorry." Mallory smoothed out some wrinkles on her comforter.

"You've got some crazy super-human strength there." He smiled.

"I'm so getting the S-A-D talk again."

Wade's brow furrowed. "Wait, you're sad about what just happened?"

"No. Not sad like boo-hoo. S-A-D like—" She bit her lip. "Oh, never mind." She waved her hand. "It's a Mom thing and trust me, you don't want to know." *Why try to explain the unexplainable.*

"As long as you're not upset about any of this, because I'm definitely not."

Mallory chewed on her lower lip, failing to suppress her grin. Being eye-to-eye with Wade made her heart pound a little harder. She studied him. A tiny white scar marked his jaw back toward his ear. A slight dimple gave his chin a distinguished appearance, and she fought the urge to poke it just to see what happened. Like when you touch the tip of a dog's nose and the tongue comes out.

Wade tilted forward and his lips brushed hers.

The sensation lingered on her lips, reminding her of the time she tried plumping lip-gloss and how it caused them to tingle. Tingle, heck the sensation was like a miniature porcupine ran laps, and her lips were the track. How his gentle touch made her feel more in a brief moment of contact than she'd felt in the last three years with Kyle amazed her. In her need to feel ordinary, she'd left herself feeling hollow and empty, depriving herself of the emotions another human being could ignite in her. A simple touch made her feel as though she'd melted and become a part of something bigger.

"What are you thinking now?"

Heat rushed into her cheeks. "That we better get downstairs, or Mom will bring up a hose."

He kissed her one last time. Then held her gaze. "Liar."

"What makes you so sure?"

He stood and grabbed Mallory under her arms, lifting her off the bed, and deposited her snug against him. He let his lips brush her ear and whispered, "Because it's not what I was thinking about."

Her knees quivered and her body ached.

"You're a work of art, Mallory Larsen."

"Oh my." She fanned herself. "We've got to go, or I'll turn the hose on myself." She yanked him toward the door. Needing the watchful gazes of her parents to douse her raging libido.

Chapter Thirteen

"Where you been?" Matt glanced up from his textbook.

"Back from hiking, I see. Did you have fun?" A day that had started off rotten had done a one eighty, and Wade couldn't beat back his grin.

"Avoiding the question, I see." Matt tapped his highlighter on the table.

"How is showing an interest in my brother's health and well-being avoiding anything?"

Matt said nothing. He waited, arching a single brow.

"I was having dessert and dinner. Does that satisfy your curiosity?" Wade leaned against the kitchen counter.

"Not with Ms. Emery again. Please tell me Candy wasn't there." He dropped the highlighter and leaned back in his chair.

"No."

"Where at then?" Matt narrowed his eyes.

"The Larsen's," Wade mumbled, turning to get a glass out of the cabinet.

Matt slammed his hand on the table. "You and Mallory made nice—finally. Poppy will be thrilled. Do you mind if I tell her the truce was because of me and gain some brownie points?"

"Have at it."

"What did you eat, and did you bring leftovers?"

"Do I look like I have leftovers? And we had pork chops and mashed potatoes." Using his glass, Wade depressed the refrigerator ice dispenser, which whirled and whined before dropping cubes into the glass. Modern technology was amazing. He filled it with water.

"You said dessert. What did you have for dessert?"

"I didn't say dessert." Wade slid his gaze to his feet. A feeble attempt to preserve Mallory's virtue, but her soft touch was still too fresh in his memory.

"Yes, you did. You said dessert and dinn—" Matt halted and leaned forward. "Wait. Was Ms. Mallory dessert? She was, wasn't she? Because you said dessert before dinner. Who eats dessert before dinner? Unless dessert's a metaphor. I'm right, aren't I?" He paused. "Look at me, older brother."

Wade did and couldn't hide the smirk on his face. His libido high-fived itself.

"I knew it. Man, when you decide to make nice, you make nice. You cad." He tossed his highlighter, and it skidded off the table.

"Knock it off. It wasn't like that." *That's right, play the knight in shining armor. Insert pat on back.*

"What was it like, because last I knew you were giving her some space?"

"That didn't work out. She's a hard woman to give space to."

"Why's that?"

"Because I truly like her. She's fun to be around and makes me laugh." Wade finished off his water and put the glass in the sink.

"You've got it bad. I'm taking credit for all of this

with Poppy, so don't blow it."

"Let's just see what happens. I don't even know how much longer she'll be here before heading back to the city."

He lifted a single shoulder. "Maybe she'll stay."

"Why would she? She's built a life elsewhere, but I hope to get to know her better before then." Gloom crept into his heart. Wade didn't want to think about her leaving.

"Do you want me to ask Poppy to pass her a note asking if she wants to go steady, and to check yes or no?" Matt laughed.

Wade scowled before walking out of the room. In theory, the note thing wasn't such a bad idea. That maneuver got him his first girlfriend in the third grade. Cecily Jones. Her mom packed the best lunches…it had been love at first bite.

Chapter Fourteen

Mallory took off her reading glasses and tossed them on the desk. "I don't know about you, Zehn, but I could use a sun fix." The dog was curled up under her desk resigned to wait for playtime. The last couple days, she'd spent analyzing market reports, reviewing customer surveys, and spending hours talking to consultants—all so Americans could look fashion forward this fall in all the latest and yet reasonably priced trends.

And the President thought his life was tough—he didn't have to worry about America falling apart if the hemlines weren't all the rage. She darn near kept the world running all by herself...and her assistant buyers, who did a great deal of grunt work, but mostly her. *You're welcome.*

The vibrating phone worked its way to the edge of her desk, interrupting her self-aggrandizing thoughts. It beeped and stilled. A text from Kyle appeared on the screen. "Great. Now what?"

He requested she meet him at a friend of the family's hunting cabin. *Not a chance.* She'd rather join the nutty folks in their polar bear plunge. Which she abbreviated to, Me: *Can't. Busy.*

The phone began its song and dance again. She sighed. Why was he even still around? Skylar's funeral was the other day.

Kyle: Need to see you now. Bring ring.

"Ha!"

Zehn's ears perked up, and he cocked his head.

"The toad wants his ring back. That's what this is all about. Why that good for nothing pond scum." She took a breath.

Me: *Come pick it up if you want it.*

Dirt bag. Cheap skate. Bottom dweller. Yep, she felt better.

And the dancing phone again. She was beginning to hate texting.

Kyle: *Do you really want me to come back to your parents? You didn't seem so thrilled the other day.*

She stared at the words. *Crap.* He's right. She didn't want him here, but she didn't want his ring either.

Kyle: *Do this, and I won't bother you again.*

Guess I didn't respond fast enough. She conceded to his request. Me: *Where is this place?*

He texted the address.

Never heard of it. Thank goodness for GPS. Me: *Be there as soon as I can.*

Mallory printed the directions off her computer. Even with technology, she still remained a bit old school. If the GPS led her astray, then she had a back-up plan. She took a deep cleansing breath—gag. The lethal gas Zehn released filled the room, and coughing racked her chest. "Have mercy, Zehn." She fanned the air with the paper the directions were printed on and leaned away from the desk.

Zehn crawled out with his tail tucked and left the room.

"You should be ashamed." She grabbed her phone

and escaped the bedroom for fresher air. "What did Dad feed you now?" she asked the humiliated dog lying at the top of the steps.

You've Lost That Lovin' Feelin' jarred her from her thoughts…thoughts of what, she had no idea. To be honest, she didn't remember thinking—she didn't remember anything about how she got from her parents' house to this winding road leading to who knows where. She couldn't be sure, but the definite possibility existed she'd just taken a power nap while driving. *We've all been there.* She grabbed her phone from the console while humming along to the ditty. "Go for Mallory."

"You're kidding, right? Have you been attending those self-esteem classes again?"

"Hey, Ella. What's up?"

"I have news."

She couldn't see her, but she could tell Ella's eyes sparkled by her voice. "Care to share? I love good news." *Whoa, that lovin' feeling.*

"No, I want to keep it all to myself. That's why I called you. Wanted to make sure you knew I had good news. Okay then, bye."

"Ha, ha. Very funny, Ella." *Now it's gone…gone…gone…woooooh. Stop it, brain, and focus.* Crazy how certain songs stick in your craw.

"Your offer was accepted!"

Did she hear clapping on the extension? "What offer?" Silence. *Time to wake up, brain, you've got work to do.* "Oh my! You're kidding. On the house?"

"No, on the swamp land in Florida. Yes, on the house. It's as good as yours…I mean once all the documents are signed, and fees paid."

Details. "You're serious. I mean, really?" Both women continued to speak in shrill tones. Apparently, enthusiasm's counterpart is squealing.

"You're excited?"

"I think so. Hard to tell with the terror monster racing through me thinking about owning my own home. He seems to be keeping the excitement at bay."

"I have an idea. We'll have a girls' night out to celebrate, and we can go pawn your ring for your down payment beforehand."

Silence.

"Mallory?"

"Uh-huh?" *Ella won't like this bit of news.*

"Thought I dropped your call. Did you hear me?"

"I heard you."

"Did something happen to the ring? Did you have a voodoo ceremony, pour acid on the ring, and then bury it with a lock of your hair? Because, if that's it, I'll be pissed you forgot to invite me."

Mallory chuckled. "No who do voodoo. That's more Hazel's style."

"What is it then?"

Silence.

"Mallory. Where are you right now?"

"Driving." Mallory leaned forward and glanced at intertwined limbs reminding her of a truss bridge

"Driving where?" A fingernail clicking sound counted down the seconds waiting for a response. "Mallory Larsen!"

Ella became relentless when she got in nosy mode. "Fine, I'm on my way to meet Kyle and return the ring."

"What!"

Mallory cringed.

"You turn that car around this instant. Better yet, tell me where you are, and I'll come get you. But under no circumstances do you go anywhere alone with that man."

Silence. The view out her windshield had the creepy crawlers running wild in her gut.

"Mallory!"

"Stop yelling at me. I'm freaked out enough." Ten minutes had elapsed since she'd passed another car, and if the road got any narrower, it wouldn't be wide enough for a dirt bike much less a car.

"Where are you?"

"He texted me and asked me to meet him at some friend of the family's hunting cabin, but man, this place is in the boonies. I don't even know what county I'm in anymore."

"You've got the ring?"

"He wants it back, and that's fine with me. He can have it."

"No, he can't. That ring was the down payment on your house. We were planning a pawn-the-asshole's-ring party."

Mallory laughed again. "I wouldn't want to use money from his ring for my house anyway. I want this to be all mine. You know?"

Ella said nothing for a moment. "I get it. I still don't think you should go alone. Who knows what that jerk will do."

"I'll be fine. If you don't hear from me, just start looking for someplace out of the movie 'Deliverance'."

"Terrific. Now, I feel much better." Ella sighed a heavy breath into the phone.

"Hey, I think I'm getting close. I'd better go. Let me know when closing is."

"I'll be calling. Count on it every twenty minutes until I know you're on your way home and done with pretty boy for good."

"Love you, Ella." Mallory smooched.

Ella disconnected.

Deliverance wasn't an exaggeration. She leaned forward, gazing out her windshield as she turned onto Hunter Run Road. Shivers, very creepy. Oak trees lined the road and Spanish moss clung to the branches like tinsel on a Christmas tree. The place had to be here. She swore she could hear the dueling banjos playing from afar.

A cabin took shape in the distance and Mallory stopped, surveying the mud pit doubling as a driveway. She backed up and parked on the side of the road. The cabin stood about half a football field away, and Mallory sighed, looking down at her white sandals. Already annoyed, she trudged forward. She glanced around but didn't see any other cabins, just woods. A very dense forest filled with critters she didn't want to think about. She strolled past a ladder-type deer stand nailed high in a Cottonwood tree on her left. Poor Bambi.

Something ashy assaulted her senses and weighed heavy in the air. She cleared her throat to relieve the burning sensation.

As Mallory got closer, she could see the open garage door, and what appeared to be Kyle's bright yellow sports car parked inside, because he said red was pretentious. Yeah, and yellow was subtle.

Smoke wafted in the air above the house. She

stopped. Why on earth would he start a fire on an eighty-five degree day? Shaking her head, she forced herself to continue on. She learned a long time ago not to ask why with Kyle. She inhaled the thick air and her lungs constricted. A coughing fit took away her breath

What in the world? Her mouth tasted like she'd licked a fireplace, and ash stuck in her throat. A warm gusty wind howled through the trees, probably screeching a warning to turn back. *Those stupid banjos.* Her body tensed with every squeak and pop the trees made. She shook off the sounds of banjos playing in her head and closed the remaining distance. She froze. A ripple of apprehension cascaded through her. He hadn't built a fire. The inside wasn't bright from lights. She gasped. Flames licked at the tops of the windows. Cute sandals be damned, Mallory bolted toward the house. "Kyle!"

"Oh my God! Kyle!" Her throat seared every time she opened her mouth. She ran up the steps and wrapped her hand around the doorknob. "Geez." She yanked back her hand. A hot burner would have been cooler. "Kyle!" She kicked the door hard, jamming her femur into her hip socket. The door was unyielding. Her heart pumped, and she gave a voiceless scream, but her throat burned like she'd swallowed acid. Unable to breathe, she convulsed into coughs.

Her eyes watered, and the heat scorched her skin, driving her from the porch. Mallory ran to the other side of the house, already fully engulfed. "Kyle." She forced out in a hoarse whisper. Her lungs seared with pain, but she dashed around to the garage, only to spot more flames.

Can't breathe. She wiped at the tears pouring from

her stinging eyes. Her body pulsed with fear. *What if Kyle's inside?* She patted her back pocket. No phone—in the car. She sprinted for her car barely aware of her feet moving. Stress muted her emotions, only autopilot directing her actions. Gasping for air, she approached her car, snatched her phone from the seat, and dialed.

"Nine-one-one, what is the location of your emergency?"

"Fire." Her voice raw from the smoke barely registered the one word forced from her. Her lungs seized up, part from running, part from smoke. Gut-clenching coughs rocked her body until she vomited the contents of her lunch.

"I'm sorry, I can't hear you."

Mallory spit and took a shallow breath. "Fire." Her voice cracked. "There's a fire. I think a man might still be inside."

"What is your location?"

Come on, brain—function. She shook her head. "Hunter Run Road."

"What is the address?" The nasal voice asked.

Mallory heard clicking of a keyboard. The voice seemed disinterested for an emergency. Address? She had programed it into her GPS but didn't remember the number. "I don't know. It's a hunting cabin." She jogged back toward the place.

"Ma'am, I need the address." The voice droned in her ear.

The road wasn't long, and looked like a dead-end. Surely they've seen "Deliverance". "I don't—for heaven's sake, man, just tell them to look for the one on fire!" She disconnected the call and broke into a run.

Kaboom.

The sound reminded her of the time her father took her to watch the space shuttle launch while vacationing in Florida. She had the sensation of being slammed into a brick wall right before the ground fell out from underneath her, and she soared backward through the air. A tree got in the way of her newfound super power, and everything faded to black.

Chapter Fifteen

"What's your name?"

Whose thumb is in my eye? And turn off that light.

"Can you tell me your name?"

There's the light again. If whoever that is doesn't stop shoving my eyeball out the back of my head, I'm gonna bite off that thumb. Mallory swatted at the intrusive thumb.

"What is your name?"

Whop. She nailed that pesky hand. "Who's your daddy?" Her brain registered snickering. She struggled to clear the thick fog in her skull that kept her from processing where she was.

"Open your eyes."

The male voice was firm, but reassuring. She strained to lift her eyelids—impossible. *Those darn thumbs must be forcing them closed.* She swatted again. No contact this time. That snickering, again. Now annoyed, she took a deep breath, and her eyelids fluttered open. *Ahhh!* Assaulted by bright lights, she clenched them closed again.

"That's it, open your eyes."

"Turn off that light!" Her voice came out forced and wavering. The rough raspy sound of someone who'd smoked since three years old wafted across her lips. Not only the Indonesian baby could enjoy a stogie every now and again.

Snickering. *That's just getting irritating.*

"I can't do that I'm afraid."

"Why not?"

"Because it's called daylight."

Huh? Who filled her head full of sand? Why didn't she know where she was? She concentrated, psyching herself up for a second try. Bench-pressing her own body weight would've been easier—not that she'd ever tried. Fighting against the pressure of her eyelids, she heaved them open, and a surge of bright light waylaid her. She blinked and covered her eyes with her arm, but she managed to keep them open.

"Welcome back."

Welcome what? Where had she gone? Her head throbbed, and the harder she tried to remember, the worse the pounding became.

"Let's try this again? What's your name?"

Oh goody, back to this game again. "Bob."

Snickering. She planned to beat whoever kept laughing. Someone pried her arm from her eyes. Bastard.

She squinted into the blinding brightness. A man's face morphed into focus.

He smiled.

Maybe mid-thirties. Hair the color of a moonless night, longer on top but short on the sides. Handsome in an intellectual kind of way. *Do I know him?* She stared. Nothing clear in her mind. She studied his white lab coat, and the stethoscope draped around his neck. The penlight he clicked off and on caught her attention, and she glared. Her brain worked enough to deduce he was a doctor. *But why am I here?* Did it have something to do with the pulsating pain in her head?

"Bob, huh?"

Mallory chuckled. Revenge.

"I haven't met a female Bob before, and that's not what I have here." He tapped his chart. "I guess I'll have to give you a memory-inducing injection. Nurse, could you bring me the six-inch-long, large-gauge needle," he said over his shoulder, to the female in the purple cow and pink hearts scrub shirt.

Say what! Pain or not, her eyelids flew wide open. "Mallory. My name is Mallory Larsen. My birthdate is November second. I'm five foot seven inches tall. My social security number is—"

He patted her leg. "That's good enough." He laughed from his core.

"That's not funny at all! Not one little bit."

"Works great with my difficult adolescent patients. Took a chance on you."

Chuckles floated over the doctor's shoulder. "She's been terrified of needles all her life."

She leaned around him. Her Mom and Dad were standing off to the side. What's going on here and why was her head so messed up? "Mom?"

"Yes, dear we're here. You gave us quite a scare."

Confusion settled, and her expression said so.

The doctor started to raise his penlight again.

"Come on, man. I answered your questions so don't abuse my pupils again."

His smile melted her insides a tiny bit. "I'm afraid I have to. You've taken quite the blow to your head."

"Good to know. I wondered why my head throbbed." He removed his thumb from her eye again so she didn't find his smile quite as charming.

"What's the last thing you remember?" He clicked

off his pen and crossed his arms.

This shouldn't be so hard. Her head felt like sand flowed through it instead of blood. "Um." She strained to remember but her thoughts were jumbled. Her head pounded as she struggled to sort through them. "Um." Her body tensed and her stomach lurched.

The doctor displayed amazing reflexes and shoved a bedpan under her in one swift motion.

Dry heaves racked her body.

"That's all right. You've sustained one heck of a concussion. Don't panic, this is all normal."

How does he know about my tendency to panic? Did my parents tell him? Traitors. Or maybe the wild-eyed terrified look gave her away. The sensation passed, and she leaned back against her pillow, clutching the bedpan. Random thoughts raced through her head, and she had no control over them. Like her brain determined it should make sense of something, and she had no say. Wait...a thought...no, a memory popped into her head. "I bought a house."

"You what!" Jim Larsen's voice reverberated in the small room and flowed out into the hallway.

Charlotte patted his arm and clutched her free fist over her heart. "Oh God, Jim. She's delusional. She has brain damage. I knew it! I knew it! I mean, look at her."

Hey, wait what? What's wrong with the way I look? Mallory's fingers traveled over her face. *Ouch.* She touched her cheek. She touched her forehead. *Ouch.* That hurts too. She touched her lip. Something stringy hung there. *Double ouch!* She yanked away her hand. She looked to the doctor for reassurance, but instead his head was bowed, and his shoulders shaking. *Terrific, I get the giddy doctor.* "What's wrong with my face?"

His shoulders heaved up and down several times, each time slowing a bit more. Once composed he looked up, his eyes still damp from laughing. "I'm sorry."

"Not very doctor-like." She frowned, crossing her arms to emphasis her pout.

"I know, but your family, my goodness." He waved it off. "There's nothing wrong with your face time won't heal. You have a few scrapes, bruising, and some swelling."

"What's the stringy thing?" She touched her lip much more gingerly this time.

"Just a couple of stitches."

"Stitches! You stitched up my face." Her breath seized inside her lungs. "Frankenstein had his face stitched up. Do you think they told him it was "just" a couple of stitches? I mean I don't have a lot going for me, but symmetry on my facial features happened to be one of them."

"It's only two. I assure you all your features are still symmetrical."

"Says the doctor with the morbid sense of humor."

He smiled.

All right, so the smile was nice. "Did I mention I bought a house?"

Her mom let out a small cry.

Mallory frowned at her mom, unsure what was wrong. She still couldn't gain any control over the random images racing through her brain, and wondered if it were true that goldfish have memories of three seconds.

"Do you remember what happened?"

"I mentioned I bought a house...didn't I?" Why did everything seem so messed up in there?

"Yes, you did."

His smile warmed her cockles, but she hadn't forgotten he'd stuck his thumb in her eye.

"Do you remember how you hit your head?"

Mallory scrunched up her face. That always helped her think. Flashes of images appeared, but in no sensible order. Something about her engagement ring. What about her engagement ring? She stared at her bare ring finger and absently rubbed it. Gradually, she lifted her head. "Fire," she whispered. Images still jumbled in her head. "There was a fire." She blinked. Memories came faster now. "Oh my gosh. Kyle."

"Kyle?" Her father shrieked. "What about Kyle?" He approached the bed, his fists clenched at his sides. "Did he do this to you?"

She shook her head. "I remember a fire, and I think the space shuttle launch."

Charlotte gasped again. "Brain damage. I knew it." She'd whispered it, but she had one of those whispers folks three miles away could hear.

Mallory rolled her eyes and shrugged at her doctor. "I'm sorry. It's all mixed up in my head. I'm sorting through it, but I can't make sense of anything. Did I mention I bought a house?"

Her father shrugged at her mom.

"Yes, you mentioned that." The doctor wrote something down in her chart and then hung it on the end of her bed. "It's okay. Memory difficulties come with the concussion."

"What about fries?"

This time she got his full belly laugh. It was nice.

Maybe she could learn to like him—if she chopped off his thumbs.

"I'll check on you tomorrow." He left the room.

Mallory stared straight ahead. His words were slow to register. "Wait! Get him back in here. What does he mean tomorrow? I'm going home now." She lunged up from her bed, and the empty stomach lurched into her throat again.

Once the heaves subsided, her Mom set aside the bedpan and squeezed Mallory's hand. "*Guten Tag. Wie geht's?*"

Her expression was soft, almost to the point of looking like pity. Mallory skewed up half of her face. "I'm fine."

"I knew it!"

"Knew what? And why are you speaking German?"

"I saw this program on cable." Charlotte released Mallory's hand.

"Of course." Malloy sighed.

"Don't judge. This lady sustained a severe concussion, and when she awakened, she spoke in a foreign accent from some place she'd never been. It's called…" Charlotte snapped her fingers. "Um…" One final snap. "I know. Foreign Accent Syndrome. You have Foreign Accent Syndrome."

"Mom, I don't have foreign accent syndrome."

"What makes you so sure?"

Mallory took a deep breath and slowly released it. "For one. I'm not speaking with an accent. Two, you were speaking German, which has nothing to do with me having, or in this case, not having an accent."

"Mmm-hmm. Your brain's working fine now, isn't

it? If you're so sure, how did you know what I asked?" She crossed her arms high on her chest and gazed down her nose.

"Maybe the two years of German I took in high school and the additional year I took in college. My dog is named Zehn, for heaven's sake."

"Humph." Her mom had nothing more to offer.

Stampeding feet and voices echoed from down the hall.

"Some folks just aren't respectful of the people resting in the hospital." Charlotte harrumphed as she tapped the button, ringing the nurse.

"What did you do that for?"

"I'll have her tell those noisy hooligans to quiet down."

"Mom. I'm sure they're just here to cheer someone up." She snapped up her head.

The stampede ended at her door. Ella, Hazel, Matt, Poppy, and Wade poured into the room.

"Well, that figures," her mom said in her loud whisper.

Mallory glared at her mom. "Stop that. See, I was right they are here to cheer someone up...me." Balloons, stuffed animals, flowers, and a box that looked like it might hold candy filled their arms. "Oh boy. The one with the chocolate come forth."

Wade grinned and visually dissed the others' selections. He stopped next to her bed, the others set down their gifts and took a spot—all except Ella, who had her head stuck out the door.

The doctor had a nice smile, but it couldn't hold a candle to Wade's sexy grin.

"You doing okay?" Wade opened the box.

Dark chocolate peanut clusters, her favorite. She grabbed for one.

Charlotte smacked her hand before she could even touch a piece.

"Hey!" Mallory pursed her lips.

"The way you've been dry heaving. I don't think so." Charlotte tapped the bedpan.

Heat surged into her cheeks. But she's right. No one needed to see her regurgitate peanuts and chocolate.

"I'll set them over here for when you feel better." Wade placed them on her dining tray.

"Thanks. I can't believe you all came." Mallory leaned around Wade to watch Ella, still half out of the room, and pointed. "What's up with her?"

Poppy crossed her arms. "We talked to your doctor before we came in here, and Ella is smitten."

"Ooh-wee." Ella walked into the room. "Smitten, my patootie. He will be my baby daddy." She fanned herself as she joined the group. "How you doing, sweetie?"

"Gosh, so nice of you to ask."

"Her attitude is intact." Ella swiped the back of her hand across her forehead. "Whew."

A nurse strolled into the room.

She couldn't be more than four feet eleven inches and carried a lot of fluff in her middle.

"Did you need something?"

Mallory shot her mom a glance. "No, I'm sorry it was an accidental push." She gave her best politician smile. The one that said like me even though I lie through my teeth.

"It happens. Ring if you need anything." She

retreated to the hall.

More than likely relieved she didn't have to clean up any bodily fluids.

"Did I tell you I bought a house?" Mallory asked and caught a glimpse of her mom shrinking back. *What's her problem?*

"Hurray, and the inspector owed me a favor so he pushed you to the top of the list. And, since the owner agreed to an earlier closing in the purchase contract we are planning to close on Wednesday." Ella pumped her fists in the air.

Charlotte's jaw dipped lower.

"What? She really bought a house?" Jim's voice boomed, and everyone startled.

"Technically, she's buying a house," Ella clarified.

"I thought she'd lost her marbles when she told us," Jim said.

Mallory pursed her lips. "When did I tell you about buying a house?"

Jim's gaze rolled skyward.

"You're staying!" Hazel gave Mallory a squeeze. "The gang's all back together again."

"Thank goodness, it wasn't brain damage," Charlotte said.

Mallory's gaze found Wade's. He didn't make a comment about her staying in town, but the intensity in his eyes told her all she needed to know. Some invisible force connected them, and her insides swooned. Oh wait…nope, that's her dry heaves returning. Way to kill a moment. She refused to hurl in front of her friends and took slow deep breaths. In through the nose…out through the mouth.

"Do I need to call back the nurse?" Charlotte

asked.

Unable to speak, Mallory shook her head. The wave passed, and she relaxed back on her pillows. "Sorry. I'm okay now. As the doctor keeps telling me, it's the concussion."

"We probably need to let you get some rest," Matt said, herding everyone from the room.

"Hang on a minute. Will someone tell me what happened? I have some of it. Like I know there was a fire, but I can't seem to dredge up the details."

"No can do," Poppy said. "Your doctor told us your brain would recall the events when it's ready."

"Can you give me a hint?" Mallory asked.

Matt was good at ushering out people and had everyone, but Wade, heading for the door.

"We'll see you tomorrow, sweetheart," Jim said.

Charlotte blew her a kiss. The random "feel better, I love you, and see you soon" blended into an undecipherable sound.

Wade hung back for a minute after everyone left. He stepped closer to her bedside and kissed her forehead. "You scared me."

Warmth spread through her knowing that. A half smile touched her lips. "I'm sorry."

"I won't ask what you were doing out there right now, but soon." He took her hand.

"That's probably a good thing, because I don't remember crap right now."

"You really staying?"

"That okay with you?" Wade's smile turned her insides into liquid lava.

His finger gently touched the stitches on her lip. "Does it hurt?"

She shook her head. "My noggin hurts more. It'll make me look like you." She touched the scar on his jaw.

"Nah. Yours will look sexy, mine just makes me look mean."

Mallory scrunched her face in her best gunslinger's expression. "Mine will make me look mean, too."

Wade shook his head and kissed her on her uninjured side of her mouth.

This time, her belly innards dropped, and it wasn't the dry heaves.

"Try to get some sleep."

She grabbed his hand. "Please tell me what happened. I know there was a fire, and it has something to do with Kyle." She turned her puppy dog eyes on him.

"We don't even have all the facts yet. Most of those will have to come from you, but you need to give yourself a chance to heal. Your brain got jostled around in there pretty badly." He tapped her forehead with his finger. Then he spun and headed for the door. "Everything will come back to you. Give it a bit of time." He smiled and left the room, leaving the image ingrained in her mind.

Chapter Sixteen

An explosion. Flames consumed the cabin. Kyle's car parked in the garage. Mallory bolted upright in bed, her hospital gown drenched in sweat. Her heart pounded so hard and fast her teeth seemed to rattle. She grasped the pitcher of water on her food tray, and her hands trembled as she poured a glass, sloshing half on the table. Clutching the glass between both hands, she mashed it to her lips. The water tasted refreshing to her parched mouth. She guzzled the lukewarm liquid and refilled. They were right when they said the memories would come back when ready. Now, she wasn't sure she was ready.

The events of the night before replayed in her head, and she desperately wanted the images to go away. Her hands clamped her head in a vise grip. "Go away!"

"Are you sure? I heard you were pretty anxious to get out of here."

She startled. The light gleamed off of his spectacular grill. Yep, she remembered him. "Hey, Doc."

"You feeling okay?"

"Nothing a benzodiazepine can't fix."

He approached and lifted the chart from the foot of her bed and made notations.

"Whatcha writing there, Dr.... I'm sorry I never asked your name, or if I did it's long gone."

"Rodriguez. And I'm noting here that you should be good to go home tomorrow."

"Thank good—wait what!" There's that cockle-warming chuckle. "Not funny."

He leaned over her and clicked on his penlight

Great. She bit back her complaint as he stuck his bothersome thumb in her eye.

Then his hands traveled behind her head and gently worked their way around to the front. He took a reflex hammer from his lab coat and held her arm as he tapped right above her elbow. "Sit up please." He gripped her hand and helped her upright until her legs dangled off the bed.

"Whoa." She swayed and pinched the bridge of her nose.

"Give it a minute." His brow furrowed as he studied her. "Headache?"

"Not the word I'd use, but yes, I feel like coal miners are at work inside my noggin."

His mouth quirked up in the corner. "You can take some acetaminophen for that." He tapped her knee with the rubber hammer.

She preferred that to the penlight.

"Let's get you on your feet."

Shouldn't be a big task since she'd been walking most her life. Mallory let her feet slide to the floor and then her body followed, or almost.

Dr. Rodriguez stopped her descent.

"Didn't expect them to feel like noodles." The way she clung to him with one hand, and the IV stand with the other made her cheeks warm.

He lifted her up.

Dr. Rodriguez smelled like baby powder...good

choice. "I'm okay now." She took a step away. "Just came as a surprise to my legs."

"Tell me your name."

Here we go again. She gave an involuntary eye roll. "Still Bob." She transferred weight from foot-to-foot, rediscovering her center of balance.

"Still have that injection ready." He gave a playful frown.

"Mallory." She looked up into his dark eyes. "You're lucky you're cute, because that's the only thing keeping me from poking you in your nose."

He couldn't hide his smile as he tucked his head, noting something else in her chart.

"Are you writing about what a terrific patient I've been and with charm like mine I should definitely be released from this hospital prison to share my personality with the rest of the world?"

He cocked his head. "How did you know?"

They laughed.

"So what's the verdict?"

"With that charm? I have to share with the world." Dr. Rodriguez flipped close the chart.

Mallory cheered while pumping her fist in the air. "One last thing. Can I lose the IV? I would like to shower and get the smoke smell out of my hair."

He nodded. "I'll send in a nurse. It's been a pleasure, Bob." He ambled toward the door.

"You know, Doc, if you keep your thumbs in your pockets, and leave your penlight at home, you and I could be friends."

He turned, and his eyes narrowed.

"I mean if you ever get the urge to ask out one of my friends, that is." She winked. Ella had not been subtle last night about her attraction to the fine doctor.

"I'll keep that in mind." Dr. Rodriguez's cheeks were pink.

How sweet. "Check your pocket."

He did and took out a torn piece of paper with a phone number. "How—"

Mallory swept her hand in front of her stomach and did a quipped bow. "One of my many talents. I'm a reverse pickpocket."

He shoved Ella's phone number back in his pocket and walked out of the room, shaking his head.

But he took her number. Mallory smiled to herself. She'd owed Ella one after finding her the perfect house. Maybe she found Ella the perfect man...perfect for Ella, that is. Mallory mentally patted her back as she drug her IV stand to go empty her bladder.

Mallory sat in a chair, flipping through the fashion magazine Hazel gave her last night. Her hair damp from her shower, but she felt almost human again.

Wade stepped through the open door.

Mallory glanced up dumbfounded. "Hey. What are you doing back here?" Her heart did a happy dance seeing him standing there. She liked this sensation, and her lips curled upward, announcing their agreement with the heart.

"Your parents had a funeral to attend this morning, so I offered to do the honors of springing you from this joint." Wade shoved his hands deep in his tan cargo shorts pockets and rocked back on his heels.

His nervousness made Mallory like him more. "Ms. Emery?" She crossed her fingers.

The corners of Wade's mouth curved downward, and he gave a brief headshake.

She snapped her fingers. "A girl can dream."

"You're terrible, Mallory. Ms. Emery isn't that bad." He took a seat on the vacated bed.

"Says the man whom she showers with baked goods."

He crossed his arms. "Doesn't hurt." He gave a small laugh. "How are you feeling today?"

She shrugged. "I'm good. Got a whopper of a headache, and my face feels like it met the tip of someone's steel-toed boot. But all things considered. I'm good." Her body flushed under his scrutiny, and she snagged her water. She drank it, instead of pouring over her head like she first desired to do.

Standing, Wade outstretched his hand. "You ready to blow this popsicle stand?"

Mallory grasped his hand, and a current vibrated up her arm. She had it bad. By the look in his eyes, he also sensed the connection. They stood, staring at each other, unable to break contact. Mallory's pulse raced, and seeing Wade step closer, she'd swear her knees knocked together. Anticipating his kiss, she tilted her chin up. A little encouragement couldn't hurt.

The door slammed open, killing the moment.

Mallory lurched backward, and her chair slid against the wall.

Ralph barged into the room.

Her eyes opened wide as she glanced at Wade, who could only offer a shrug.

"You enjoy seeing me?" Ralph asked.

"Not particularly," Mallory said through clenched teeth.

Ralph studied Wade. "What are you doing here?"

Wade raised his eyebrows. "That's easy. I, in fact,

did miss seeing you."

She snorted and tucked her chin to her chest. Mallory composed herself enough to look up, and Ralph's glare burned into her.

"Trouble is your middle name, Ms. Larsen." Ralph gritted his teeth.

"Ms. Larsen is it now? How very formal of you, Ralphie." She deliberately goaded him, but she also couldn't find the energy to care.

"Detective Shimkus!" He swung back his arm and sent her chart flying off the end of her bed and clattering to the floor.

Mallory stepped back.

Wade took a protective step in front of her. "What do you want?"

Ralph took a deep breath, reining his temper back to a gentle boil. "Why am I here?" He screwed up his face. "Why do you think I'm here? People die. Places explode. And you, Ms. Larsen, are right in the middle."

Now she understood. This was another nail in her coffin, and if Ralph had his way, he'd put her in the ground by nightfall. She blinked. No words found their way out of her mouth.

"Bodies are piling up, and they're all people you don't like. Convenient."

Okay, now she regretted her Ms. Emery comment. *Wait.* "I'm sorry, did you say bodies? As in plural?" Her voice quivered, and she took a step closer. She rested her hand on Wade's forearm.

Ralph sneered but didn't reply.

"Did you find Kyle?" Her hand trembled. "Please tell me."

"Why would you think we found Kyle?" Ralph

asked.

Great, he planned to make this difficult. "Because I remember heading to meet him. Some of the details are still foggy, but I was supposed to meet him at that cabin. I didn't find him before…" Tears welled up in her eyes, and she glanced away.

"Save the water works for the jury." Ralph jammed his finger toward her face.

"Where's Detective Alvarez?" Wade folded his arms across his chest. "I think any questions should come from her."

"She's working another angle of the case. And you don't get to decide who asks the question."

His jaws chomped like a beaver building a dam. *I wish I had a log.* Mallory snickered then pressed her lips together ceasing a full-fledged laugh.

"You're not impartial. You have an obvious conflict with my client, and you should recuse yourself from any further contact."

Ralph took a large stride, putting himself less than a foot from Wade.

Which, if it hadn't been for the situation, would've been amusing. He had to look up to make the eye contact needed to issue his implied threat to Wade. "What do you want, Ralph…Detective Shimkus?" She just wanted this to be over, and she didn't want the tension she detected in Wade's forearm to escalate into an all-out brawl. "Ask your questions and go."

Ralph relaxed his posture and took a step back. He moved his gaze to Mallory. "Why were you at the cabin?"

"I already told you, I was meeting Kyle."

"Why were you meeting Kyle?"

She sighed, steeling herself for the humiliation. "He wanted his engagement ring back and asked me to bring it to the cabin."

Ralph narrowed his eyes and gnawed on his molars again. "So instead of dropping by to pick it up, he asked you to drive all the way out to some remote cabin to deliver it? How convenient." He withdrew his notepad and made a notation.

Mallory squinted, wishing she could see through the notepad. "It wasn't like that. He didn't think I'd want him showing up at my parents' again."

Ralph raised his eyebrows. "Again?"

The Dodge Charger had been parked down the street when Kyle stopped by her parents, and she assumed he'd run his plate. So, he knew darn good and well Kyle had been there. "Yes, again." Back to the notepad writing. Annoying.

"Why wouldn't you want him there?"

Ralph's condescending tone wore thin. "Knock off the act, Ralph. I'm ninety-nine percent sure you're aware he'd been to my parents' house. And I don't think it would take Einstein to figure out why I wouldn't want the fiancé who cheated to show up there. He's not exactly on my family's Christmas card list. So, next question." Mallory paused, folding her arms across her chest and letting out a deep slow breath. "Please."

"Fine." Ralph nodded. "So, why meet him at a remote cabin?"

"It was the place he said he was staying. Apparently a buddy's hunting cabin."

"And that's where he chose to stay?"

"Well, you need to ask him that." A coldness flowed through her veins. If Ralph could ask him. She shook off the thought. "Look, Kyle was always cheap. If he thought he could save a couple of bucks on room and board, he would."

Ralph remained silent, tapping his pen against his chin.

"What?" Mallory's headache grew worse.

He stopped tapping and pointed his pen. "Let me tell you what I think went down. You found out where your ex-lover was staying. Concluded it would be the perfect spot to get rid of your little problem. So, you drive out there, surprise him, and tie him up. You turn on the gas stove, and KABOOM." His hands jerked wide, and his voice pierced the air.

Mallory's heart slammed into her chest wall, and she staggered backward. "Geez, Ralph." She steadied herself and flattened her hand to her chest. "Was that necessary?" Another chill. "Wait, you said tied up? Did you find evidence of a body there?"

"Mallory, this doesn't look good for you. Kyle allegedly calls you, and he instructs you to meet him somewhere that just happens to blow up." Ralph shook his head.

"I have proof he called me. I mean texted me. The texts would be on my phone." She looked around the room. "Where is my phone?" She couldn't recall the last time she had it. The palm of her hand hit her forehead. "The explosion. I held it in my hand right before the explosion." She looked from Wade to Ralph. "It must have been knocked from my grasp."

And Ralph wrote in his notepad again. Only this time, he added a sneer. "Convenient."

Mallory had a lump in her throat. This didn't look good. "It's the truth. I might not have wanted to marry

Kyle, but ultimately, he was out of my life. I didn't need to…" she swallowed hard, "hurt him to make that happen."

"What make you think he's…hurt?" Ralph asked.

"You do. You've totally implied Kyle was inside the house, even if you've refused to out-and-out say it." Her eyes misted over. "Why won't you tell me? Especially, if I'm being accused of something."

Ralph narrowed his eyes, and then put his notepad back in his pocket. He turned toward the door and took a couple of steps. Without turning back. "There was a body in the trunk of the car in the garage. Hands were bound behind his back. The body is severely burned, making identification difficult. The medical examiner will do this by dental records." He took another step. "When it's confirmed that it is your fiancé"—he blew out a whistle—"you'll be subjected to a lot more questions." He stopped at the door.

"Wait. There has to be a way to retrieve my texts with the phone provider." A flicker of hope smoldered in her chest. She prayed Wade wouldn't extinguish it as she glanced his direction. "Isn't there a way?"

Wade rubbed her back in a reassuring gesture. "I'll make some calls."

"You'd be wise to put some distance between you, and Little Miss Trouble Magnet. If you don't, we might find you in a river with a cinder block tied to your ankles."

"Thanks for the useless advice." The muscles flexed in Wade's neck and back. "Get out, or I'll file a complaint with your department regarding harassment of my client. Did you know my Great Aunt was Sheriff Stovall's godparent, or as she liked to call him Jerry

Beary?"

"You can't hide behind your connections forever." Ralph left, a guttural chuckle in his wake.

"Was your Aunt really the Sheriff's godparent?"

Grinning, Wade shrugged. "Anything is possible."

Mallory dropped her head into her hands. "He's right, you know. You need to distance yourself from me."

"Nope." Wade dragged her hand from her face.

She fought against the motion. "I mean it. Trouble does seem to find me, and I don't want you caught up in this fiasco. Distancing yourself is for the best."

"Things could be worse." He pried one hand from her face.

She rotated her head to see him. "Ha!"

Wade gave a half grin. "Okay. I admit it's pretty bad right now, but that doesn't mean I'll desert you."

"You don't owe me anything." She slid her hands through her hair…and flinched. "Ouch." She shook it off. "We aren't even a couple. We are…we are…" She sighed. "I don't know what we are."

He stepped toward her. "It's my looks, isn't it? You're blowing me off because of my appearance. I'm not handsome enough. I can grow a handlebar mustache like Ralph, if that's what it takes." He pursed up his lips and traced his pretend mustache with his fingers. "I'll do it, I swear. The look worked for Yosemite Sam."

She laughed. "Please don't." She shook her head. "We'll talk about this later, after you've had some time to think about it."

He followed her to the door. "I won't change my mind." He grasped the handles on the wheelchair.

She didn't respond. *Neither would she.* "Let's go.

You need to take me for coffee before we go pick up my car, and look for my phone."

"Did your doctor clear you to drive?" He glanced at the nurse walking beside them.

Mallory shrugged. "He didn't say I couldn't."

"Aren't you on pain medication?" His footsteps faltered.

"Keep going, man. I'll need my mocha by infusion if we don't get a move on it."

The soft thud of his rubber soles sounded on the tile again.

Chapter Seventeen

A coyote dashed across the road, and Wade slammed on his brakes. He stretched his arm across the seat, stopping Mallory from jerking forward. "Sorry."

"My mom used to do that same move when I was young. Very maternal of you."

"You okay."

"I'm good." She held up her mocha. "Didn't spill a drop."

He accelerated again and surveyed the trees hovering over the road. "Are you sure this is the correct way?" This area creeped him out, and he couldn't imagine her driving out here alone.

"Sure am. Do you hear the banjos?"

He snorted. "Loud and clear. They're saying turn back."

They drove in silence for another ten minutes. Both seemingly lost in their own introspection. Wade wasn't sure what Mallory was thinking about, but he could tell the stress wore on her—even if she smiled through it. He sensed she planned to force the issue of not pursuing a relationship with him, but he wouldn't let that happen. If he could enjoy her company so much with all this crap going on, imagine how much fun they'd have once this dark cloud disappeared. The emotions filling him when together told him this relationship was worth the fight...even if she didn't see it, he would fight for both of them.

"Turn right up here."

"You're kidding?"

She gave him a look confirming she wasn't.

"I can't believe you drove out here by yourself." He squeezed the steering wheel. "Of all the crazy, stupid, insane—"

"All right, Dad." She held up her hand. "I think my night in the hospital proved this was a dweeb move."

Mallory stilled as they turned into the driveway, his truck cruised through the mud effortlessly. Two sides of the structure still partially stood, but no roof remained. He visualized thick black smoke billowing toward the sky. Wade put the truck in park, and they got out.

Silent, Mallory shuffled toward the house, almost in a trance.

He followed. The foundation and remaining walls were scarred with scorch marks, and the appliances were still identifiable in the exposed kitchen. Strange how a house's energy disappears after something like this. Like the house itself died.

At the yellow crime-scene tape, Mallory stopped. Tears visible in her eyes began to trickle down her cheeks.

Even the wildlife mourned in silence. No wind through the leaves, no birds chirping, no sounds of the tree frogs. Just stillness. He couldn't take her distance and wrapped his arm around her.

Mallory leaned into his embrace. She focused on the garage.

The car had been taken away, but he sensed she was remembering.

Mallory blew out her breath, vacated his embrace,

and brushed away the tears. She wiped her nose on the back of her hand. "Do you think Detective Shim—Ralph—was telling the truth about the body in the trunk?"

"I don't know why he would lie. It'll probably be in all the papers tomorrow."

"Great. I can see it now, Mallory Larsen suspect in the murders of her ex-fiancé and her maid of honor." She wiped her nose again. "I'll have to relocate, and I haven't even signed the paperwork on my new home."

"You're not going anywhere." He bumped her with his shoulder, in a gentle rocking motion.

She glanced at him, eyes still moist from tears. "It's Kyle. I can feel it in my bones. Kyle was in the trunk." She shivered.

He slipped his arm around her shoulder.

"Why would someone kill Kyle?"

He could tell her brain worked overtime on something, the way her eyes flitted back and forth.

"None of this makes any sense. He texts me to come out here, and by the time I get here, I see the cabin on fire and he's already in the trunk?" She walked along the yellow tape, letting her fingers drag along it. "Do you think there's a chance Kyle didn't send me the text?" Her body turned rigid. "What if whoever killed him timed it so I'd be out here, and near the house when it exploded."

"There's no way anyone would've known when you'd arrive." Even as Wade said the words his stomach soured.

"What if they were watching?" Mallory pivoted, checking her surroundings.

"I don't know?" Wade didn't like any of this.

"They wouldn't have known I'd park so far away. Or, that I would've forgotten my phone in the car and had to run back and grab it." She shook off the thought and turned toward him. "Kind of far fetched, I know. I think my concussion still has me thinking crazy thoughts."

Wade nodded, but he wasn't so sure. He planned to keep close to Mallory until this mystery resolved itself. "Let's look for your phone."

She spun in a circle once, twice, and then a third time.

Wade put a hand on her and stopped her motion before she fell.

Her brow furrowed, and she glanced back over her shoulder toward the road. "Where's my car?"

Wade followed the direction of her gaze. "You sure one of your folks didn't pick it up for you?"

She tucked her chin and looked at him out of the corner of her eye.

"What? Was that a dumb question?"

She snickered. "It was the visual of my parents driving a five-speed. They're lucky to find reverse on an automatic."

He nodded. "Maybe Hazel, Poppy, or Ella?"

"I'd think they would've mentioned it, and they would have needed directions out here."

"True." He glanced at the thick woods encroaching on them. He could only imagine how many sets of eyes watched them under the cover of the trees.

They walked back to where she'd left her car and searched for her phone. After fifteen minutes, they gave up.

"I knew I should've gotten the protection plan."

Wade opened the passenger side door, and they paused watching a police cruiser drive up behind them. A tall lanky patrolman stepped out of his car. He couldn't be more than twenty-one, and had a short crew cut, making him look even younger.

As he approached, he tucked his thumbs in his duty belt. "Can I help you folks?"

"No," Wade said. "We were just leaving."

"I know everyone gets curious about the scene of a crime, but I could write you up for trespassing."

The man appeared to be imitating the Duke's swagger, and Wade fought the urge to say "well, partner," but he didn't get the chance because Mallory stepped forward.

"I'm the one who called 911. I was here when the place exploded."

The deputy relaxed and dropped his hands to his sides. "I thought you might've been with the press. A statement was issued earlier today, and calls have been wild at the station."

Now the deputy is their best friend.

"Do you know what caused the explosion?" Mallory asked.

The deputy hesitated, apparently deciding how much to say. He shrugged. "Someone started a fire in the back of the cabin, and then left the gas stove on. It was just a matter of time until the cabin blew. If you were here, you're lucky to be alive."

Mallory nodded. "You said someone started it. How do you know someone started it?"

"I was here when the fire investigator showed up." He walked past them and ducked under the crime-scene tape. "I don't know if you can see from this distance,

227

but over in that area is a localized burn pattern with clear demarcation between the burnt and unburnt areas." He pointed to a char pattern on the foundation.

"I think I can." Mallory squinted.

"That means some type of accelerant was used to start the fire." They ducked back under the tape. "Now I'm no fire expert, mind you, but we're taught the rudimentary things to look for. The fire department investigators would be a lot more specific."

Wade extended his hand. "Thanks for talking with us."

"You guys should head on out. I'm glad you're all right, ma'am." He turned to leave.

"Thank you—hey, do you know what happened to my car?"

The deputy looked over his shoulder. "The matchbox of a car that was parked at the entrance."

Mallory scowled.

Wade chuckled. Earning him an elbow to his ribs.

"It's a very popular vehicle. Not to mention hip to be driving."

The deputy and Wade exchanged a glance, the unsaid meaning clear. A pat on the head, and an okay dear whatever you say.

Mallory folded her arms across her chest. "So we know you both have lousy taste in vehicles, let's move past that and back to, do you know where my car is?"

"Sure. Detective Shimkus impounded it as evidence."

Mallory's eyes narrowed. "Why, that good-for-nothing pile of dog—"

Wade bumped her, and she lurched forward to regain her balance. The bump was a bit stronger than he'd intended, but it stopped her rant. "Can you tell us where he had the car taken?"

"The lot on the corner of Fourth and Madison. Right around the corner from the station."

"I know where that is." Wade thanked him.

"You might consider getting yourself a fine-looking truck like your boyfriend here. Now that's a vehicle."

Wade and the deputy once again exchanged appreciative glances over the male version of respect for an excellent automobile selection.

"He's not my boyfriend."

"All right, pumpkin head." Wade put his arm around her and squeezed her close.

She gave him a firm shove and stomped to the truck, climbed in, and slammed the door.

Wade closed the driver side door.

"Well, of all the low down dirty rotten things." Mallory sat, legs crossed, briskly jiggling her top foot.

The movement reminded him of an upset cat swishing its tail. "We were just teasing about your car."

Mallory rolled her eyes. "I'm talking about that butt wad, Ralph. He knew good and well that was my car and impounded it out of spite. Not to mention he didn't say a word at the hospital. No, can't save us the drive all the way out here. Next time I see him, I'll kick his scrawny little patootie into next week." She slapped at a strand of hair that had fallen over her eye."

"Language, Mallory. Geesh."

"Huh? Oh." She giggled.

Wade's stomach complained about missing lunch. He waited on the Larsen's front porch for Mallory. After they retrieved her car she caught a red light, so he beat her home.

She parked, got out, and her steps faltered as she made eye contact, but then walked toward him.

"Your parents aren't home yet." He offered in way of an explanation for being on her steps.

"If they went to a funeral, they'll make a day of it. They treat the funeral dinner like an after-party." She smirked. "I think it's generational."

They stared at each other. A knot formed in the pit of Wade's stomach. He sensed her walls going up. The dreaded brush off.

"Thanks for everything you did today." She paused. "And every other day." She stepped past him and unlocked the front door. Zehn shot past her like a rocket, quick to find the perfect-sized bush to relieve himself on. "Guess he didn't miss me."

"Nah. He just had more pressing matters to take care off." They both watched as though a dog urinating was the utmost fascinating process they'd ever seen.

Zehn pawed with his hind feet and sent up chunks of grass into the air. He ran back up the steps and leaned against Mallory's legs. "Hey, big guy. You did miss me." She scratched his head. "I better get in. I'm feeling a bit tired and think I need to lie down."

"Sure, let me know if you need anything." Wade shoved his hands into the pockets of his cargo shorts. He stepped toward Mallory, intent on giving her a kiss.

"Okay. Bye." She slipped through and closed the door.

Wade's gut rocked and tensed. She gave him the bum's rush, but he refused to concede.

Chapter Eighteen

"Have mercy." Poppy studied the navy blue-and-white-striped short scuba dress. A floral imprint of pink and peach layered over the top of the stripes. An absolute hot sleeveless number, with a high racer-neckline, and backless to the waist. The high-density Lycra fabric would wear fabulously on a toned physique. "If I come out wearing that number when Matt and I take our trip into Chicago, we'll never make it out of the hotel room." The intensity in her gaze looked to be enough to suck that dress right off the mannequin and through the window they peered into.

"No self-esteem shortage in that ego," Hazel said.

"A lady's got to work her assets." Poppy glanced over her shoulder.

"Your assets will almost be hanging out based on the length of that dress." Mallory took a step closer.

An evil grin crossed Poppy's face.

"And let's rewind a smidge. You're going away together for the weekend?" Mallory asked.

"Totally missed that," Ella said, dragging herself away from the luxurious rich brown soft leather handbag, and the pool of drool left on the floor. "You and Matt taking a little get away?"

Poppy nodded, biting at the corner of her lip.

"Getting serious between you two?" Mallory asked.

She shrugged. "I really like him." The ladies all turned in, forming a circle. "He's different than other guys I've dated."

"How's so?" Hazel asked.

"I've never truly connected to someone before. Do you know he came over the other evening, and we stayed up all night talking?"

The smile taking over her face could light up the mall.

"Seriously. Just talking, and we never ran out of things to discuss. I can't wait until the next time I see him, and my heart skips a beat every time I picture his face." Poppy sighed.

"Might want to get that looked at. My Uncle Fester said that exact same thing, and it didn't end well for him." Hazel made the sign of the cross.

Mallory elbowed her hard enough Hazel stumbled to the side.

"What?" Hazel staggered back.

Mallory narrowed her eyes. "You know what." She turned her attention back to Poppy. "Matt's a terrific guy. I'm so happy for you two."

"Hey! We might be sisters-in-law. Wait." Poppy scrunched up her face. "If I marry Matt, I'm Wade's sister-in-law…right? Then if you marry Wade, you'd be Matt's sister-in-law, and if I'm his wife…what would we be?"

Mallory grabbed her hand and yanked. "Committed to a nut house."

"Where are we going?" Poppy asked, her feet sliding along the tile as Mallory drug her.

"You and Wade are getting married!" Hazel said.

"No. Wade and I aren't even seeing each other."

"What are you talking about?" Poppy asked. "You two are terrific together. We worked all this out not so long ago."

Mallory stopped. "Look, we aren't at war or anything, so there's no issue with you having to choose between spending time with me or Matt. But, Wade and I are not a couple, now or ever."

"But why?" Poppy stomped her foot.

"It's not in the cards for us." Mallory rotated to face the group. "He's a great guy, and I do like him, but understand my life's a disaster right now. To ask someone to jump into the middle isn't fair."

"What if Wade wants to be in the middle with you?" Ella asked.

"He's already helped me out in so many ways. He's done enough, and I need to get through this on my own. I refuse to drag anyone else into the quagmire. Especially, if chances are good I'll end up in jail." Mallory rubbed the back of her neck.

Ella's jaw slackened. "That's not a real possibility, is it? I mean you didn't do anything wrong."

The ladies huddled around Mallory, who desperately tried to squash the fears rising to the surface. "If Ralph gets his way." She looked away to hide the tears forming in the corner of her eyes.

"Oh, sweetheart." Poppy embraced her. Ella and Hazel piled on. Their feet got all tangled up in the cluster, and they collapsed to the floor in hysterics.

"You guys are the best friends a girl could have. You always make me smile, no matter how crappy of a day I'm having." Mallory wiped away the tears as she sucked in her giggles.

A group of older shoppers, who looked liked they

might have been a part of the ensemble who'd arrived at the mall on the large bus blocking the food court entrance, side-stepped the mosh pit of females congregated on the floor, hugging and crying. They didn't act surprised by the spectacle. Might be an everyday occurrence at the assisted living facility.

"Honey," Ella said. "You never talk about the situation. You always come off so positive and strong. I forgot how scary this must be."

"I don't want you guys worrying about me." Mallory made eye contact with each of her friends. "Okay? Please. You're my chance to forget for a while, so please don't pity me. Let's just have some fun."

"I'm gonna kick Ralphie's butt when I see him." Hazel put up her dukes. "Picking on our Mallory. He doesn't know who he's messing with."

Mallory gave a weak smile.

Poppy put up her hands. "We won't talk about this anymore for now. If"—she said, pausing—"and only if, you promise you'll come to us when you need to vent."

Mallory nodded. She scrambled to her feet, and it took both Hazel and Mallory to lift Poppy up.

"Stop wearing hooker heels." Hazel placed her hand on Poppy's shoulder steadying her.

Poppy stuck out her tongue.

"We're here to celebrate you signing the closing papers on your new home this morning," Ella said. "So on with the celebration."

Mallory yanked Poppy toward the boutique's door.

"Where are we going?" Poppy asked.

"To see how fabulous you'll look in your new dress."

Poppy gave a squeal and sprinted into the store in

hooker-heel fashion.

The vibration of the vehicle lulled Mallory to the brink of sleep, but the throbbing of her feet after an eventful afternoon of shopping squashed that possibility.

Hazel dumped off Mallory and Poppy in front of the Larsen's house. "I won't be dropping you off at your parents' house for much longer."

Mallory and Poppy stood next to the driver's door. Mallory armed with her new cell phone, and Poppy with a white plastic bag containing her new dress draped over her arm.

"When will you have us all over to your new place?" Ella leaned over from the passenger seat to ask out of Hazel's window.

Mallory rested her hand on the doorframe. "Right after I have my moving-in party where everyone helps me get my crap out of storage." She mouthed hurray.

Ella scowled. "I don't like to sweat."

"You'll survive. If I can get my big ole badonkadonk in and out of a moving truck, I can assure you your tiny ass will float," Hazel said.

"I have someone coming out to do a thorough cleaning tomorrow." Ella winked. "My gift to you. So, you can move in anytime after that."

"You're the best, Ella." Mallory glanced at her friends. "All of you."

Poppy rubbed Mallory's arm. "We're really glad to have you home. So you name the time and place, and we'll make a day of it."

"Maybe Labor Day. I'll work on moving some smaller stuff myself, but then if you guys can each come and round up some muscle we can move in the big stuff, and then have a barbeque to celebrate."

"Girl, you not gonna grill up some tofu?" Hazel curled up her lip.

"That was the plan." Mallory gave her best sincere face. "Maybe some zucchini."

"Eww." Emerged from Hazel, Ella, and Poppy in various octaves.

"Unless that zucchini is in some bread with four cups of sugar and nuts, forget about it," Hazel said.

Mallory's face erupted into a grin. "I was thinking about the three 'B's'—brats, burgers and beer."

"You add mac-and-cheese and you got a deal." Hazel stuck her hand out the window.

Mallory shook on it, and she and Poppy watched Hazel drive away. "So what are you and Matt doing?"

"We're going to a movie. I planned to ask you, and Wade, to join us…"

A hollowness filled Mallory. Something she'd have to get used to. Her face must have reflected the pained sensation, because Poppy tilted her head to the side and flattened her lips together.

She put her arm around Mallory. "Honey. This mess will blow over. You don't have to drive off Wade. He's a big boy and understands what you're facing. Let him be there for you."

As Mallory stepped away, she gave a small shake of her head. Her mouth opened but being too choked up to speak, she closed it.

Poppy swapped her bag to the other arm. "I get that you don't want to talk about this, but I've been around when Wade talks to Matt, about you."

Mallory pivoted toward her. A little lightness found its way into her belly. "He talks about me?"

"All the time." Poppy held her stare. "He talks about how much fun you are to be around. You make him laugh. He never knows what you'll say or do, but knows it'll be hilarious in a totally unintentional way."

"That's humiliating."

"No, it's sweet. He's afraid you'll push him away before he can convince you to give you guys a chance." Poppy tapped her foot. "I have to tell you if what he said was any indication I don't think he's giving up easy."

"It's infuriating that makes me happy to know." Mallory blew her bangs out of her eyes. "It's not that I don't have feelings for the guy. I like him…I really like him, and it's because I like him that I won't let him close—I'm no good for him."

"Bull. You're scared, plain and simple. You're using this crap going on in your life as an excuse, because Kyle burned you. And perfect Kyle was supposed to be safe. You've always picked the safe guy because it wouldn't hurt your heart if things didn't work out. Kyle was that guy, and he cheated. Since your feelings for him didn't go much beyond caring—"

Mallory opened her mouth to protest.

Poppy silenced her with a finger. "I've been quiet about this for too long so I'm saying my piece, even if you hate me in the end. Since you weren't in love with Kyle, walking away was easy when he crapped on you. Your ego was bruised, but your heart wasn't broken. Now this terrific guy is crazy about you, and wants to try a relationship, and you're running scared because this time your heart is involved." Poppy took a deep breath. She talked so fast she'd run out of air.

Mallory opened her mouth again and closed it

without provocation from Poppy. She'd hit the nail on the head. The emotions stewing inside her when Wade was in close proximity scared her to death. She had no argument, and that made her mad. "You suck." Mallory spun and stormed up the sidewalk to her parents' porch.

"Love you, Mal, even if I'm saying things you don't want to hear."

Poppy's laughter followed her as she closed the door. Mallory leaned her back against the door and shut her eyes. Poppy was so right. Stupid friend. How dare she call her out? Zehn bumped her hand. "Hey, baby." She squatted down and got bombarded with Zehn kisses. She hugged his neck. "I'm so glad I have you." *Toot.* Mallory scrunched up her nose. "Even if you have a weak intestinal tract." She stood, searching for fresher air. "Oh, honey." She waved the air in front of her nose. "Dad has got to stop feeding you the junk he doesn't want."

****

"Mallory." The sound of her mom's voice drifted up the stairs and into Mallory's subconscious. "Dinner's ready."

Mallory shoved up the facemask and squinted in the blinding light. That's what happened when napping in the middle of the day. She intended to get some work done, but Poppy's lecture circled her brain so long she couldn't focus on anything else. So, instead she did the mature thing, curled up in the fetal position, and fell asleep.

She twisted until her feet hit the ground. Mallory looked down at her cut-off sweatpants and T-shirt big enough for a sumo wrestler, as she stumbled to the bathroom, and splashed water on her face. After drying off, she hung up the towel and cringed at the reflection glaring back. She rubbed the "Z" like imprint the mask left on her face and hair. Mallory ran her fingers through her hair, and it sprung right back into standing position. "Oh, who cares anyway?" She shuffled down the stairs in her elephant slippers and stopped when she saw her mom coming up.

"I wasn't sure you heard me." Charlotte's gaze focused on her hair.

"Don't say it." Mallory started past her. "What are we eating?"

"Meatloaf."

Mallory did an about-face and headed back up the stairs. *Woke me out of my nap for meatloaf.*

"I made a white bean casserole."

Her ascent stopped, and she glanced over her shoulder. "Aw-shucks. You did that for me?"

Charlotte rolled her eyes. "It paired well with the meat loaf."

"Sure, Mom." Mallory, pleased with her mom's thoughtfulness of going to the extra trouble, started back down the steps.

"You might consider combing your hair."

"I said, don't say it."

"I thought you were referring to the Zorro imprint on your face." Charlotte's genial smile was insincere at best.

Mallory glanced at her mom's perfect hair, and pearl earrings and sighed. "What's the point? You know what I normally look like."

"I'm just saying. Looking presentable isn't a bad thing. You never know who might show up."

She crossed the threshold of the kitchen and

ground to a halt.

Wade eyed her up and down. A single brow rose.

You've got to be kidding me. A hand instinctively slapped down the hair standing on end.

"Hey, Mallory." Wade gave a wave. "Nice shoes."

She glanced at her feet. Okay, so she could've put on socks instead of stuffed slippers. "What are you doing here?"

"Mallory, that's rude." Charlotte bumped her from behind. "Now take a seat before the food gets cold."

Mallory scowled and begrudgingly plopped into her chair.

"A package of your mother's was inadvertently delivered to Wade's house, and he was kind enough to bring it over," Jim offered as way of an explanation for Wade's presence.

How that got him to their dinner table she wasn't sure.

"We have so much meatloaf I insisted he stay." Charlotte sat and scooted her chair closer to the table.

Of course she did.

"The food smelled amazing. Couldn't turn down an offer like that." Wade winked at her mom.

Mallory stayed quiet and hoped the conversation would take a turn for the better.

Charlotte snapped her napkin and gingerly placed it on her lap. "And you never eat any. I'm thrilled to have someone who appreciates my cooking."

Guess quiet didn't work. "Mom, I appreciate your cooking just fine. I appreciate anything you cook that didn't have a face before it arrived on my plate."

Charlotte gagged. "Mallory! We're eating. Don't be gross."

"Hey, you're the ones eating Bessie the big-eyed cow. I'm just calling a spade a spade." Mallory gave a silent headshake and reined in her attitude. Wade sitting so close provoked her edginess.

"What was your package, Mom?" She passed the meatloaf to Wade, who piled three slices onto his plate. Guess he wasn't fond of Bessie either.

"Oh, just this thing." Charlotte scooped a spoonful of mashed potatoes and passed the bowl to Mallory.

Now I've got to know. "What thing?"

"This thing for my face." Charlotte placed her napkin in her lap.

"Where did you find this thing?" Mallory couldn't stop herself.

Charlotte's fork slipped and clattered onto her plate. "An infomercial on cable."

I should've guessed. "Is it a cream or something?"

"No." Charlotte looked everywhere but at Mallory.

Jim put a miniscule spoonful of the bean casserole on his plate. "For heaven sakes, Charlotte. It's some electronic gizmo she bought for facial wrinkles."

Wade hesitated before dumping corn over his mashed potatoes. He failed to hide his smile.

If Wade wanted to have dinner with her eccentric family, he could deal with the fallout. "You're planning to electrocute your face to look younger?"

"Oh, Mallory it's not like that, it works the facial muscles you can't exercise on a treadmill." Charlotte nodded as she spoke. "The lady on cable said I'd take ten years off my appearance."

Defensiveness tinged her mom's voice, and Mallory sighed. "Of course she did."

"It was on cable!" Charlotte smacked the table.

Mallory put up her hands. "Hey. It's all good, Mom. If they said on cable that's what it does, then it must be true. Just promise to let me borrow it." Like she'd shock her face, but this appeased her mother.

"Of course. It would help those crow's feet." Charlotte pointed back and forth to Mallory's eyes.

What? Corn fell out of Mallory's mouth.

Wade snickered.

She wiped her mouth and put her napkin back in her lap. Mallory trailed her fingers across her eye area.

"Everything is absolutely delicious, Mrs. Larsen," an overzealous Wade proclaimed.

Suck up.

"Please, call me Charlotte."

Wade shoveled a spoonful of potatoes into his mouth and swallowed. "Charlotte. I haven't had a home cook meal since—"

"Since you had lunch with Candy at Ms. Emery's?" So, Mallory was still bitter.

Wade coughed and locked his agitated gaze on Mallory.

Pleased with herself, Mallory grinned.

"Nothing like this feast. I assure you." Wade squeezed Mallory's knee.

She stiffened, shot him an icy stare, and kicked his ankle.

He flinched. "Can you cook like your mother?" His hand slid mid-thigh, and his fingers brushed under the hem of her shorts.

She jerked back, and her chair tumbled, plummeting her to the floor.

"Good Lord, Mallory. What's the matter with you?" Jim asked.

She locked gazes with Wade, and she'd swear she saw a flash of guilt. "Charley horse." She uprighted her chair and hung onto the back as she hauled herself to her feet.

"I watched a program on cable that said charley horses can be a result of low potassium. You need to eat some red meat." Charlotte nodded as she tore a piece of white bread in half and buttered it.

Mallory did a mental eye roll. "White beans, dark leafy greens, mushrooms…all high in potassium. But, I can assure you whatever is causing my muscle cramp, I will seek out and eradicate from my life." She sank into her chair and glared at Wade.

He choked on a bite of meatloaf and guzzled his tea.

"I'm glad you're enthusiastic about your health, but that language seems awfully extreme," Charlotte said.

"It's all about taking control, Mom." Mallory survived the rest of the meal without any further "charley horses".

"The meal was scrumptious." Wade patted his stomach.

"Bring the boy another piece of apple pie, Charlotte." Jim shoveled a huge bite into his mouth, chasing it with vanilla ice cream.

Wade put up his hands. "Can't do it. If I eat another bite something will rupture."

"Well, I'll wrap you up another piece to take home for later." Charlotte cut into the pie sitting on the counter.

"I won't object to that." Wade gave her a wink.

Mallory sat unspeaking, watching the show. He

didn't seem fazed by her dysfunctional family, and it annoyed her how he fit right in.

Wade stood. "I better be getting home."

Charlotte handed him his pie wrapped in five pounds of plastic wrap. "Mallory will show you out."

"He knows where the door is." The snippy remark slipped out, but too late to take her comment back now.

"Mallory Larsen!" Charlotte spun, hands on her hips. "I raised you with better manners than that. If you lost them in the city you were living in, you need to go back and find them. Now, young lady, you will show out Wade." A foot stomp ended the rant.

Mallory's eyes were wide. *Okay, I've been sufficiently chided.* She glanced at Wade who displayed a shit-eating grin. Great, called on the carpet in front of him. She'd behaved like a spoiled child. Swallowing her pride, she stood and strode past Wade. His flip-flops smacked his heels as he followed. "Here's the door." She grasped the door handle and yanked.

Zehn shot outside.

Where did he come from? Mallory sighed and stepped out onto the porch to watch Zehn.

"I didn't mean to get you into trouble." Wade moved close.

The warmth of his breath on her neck made the baby fine hairs stand. She shrugged and stepped forward.

"You were being rude." He advanced as she spun.

She slammed her palms into his chest, and his warmth flooded into them halting the shove.

"Mallory?"

She focused on her hands. The heat radiating into her palms felt like sunshine reflecting off the ocean on a perfect day. She closed her eyes, allowing the warmth to encircle her body. His pecs flexed under his snug shirt, mesmerizing her. And she'd never admit it but wanted to see what treasures his shirt hid.

"Mallory?" His free hand covered hers.

She blinked. Tilting up her chin, Mallory's unfocused gaze redirected to his eyes.

"Mallory. I enjoy a good grope as much as the next guy, but unless you're ready to act, you need to stop."

"Huh?" She blinked. Her senses rushed back. Oh, God. She'd felt him up. Her cheeks flamed, and she snatched away her hands. She cleared her throat and stepped back.

"You're cute when you blush."

"I'm not blushing." She cast her gaze downward.

Using the side of his knuckle, he raised her chin. "Yeah. You really are."

Shaking her head, she swatted away his hand. "Bye."

"Back to rude, are we? You run so hot and cold. One minute you're talking to me like I'm dirt, and the next there's enough electricity to power a town. You've got to figure out what you want, because it's driving me insane." He closed his hand on her upper arm.

She jerked back. "Don't touch me."

"Did I hurt you?"

"No." She spun and sat on the steps. "I can't think when you're close."

Wade sat beside her. "I get it. I do, but there's no need to push me away."

She dropped her head to her knees. "If you get it. You'll just go away."

"Okay."

She snapped up her head. That was too easy, and her gut contracted. She'd gone and done it now. He'd given up. She must have been scowling because he smiled.

"You're a lesson in contradiction. You say what you believe you should, but your body expresses exactly what you feel."

Now he's obnoxious. She had nothing to offer in rebuttal. She tried hard to do the right thing, but she didn't like the thought of never seeing him again.

"Relax. When I said okay, I didn't mean I was walking out of your life."

Her heart did the dreaded happy dance, and she mentally scolded it. "Care to explain?"

"Let's be friends. I might want more, but I'll settle for friendship…" He stared intently. "For now."

Mallory's innards knotted. This made her glad to hear, but also terrified her. "Do you think we'll work as friends?"

"Probably not, but I'm not willing to let you walk away. Look, I get you're scared, but you've got to let people support you."

"I feel toxic to those around me. Heck, if I didn't know I hadn't killed my fiancé and his girlfriend, I'd suspect me too." She watched Zehn taking a nap in the sunshine. "All this feels so contrived to me."

"I agree, and we'll get to the truth." He shifted, glancing across the street. "I have Skylar's emails for the past eighteen months I've just started going through."

"She didn't delete them?"

"She did, but her ISP backs up their server, so I obtained them through a back door. I'm working on getting her texts too. I have someone who has software that helps retrieve deleted texts, so we're making progress."

"Why are you doing all this?" She gnawed on her nails. She hadn't bitten her nails since she was eight, but it was becoming habit.

"Because we're *friends*…aren't we?"

Standing, she yelled for Zehn to come, or at least wake up. "Let me think about it."

Wade threaded his fingers through his hair but didn't argue. He stood and walked away.

A miserable empty sensation filled her again as he crossed the street without another word. What was wrong with her? Why wouldn't she let herself be free to do what she wanted?

Chapter Nineteen

The screen door slammed behind Mallory, and coffee sloshed from the mug Jim held. "Sorry, Dad. Mind some company?"

Jim sat in the padded chair reading the newspaper. The first golden rays of the morning kissed the ocean blue sky and reflected glorious shades of rose and yellow off his glasses.

Mallory handed him the napkin she held her bagel on.

"Nice morning. I could get spoiled if we have too many of these low humidity days." He mopped up his mess.

She took the seat opposing her father and set her coffee mug on the table. The scent of Old Spice wafted in the breeze. How is it a smell could be so reassuring...so Dad. "Mind sharing the paper?" She chewed her bagel.

"Nothing interesting in here. But check out Marmaduke. That dog should be called Zehn." He handed her the colorful section of paper.

Pressure built and commingled with agitation deep within her gut. "Dad...Dad...DAD."

Jim jumped. "What?" He peered over his bifocals.

"What's in the paper that you don't want me to see?"

"I don't know what you're talking about." He

paused. "Well, there's an article on increasing gas prices. That ticks me off."

"You're a terrible liar. Now hand it over." Mallory held out her hand, but Jim didn't look up from the paper. "Either hand it over, or I'm going across the street and steal Ms. Emery's off her sidewalk. The woman already hates me. What do I have to lose?"

Jim's shoulders slumped. He took off his glasses and placed them on the table. He handed her the paper. "You know I only want to protect you."

"I appreciate that, but hiding things doesn't help." She looked down at the front page and the boldfaced heading.

Scorned Ex-Fiancée Possible Suspect
in Double Homicide

Bile rose in her throat.

"*A body found early last week has now been identified as Kyle Malloney.*"

She'd known the body in the trunk was more than likely Kyle, but to see the fact confirmed shook her. She was sure a tear would slip from the corner of her eye if it weren't for the fact her insides had turned to ice.

"*A source at the sheriff's department revealed that local resident, Mallory Larsen, is a person of interest in this case. Prior to Mr. Malloney's demise his current girlfriend Skylar Masterson, also Ms. Larsen's former maid-of-honor, had been found stabbed to death in an alley behind Grayson's Club. The common denominator between both murders is Mallory Larsen. Not only was Ms. Larsen Mr. Malloney's ex-fiancée, but was also the first person to report both murders. Coincidence? Or could this be a case of an ex-fiancée scorned?"*

Mallory slapped the paper down on the table. "Source at the sheriff's department my ass hurts." She couldn't stop her gaze from gravitating up the street, to where the black Dodge Charger once again parked at the curb. The ice in her veins had been replaced by the fire in her fury. "That's it." She sprung to her feet and launched her remaining bagel into the yard, as she sprinted down the sidewalk.

"Mallory. Stop," Jim yelled.

But, anger plugged her ears.

"Mallory. This is exactly what he wants."

Her strides were long and determined as she made a beeline for the car. Ten feet from it, brake lights flashed, and the car peeled away from the curb. Huffing hard, she stared after it. Her fingers raked through her hair secured by a ponytail. With nowhere to release her anger, she hung her head defeated and ambled back to where her dad waited.

"It's for the best."

Mallory's gaze met her father's. Her eyes blurred with tears. "I'm just so tired of dealing with this mess. Ralph wants to ruin me, and it's not fair." She plopped into her chair and dropped her head into her hands. "I'm not even sure the police are looking for the real killer."

"You have good people helping you."

She tilted her head and followed her dad's gaze across the street. "I don't want to drag anyone else into this. I feel toxic."

Her father plucked her hands from her head and squeezed. "Don't. You're a wonderful girl, and the truth will come out in the end. Be strong, and lean on your family and friends."

"Do you believe that?"

"Yes, I do."

Mallory pushed away her cold coffee. She studied the house across the street.

"Why don't you go see if Wade has found anything out on those emails."

Mallory's surprise must have registered on her face.

Jim patted her hand. "He mentioned it last night."

She nodded. "You're right. Maybe I can help him go through them or something. I need to feel like I'm doing something." She stood.

Jim rose and embraced her. "You don't have to go through this alone."

Such a typical dad comment, and she loved him for his loyalty. Mallory gave a weak smile, and swiped at the escaped tears. Her family might be eccentric, but they were also loving and supportive. She wouldn't have traded them for the world. She might have said otherwise as a kid in high school, but most kids grow up and realize what they have in family. "Don't give Zehn any table food." She pointed at his nose.

He held up three fingers.

"Unless you were a scout and female, that means nothing."

"I was too busy chasing greased pigs when I was growing up. Never did the scout thing."

She decided not to get into a conversation on why he'd chased greased pigs. "His gas has been terrible lately. I have him on a bland food diet of pureed turkey and sweet potatoes. That's all he gets."

Jim snarled up his lip. "A man nor dog can live on

sweet potatoes alone."

"Promise me. I nearly died last night from his continuous leak of obnoxious gas. If I'd been a smoker, I would've been a goner."

"Fine." Jim made a frownie face as he trudged into the house.

Only because he lost his garbage disposal for all the things her mom fed him that he didn't want.

Another ten minutes passed before Mallory worked up the courage to cross the street. Her knock on the door sounded no louder than a sock falling. *Guess he's not home.* She was walking down the steps when the door creaked open.

"I thought I heard someone out here." Wade leaned against the doorframe.

Dude's got excellent hearing. "Good morning." Now what, she wondered?

"Would you like to come in? I planned to call you in a bit anyway."

"Got coffee?"

"Think I can manage that." He opened the screen door.

They brushed arms as she passed. Those stupid sparks.

He poured two cups of coffee and set a mug in front of her. "What brought you to my doorstep?"

"Why were you going to call me?"

"You go first." He sat across from her.

"You see the paper yet?"

Anger flashed across his eyes.

"Guess so." Mallory shrugged.

"I'd sue that department if I were you."

She stirred a couple spoons of sugar into her coffee

and chased it with a bit of milk. "I'm running out of fight, I guess."

"Wouldn't have guessed as I watched you sprint down the street earlier."

She snickered. Part from embarrassment. "Saw that did you?"

One side of his mouth arced upward, making his laugh lines more predominant. "Remind me never to get in a foot race with you."

"Ran track in high school and college." She glanced over her mug. "Scholarship."

His lips arched downward, and he nodded.

Obviously impressed.

"Back to my original question. What brought you over? I mean you've been avoiding me, and now you're on my doorstep."

She shrugged. "I decided to take you up on your offer of friendship."

Wade's eyebrows rose.

"I could really use one." She sighed and set down her mug. "I need to feel useful. You said you'd obtained emails of Skylar's, and I thought maybe I could help look through them."

"Like my assistant?"

"No, more like your boss."

Wade let loose a belly laugh. "Funny you should mention it. That's why I planned to call you. Grab your coffee and follow me."

"You were going to call me about being your boss?" She shuffled behind him, clutching her mug in both hands.

The back of his head shook side-to-side. "Just follow me."

"I—"

He stopped.

Mallory slammed into the back of him. She cupped her mug, containing the spillage. "Am."

He looked over his left shoulder and rolled his eyes.

She gave a sheepish grin and shrugged.

Wade opened his office door and stepped behind his desk.

The elegance of his office surprised Mallory. An antique roll-top desk sat in the middle of the room, containing stacks of papers, and books. An "L" shaped section angled off the corner of the desk. It wasn't antique, but the wood grains matched perfectly. Two large computer monitors sat side-by-side. One entire wall held a bookcase loaded with not only law books, but also novels. A muted tri-colored area rug covered the wide plank hardwood flooring. Some type of dark hickory, she guessed. Impressive. Her office existed in some drab corner of her bedroom and consisted of a desk made out of particleboard.

Wade brought a chair over for Mallory, and then rolled out his chair and sat. He plucked the sheet of paper marked with a blue flag from the middle of the stack.

"What's that?" The chair screeched as she drug it closer so she could peer around the side of his shoulder.

He turned his head, and they were nose-to-nose.

Focused on the paper, she ignored the fact he studied her face. The word "lover" jumped out. "Oh, geez. These aren't from Kyle, are they? The only sweet note he ever left for me was to tell me we were out of beer."

Wade turned his attention forward. "No."

"Whew. I saw lover, and just assumed it was a personal thing." Mallory folded a leg underneath her so she could come closer. Wade stiffened, but she disregarded it. She inhaled his scent deep into her nostrils. Kind of a citrus smoky fragrance, definitely fell into the yummy category.

"Yes. I mean no. I mean. Will you sit back so I can concentrate?"

Her ponytail brushed over his shoulder as she turned and gave him her best "What?" expression.

"Sit, and I'll read some of this to you. I think you'll get it, but you've got to give me some space."

"Do I stink or something?" She tugged at her shirt and sniffed.

He made a grumbling noise. "Yeah, you smell bad. I can't stand the smell of strawberries and cream you must have bathed in."

"Hair."

He squinted.

"Hair." She pointed to her head. "I washed my hair with a strawberry-scented shampoo. You hate it?" She tugged on a section of her ponytail, bringing it around and giving it a good sniff.

She wasn't sure what described the noise he made next, but the quickness of his movement startled her. One hand snaked around her neck, and the other encircled her waist. One yank, and she landed half on the arm of his chair, and half in his lap. Mallory opened her mouth to speak, but his lips claimed hers. The kiss wasn't gentle. It was raw, and filled with pent-up sexual frustration. Her defensive walls crumbled, and she wrapped her arm around his neck thrusting closer. She wanted this, and her body had taken over for her mind. A fire burned in her gut, and heat surged head-to-toe.

Something mashed against her shoulders, driving her back. She fought against it, and she dug her nails into the back of his neck. Her brain kick started, and she realized he forced her back. She released her death grip, relaxed her body, and promptly slammed her back into the desk.

"Oh, God. I'm sorry. Are you okay?" His hand stroked her back.

She nodded, unable to speak.

He tugged her forward and rested his forehead to hers. Their breaths rapid pants. "You're killing me. You even taste like strawberries."

Her fingers touched her lips, and they were so close they brushed his face. "Lip gloss." She smiled. "Gone now."

He laughed. "Guess so."

"Why did you slam me into your desk?" She sat up a little straighter. "Kind of hurt."

"Friendship."

"What?"

"I promised you friendship, and instead I'm taking advantage of you in your vulnerable state."

"I'm okay with it. Take away."

"You run hot and cold." He still had his arms around her waist.

"I know." She blew out her breath, scooted from his lap, and returned to her cold lonely chair. "I get conflicted between what I want and what I think I should have."

"What is it that you want?" He tilted his head, studying her.

A sly smile played on her lips. "That's a loaded question. I think the answer is obvious."

Their gazes locked, and the air sizzled with the memory of seconds before. Mallory dropped her chin to her chest, breaking the connection. She sighed. He's correct. Friendship is all she could handle right now. Playtime had ended. Time to get down to business. "So, read to me."

"Are you ready for this?" He picked up the sheet of paper.

"Why wouldn't I be ready?"

"Just wait."

"I've never enjoyed a game of pool as much as I did last night, lover. I've thought of little else."

"I didn't even know Kyle played pool?"

"Shush."

"Oh. Sorry. Please continue." Mallory sat back in her chair, arms resting on her stomach.

"To watch you bend over and stretch across the table. The way the pool stick slid back and forth between your fingers."

"Humph. Now I know why Kyle liked pool."

"Will you be quiet?" He glanced over his shoulder.

With her finger, she made a gagging motion.

"Now, where was I?"

"The way the pool stick slid back and forth between your fingers. The balls cracked and scattered. I didn't have any idea if you even pocketed one. All I knew was your flawless body looked amazing as your schoolgirl outfit hiked up toward your perfect—"

"Holy crap. Kyle was in to role-play? I had no idea. That kinky bugger." Mallory folded her leg under her again and rose to read over his shoulder.

"Do you want to hear this?" Wade shook the paper.

"If you would get to it, then I wouldn't have to read over your shoulder."

"You keep—"

Mallory straightened out the paper scrunched in his hands. *"Thought of little else.* Blah…blah…blah. *Pool stick slid.* Blah…blah…blah. *Schoolgirl outfit*—okay, here we go—*perfect ass. When I bent you over that table and slid your skirt—"*

Mallory fell silent, but her gaze continued to scan the page. She fanned herself with a magazine. She skimmed faster, and she fanned harder. She couldn't believe what she read. She'd read erotic novels that didn't contain such raw illicit material, but she couldn't stop reading. She needed to stop reading.

"Mallory?"

She jumped. Almost forgot about Wade being in the room.

"Are you still with me?"

"Is that even possible?" She pointed to a section on the paper. "I mean how could someone get their body into that position?"

Wade shrugged. "Want to give it a shot?"

She snapped up her head, meeting his devious gaze. She flicked the tip of his nose. "Behave…friend."

"Just taking one for the team."

"I bet."

She set down the paper. "I never had any idea Kyle was that kind of guy."

"He's not." Wade tapped the paper. "Look at the date."

She narrowed her eyes and scanned the email again. April 2013. She'd moved home March 2014.

"How is that possible? I didn't introduce them until about three months before I moved back." Then she got it. There was someone else.

He extracted another page out with a blue flag. "Here, read the one about Neapolitan ice cream."

"What could they do with ice cream anyway?"

Wade snorted as if saying find out for yourself.

She rested her forehead on the palm of her hand as she read. At some point, her jaw dropped. "Well, that must have been very sticky, but nice of him to clean up." Her cheeks flamed, but she read on. "I have never heard of using that for a bowl."

Wade erupted in laughter.

"It must have been very cold."

He couldn't speak. Tears rolled down his face.

"But I have to give them credit that was totally ingenious how they separated the flavors."

Wade pinched his sides and another wave of laughter hit. "Stop—talking," he said through fits of laughter. "Please."

Laughter's contagious, and Mallory caught his. They continued for a few good minutes before they subsided into giggles, finally tapering off. They were both winded.

"I wouldn't have wasted all that time jogging if I knew I could get the same workout by sitting and laughing," Mallory said.

"Feel better?" Wade asked.

"Much. What's next?" *Time to get back to work.*

Wade picked a sheet from the stack flagged by a yellow tab. "These are the ones to and from Kyle. Do you want to see them?" His brow furrowed as he studied her face.

Mallory nodded.

"They start about three months before you moved back here. Which obviously fits with when you said you introduced him to Skylar."

Mallory's stomach rolled, but she needed to come to terms with this.

"The tone completely changes and unlike the other emails with no signature, he always signed them 'XO Kyle'."

"How sweet." Okay, so she's a little resentful. "Go ahead."

"This is from Skylar to Kyle."

Skylar: *"I was so glad you called me. I also felt the connection you mentioned and would love to see you again. I know Mallory only left us alone for an hour, but it was long enough for me to see what a special man you are. I don't want to hurt her, but the thought of not seeing you again is more than I can take. I don't know what spell you put on me, but I can tell you're a man I could fall hard for. I'll be waiting to hear from you."*

"Oh gag." Mallory mimicked a dry-heave. "I love you…I love you…yuck!"

"Here's his response."

Kyle: *"I didn't know if you'd contact me back, but I'm pleased you did. Mallory is leaving town for business on Tuesday evening. How about coming to spend some time with me then? Please don't say no."*

"Her reply."

Skylar: *"I'll be there Wednesday afternoon. I can't wait to see you again."*

Mallory rolled her eyes at the smoochy face emoticon.

"And his."

Kyle*: "I'll have the Cabernet Sauvignon chilled and waiting...until then."*

Mallory surged to her feet. "That son of a—that was the hundred-and-fifty-dollar bottle of wine my client gave me for closing a big contract. He told me he accidentally knocked if off the counter. That worm!"

"I think we've read enough. Cool down a bit."

"Cool down! Do you know how tasty that wine is?" She snatched the page from Wade and ripped it in half.

Wade patted her shoulder.

"Don't placate me with a pat. I'm mad." She made fists in front of her, still clutching part of the page in each hand.

Wade put up his hands. "You're not going to hit me, are you?"

Mallory tilted her head. Okay, a little melodramatic, but reading what a low-down, thieving cheater Kyle was flooded her with feelings of past insecurities. Her tirade stopped. Adrenaline dissipated from her body, leaving her sluggish. "No. I won't hit you."

"Good, I'd hate to have to tackle you."

Mallory smirked. "On the other hand."

Wade shook his head. "I'll make you a deal. On our first date, I'll see you get a glass of this amazing wine."

She plopped into her chair. "You will? That's really sweet of—wait, date?"

"Sure. I know you keep flipping that hot-cold switch, but I anticipate a first date."

A frown crossed her face. "What if I'm in jail?"

"There're always conjugal visits." He waggled his

brows.

Her smile returned. "You're awful, but it's a deal...on the wine. If I'm not in the big house."

Wade shifted in his seat. "One more thing I want to show you." He selected a sheet flagged with a red tag. "These were from our mystery man beginning about two months before you moved home."

Her hands covered her ears. "Please no more schoolgirl role playing."

"Listen to this."

"Why aren't you responding to my emails? What's going on? You aren't returning my calls. I stopped by to check on you, and you wouldn't open the door. I could hear the television on inside, but the door was locked, I used my key, but you had the chain on. Is something wrong?"

"After about five more of this type of email, she finally sent this back."

Skylar: *"Stop calling me. No more emails or texts...please. I need some space from you. Give me this time."*

"He's mad now."

"What do you mean stop calling you? You're my girlfriend I'm supposed to call you. Are you seeing someone else? If there is someone else—"

Mallory read over his shoulder again, watching as he flipped through the emails.

Skylar: *"If I didn't know better, I would say that sounds like a veiled threat. Get it in check, little man, or I'll show you what a real threat looks like. We're through, now move on."*

"Ooh-wee, she's ticked off," Mallory said.

"You think you can just walk away after what we

had? Think again, we're far from over."

"The last email was less than four weeks prior to your move home. You know what all this means, don't you?"

She boosted the rest of the way out of her chair and faced Wade. Her butt rested on his desk. "Means he got away with stealing my wine."

"No, dummy."

Ouch. Little bruises emerged on Mallory's tender feelings. She stuck out her lower lip.

"Only kidding…sort of." He gave a sideways glance. "Think about it. She had a boyfriend she dumped for Kyle."

Her eyes widened. "I am a dummy." The heel of her hand struck her forehead. "There's a suspect…a real suspect." Mallory's excitement couldn't be contained. "Do you think you can find out who wrote those emails?" Exhilaration nearly vibrated Mallory's butt off the desk.

"I'm working on tracing the email address. And I have someone trying to get her cell phone records."

"This is the best news." Mallory sprung to her feet. "For the first time, I have some hope this predicament I'm in might get resolved." Mallory launched herself at Wade, and his eyes flew wide open. He got his arms up in time to catch her, and she flung herself into his lap.

The chair rolled three feet before falling over and dumping them on the floor. Mallory thanked him in between planting kisses all over his face.

Wade laughed, as he grabbed her face between the palms of his hands. "We still have a lot of work to do. We need a name, and there's no telling if this guy is even involved. So don't get too excited yet."

"I know that, but now, Ralph will have to admit other possibilities exist, and maybe he will stop parking at the end of the road." She sighed. "That's a lot to hope for, but a girl can dream."

She smiled down into his eyes. The heaviness of the air in the room stifled her ability to breathe or think. She marveled at the darkness of his iris against the sclera. Impossible to ascertain where the pupil ended and the iris began. She traced her finger down the small scar on his jaw.

He released her face and grabbed her hand. "You need to stop this." His voice barely audible. "If you want to be friends."

Her heated gaze snapped to his. "How did you get this?" She yanked her hand, but he wouldn't let go. Instead, she improvised and traced it with her tongue.

A sharp intake of breath broke the silence, and his body shuddered. "My brother hit me with a board."

"That wasn't nice." She kissed the scar.

"Accident."

A hand slid behind her head, and his fingers tangled into her ponytail. A slight yank and her neck bent back until they were eye-to-eye again. If possible his eyes darkened even more, and his lips parted the second before he tugged her close.

The air crackled and every bit of sense Mallory had remaining flew out the window with her conservative values in tow. She seized the hem of his T-shirt, and yanked it over his head, sending it soaring to who cared where. Her fingers slid across his abdomen, and his body tensed. His reaction to her touch pleased and encouraged her. Her hands journeyed up his chest and glided across his perfect pectorals.

Strong arms wrapped around her waist and rolled her. The soft rug hugged her back. Warm air hit the hollow of her neck followed by the tantalizing flick of his tongue. A moan escaped from the back of her throat, but she didn't care. Wade's hand, pure fire on her bare belly. He circled his thumb around her pierced navel, skillfully teasing. He wasn't close enough. Mallory's arms clung to his back. She dug her nails into his shoulders, drawing him closer. She let her toe migrate up his calf to the back of his knee and anchored in place. His hip crushed, unyielding onto hers. Not even air could seep between their bodies' point of contact. Much better. They were a fiery mishmash of body parts, so much so she could almost smell the smoke.

"Geez, Wade. What are you thinking?" A deep voice boomed, followed by hurried footsteps breaching the room.

Wade launched off of Mallory, and her head ricocheted off the floor. "Ouch." She scooted up onto her elbows. Wade succeeded in getting all but her middle button undone. Tricky. She fumbled with her buttons and managed to fasten two more before the footsteps stopped.

"For heaven sake, man, are you trying to burn us down?"

Mallory looked up as Matt jerked Wade's shirt, still smoking, off the lampshade.

Matt folded the shirt over onto itself, smothering it. He dropped his gaze to the unmoving couple lying on the floor, and a smug irritating grin crept across his face. "Explains the shirt." He chuckled.

"Everything okay?" Poppy walked up next to Matt. "Oh my. Guess so."

Mallory narrowed her eyes, annoyed at the smug grins on both their faces. Those two were perfect for each other. No one spoke for a moment, but bless Poppy she always found something to say.

"Looks like you two are getting it on better." Poppy waved off the comment. "Oh, excuse me, I meant getting along better."

"Seems so." Mallory sat up completely and scooched to lean her back against the bookcase. Gut-wrenching humiliation made her wish she could crawl away anywhere to escape their piercing stares. She stole a glance in Wade's direction, where he sat bare-chested, and if the redness climbing up his neck was any indication, his embarrassment equaled hers.

"Want to throw me my shirt." Wade held up his hand.

"Nope, this one is going to the rag pile." Matt held it up. "Got a big hole in the middle now."

The light bulb burned right through the soft olive-colored material, leaving a black melted edge.

"Aw man. That was my favorite shirt." Wade winked at Mallory. "So worth losing it."

Mallory's face flushed so hot she'd swear she'd entered early menopause. *Kill me now.*

"Got somewhere you need to be, Matt?" Wade asked, rising to his feet, and then helped up Mallory.

"Nope."

Poppy elbowed him hard.

"That hurt." He sighed. "I need to throw some water on this shirt to make sure it doesn't set the garage on fire."

Poppy put her hand on his upper arm and spun him toward the door, following with a gentle shove.

The ponytail holder had worked its way to the ends of Mallory's hair. She finished its descent with a tug and slid the holder over her wrist, bracelet style. She blew her bangs out of her eyes and had an unobstructed view of Poppy and Matt retreating. Mallory couldn't discern their mumbles but assumed they involved her and Wade.

"Oh, and Mallory," Poppy said, without looking back. "You might want to do a better job with the buttons on your shirt before heading home."

Mallory glanced down at the good-sized gaps on her misbuttoned shirt. "Terrific. I wasn't mortified enough."

Wade stepped closer, flattened her against the bookcase. "Where were we?" He leaned down to kiss her, but she ducked under his arm.

"I was leaving." She fixed her buttons as she walk-jogged toward the front door.

"Where you going?" He play-chased after her.

"Home before I lose the last of my dignity." Arms enclosed her waist, halting her progress. She bit off a high-pitched giggle before the sound carried to Poppy and Matt's ears.

"It was just getting good," he whispered into her ear.

Her insides smoldered, and her knees wobbled at his touch. She faced him and scanned his bare chest, her hand tracing where her gaze looked. "I've got to get out of here." She yanked from his grip.

"Why? Are you flipping the I-hate-Wade switch again?"

She stopped, hand on the door. "I don't think I could if I wanted to."

He stepped close. "How come?" His lips brushed her neck.

Mallory stretched her head to the side. She leaned into him, and her stomach swooned. "Because you're so darn good at that." She turned, wrapping her arms around his neck and sought out his mouth. Liquid fire careened through her, and her senses took a hiatus. Once his fingers found the buttons on her shirt those miserable senses rushed back. Her hands drifted down to his chest, and she shoved him back. "Stay there." She pointed with one hand and clutched the doorknob with the other.

He opened his arms wide. "Where you going?" He advanced.

"Ah-ah-ah. Don't you dare." Mallory opened the door. "Stay," she said, as though commanding Zehn.

Wade didn't obey as well as Zehn, and he lunged.

She simultaneously shrieked, ducked, and leapt out the doorway. Feeling safe in the out-of-doors she stopped and waited.

"Really leaving?" He leaned against the doorframe.

"I think it's best."

He nodded. "You're running scared again, aren't you?"

"Not in the way you mean." She chewed on her lower lip.

His eyebrows rose, asking the unspoken question. In what way then?

She waved him off. "Don't look at me like that." She kicked at a stick on the porch. "I know we got a bit carried away in there—"

Wade rolled his eyes and stepped out onto the porch. The screen door slammed behind him. "Here we go."

"Stop that. You don't know what I plan to say." She jutted her hands on her hips. "I only want what is best for you."

"Hey, that's great news. Let me call my mother, and let her know she's been replaced. One more item off her plate. She'll be so thrilled."

His bitterness didn't come as a surprise, but this was for the best. The trouble was making him realize it. "I'm not being like your mother. I think what happened a little while ago proves that." *Okay, that's gross...moving on.* "If you let me finish I think you'll see the wisdom in what I'm saying." Her words sounded a bit pompous, but too late now. Just plow forward and hope he didn't notice.

"Please go ahead." He made a sweeping motion with his arm, finishing in a bow.

So, he noticed. His attitude made her pissy, but she ignored it. "As I was saying, I know we got carried away, but that doesn't mean I want to put on the brakes...altogether. I just think we need to slow down a bit."

Wade's posture relaxed a smidge.

This gave her the courage to carry on. "Things are complicated right now, and I have this constant black cloud hanging over my head. I enjoy spending time with you, I really do, but I want the bad stuff behind me." She dipped her chin into her chest. Allowing emotion in didn't come easy. She struggled every day not to worry about Ralph wanting her in jail, but it was getting harder to do. "I want to give us a real chance, and I'm afraid if things get too far too fast, you'll run for the hills when you get tired of all this turmoil."

Tears escaped the corner of her eyes, and she turned her head to hide her weak moment from Wade.

Strong arms encircled her, and the stupid tears overflowed, rendering her unable to speak.

"I'm sorry," Wade said. "I've been insensitive."

Mallory shook her head.

"Yeah, I kind of have. You appear so strong. Like nothing ruffles your feathers, and I guess that made it easy to forget how hard this must be on you. Two people you were once close to were murdered." He gave her a squeeze. "You have this tough exterior and never seem fazed."

She sniffed. "Zehn lets me cry on his coat at bedtime. He gives great hugs."

"So do I." His lips brushed her cheek. "You can lean on me."

She gave a short laugh and then sniffled. "That's just it. I don't want you to see me as some weak pathetic creature you have to take care of." Her voice lowered. "That's how Kyle saw me."

"I could never see you like that. I think you're made of some of the sturdiest material I've come across. I'm not sure I would've held up as well as you with all the crap being thrown at you. I mean you were nearly blown up, for Pete's sake."

She rested against him. Being held felt nice, and the embrace did take away some of the burden. "I don't want to start off whatever this might be with drama. Not to mention if I end up in jail, I don't want to patch the hole in my heart when I find out you're dating Candy."

Wade gave her ear a playful bite. "You always cover up pain with humor, don't you?"

She blew out a long breath. "It's a problem of mine." They both laughed, and then fell silent.

After a minute, Wade spoke. "I'll make you a deal." He turned her toward him and wiped away the last of her tears with his thumbs. "We'll slow down. Now, it won't be easy."

A slow sexy grin spread across his face, and she considered dragging him back into the office. This would be a challenge.

"But, you have to start trusting me. I can handle the things going on in your life, and I want to be there for you if you'll let me…can you do that?"

She looked up, heavy-lidded from crying. "I'm a mess." She leaned her forehead to his chest.

"You're a beautiful mess though. Relationships are tough, and we have to be honest with one another."

"Relationship?" She leaned back and looked him in his eyes.

"That okay with you?"

Knots formed in her stomach. That word scared her. She gnawed on the corner of her lip. Fear paralyzed her vocal cords. Her relationships were always epic fails. Casual dating was safer territory with less pressure.

"Stop thinking and just feel, Mallory." He lifted her chin with the side of his finger. "What is it that you want?"

She blinked. Thoughts rushed through her brain. She analyzed everything that had happened up to now. She wanted to sort out her head from her heart. Bile rose high in her throat. She probably had an ulcer.

"Stop thinking. Answer me now…right now. What do you want?"

"You." The single word slipped out before her brain could pick up where it had left off in its analysis of the situation. Surprise must have registered on her face because he chuckled.

"Good. Now that that's settled." He kissed her.

Chapter Twenty

"You could use the office to study in." Wade looked at the laptop and four textbooks spread out on the kitchen table.

"This is closer to the refrigerator, and you never know when I'm gonna need to refuel." Matt finished typing and looked up from his computer.

"Where's Poppy?"

"Where's Mallory?" They both asked at the same time.

"You go first," Wade said, as he looked in the refrigerator—for what he had no idea. When nothing jumped out screaming "it's me you want" he closed the door.

"Poppy's in the bedroom going through my closet. Apparently, the pants I packed didn't blend with the dress she's taking this weekend."

Wade screwed up his face, peeking over his shoulder at Matt. "Do your pants have to blend?"

Matt threw up his hands. "Exactly what I asked, and apparently so, because she looked at me like I was dumber than dirt."

Wade snickered. He snagged a bag of chocolate chip cookies from the cabinet, then walked over and sat at the table. "You two seem pretty serious."

Matt tapped his pen on the table. "She's a great girl."

"Is that all?" Wade bit into a cookie, still clutching the bag with one hand.

"Give me one of those."

Wade tipped the bag in Matt's direction, and he took a cookie and returned three times. "I can't imagine not having her in my life. So, she's a bit of a fashionista, but she's warm, giving, smart, and has a terrific sense of humor." He exhaled. "I think I'm—"

He appeared a bit green around the gills, and Wade wondered if he would get sick. He set aside the cookies. "I can't believe it."

Matt locked gazes with him.

"You're in love with her." His voice could've rattled the windows.

"Shhh!" Matt swung around to check over his shoulder.

"Relax. She's not in here."

Little beads of sweat formed over Matt's upper lip. "What should I do?"

"I don't know? What will you do?" Wade chewed his cookie.

Matt exhaled hard and ran his hands through his hair. "I think I've got to ask her to marry me."

The half-eaten cookie hit the table, and Wade's gaze followed it. Matt's words echoed through his brain.

"Say something, man." Matt wiped his upper lip.

When Wade looked up, he wore a huge grin. "Matt, that's fantastic. I never thought you would—"

"What's fantastic?" Poppy strolled into the room and placed her hands on Matt's shoulders.

Matt's mouth opened and closed. His eyes were wide, and pure panic was all Wade could see in them.

"Cookies." Wade held up the bag. "Delectable. Want one?"

She eyed the bag. "Love one, but I'm afraid if I do, I won't fit into my dress for this weekend."

Matt's arm snaked around her. "Tight. I like it."

"Babe, I'm leaving. I have a few errands to run. Call me when you're done with class this evening, and we can grab a bite." She leaned over and kissed him. Her thumb wiped away the crimson lipstick left behind on his bottom lip. "See you, Wade. Oh, and Wade, be good to Mallory, or I'll hunt you down and gut you like a fish." She wiggled her fingers in a toodle-oo gesture.

"She can be a real charmer, can't she?" Wade asked, after the door clicked shut.

Sweat beaded on Matt's forehead. He nodded. His finger tapped the mouse and the mechanical hum of his computer waking up filled the room. "I don't know how this happened. I met her at Grayson's and now several months later, I can't imagine my life without her."

If Matt's color didn't improve soon, then Wade might have to take him to the hospital. "When will you pop the question?"

"Probably this weekend while we're away." He fidgeted in his chair.

"I can't believe my baby brother's getting married." A moment of jealousy sucked the wind out of Wade. He's the older brother, shouldn't he be the one to marry first? Isn't there some unwritten rule about that? Wade took a deep cleansing breath, his edginess subsided and made room to allow in the happiness this joyful occasion deserved. "Brother, this is great news. I'm so happy for you."

Matt put up both hands. "Don't be too ecstatic yet.

The lady must say yes first."

"I don't think that will be an issue."

"You never know. Anyway back to you. I need to get my mind off this. I'm more nervous than I've been in my life." He closed the lid on his computer. "Where did Mallory run off to?"

Wade grabbed another cookie and took a bite. "Ome—" Coughing overtook him and sent cookie bits all over the table.

Matt lunged to save his papers from the flying debris. "Get a drink, dude."

Wade, already on his feet, seized the milk jug out of the fridge and guzzled.

"You know, Mom would tell you to use a glass."

Wade set down the jug. "It was a matter of life and death." He grabbed a glass and filled it before putting away the milk with cookie pieces floating on top.

"Was it something I said?"

Wade sat again. "Home. She went home."

"Looks like you're making head way with her."

"Let's just say I think I'm starting to understand her." Finished with the cookies, he slid the bag away, which Matt snagged. "One minute I think she's into me, and the next I think she hates me, but I realized after talking to her today she's just scared."

"Of you?"

Wade shook his head. "No, of everything she's going through. She smiles and tries to laugh off everything, so no one worries about her. But in all actuality, it's a shield. One she lets down only when she's alone."

"I've been amazed at how well she's held up through all this. I mean she gets hospitalized after an explosion and acts like it's nothing."

"That's what I'm talking about. She doesn't want to drag anyone into her mayhem and feels it's better to keep everyone at arm's length with the intention of protecting them. So she hides behind this false front and instinctively pushes me away."

"And now?"

Wade half smiled. "Let's just say I think the walls are cracking."

"Is there a real chance she might go to jail?"

His heart throbbed at the uncertainty. "I would say not based on the information out there right now, but it sure seems like someone is pointing the evidence in her direction. If they keep dredging up stuff to stack the decks against her, the evidence could tip the scales." He waved it off. "Bottom line is she didn't kill anyone, and we have to believe the justice system will work."

"You really like this girl."

Wade's brow crinkled. "Of course, I like her."

"No, I mean you 'like' her '*like*' her. You haven't worked so hard on getting a girl to fancy you since Lucy Brown in high school. Remember her monogramed sweatpants. They said LOOSEY across her butt. You were all over that."

"I was also a teenage boy who thought with his—"

"Hormones?" Matt offered.

Wade snickered. "Yeah, hormones." He paused, wiping away the sweat ring from under his milk glass with his napkin. "I do like Mallory. I have a great time when I'm with her."

"I couldn't tell."

Wade nodded. "I'll help her figure this situation out, and then we'll see where things lead."

"Well if earlier was an indication—"

Wade threw his napkin and hit Matt right between the eyes. "Mind your own business."

Matt chuckled. "Who would've ever thought we'd be dating best friends?"

"I don't know that I'm actually dating yet, but I hope to be soon."

"What's that?" Muffled music reverberated from the distance. Matt glanced around the kitchen.

"I think it's *You've Lost That Lovin' Feelin'*." Wade and Matt got up, tracking the sound growing louder. "I think it's in here." Wade opened the office door. Sure enough, the music resonated from there. They searched the room and pinpointed the sound under the desk. Wade shoved aside the chair, knelt, and retrieved a cell phone. "Must be Mallory's."

"Must be." Matt agreed.

Hesitating for a second, he tapped the answer button. "Mallory Larsen's phone." Mallory might be calling to locate her phone.

"This is Detective Alvarez. I need to speak with Ms. Larsen."

"She's not available right now. This is her attorney, Wade Porter. Can I help you?" He was certain this crossed an ethical boundary, but too late now. Silence hung on the line, and he assumed she was deciding how much to tell him.

"Detective Shimkus has some questions and needs her down at the department ASAP."

"What's this about?"

"That's all I'm at liberty to say. We'll expect her within the hour."

Wade replied to the disconnected line. He glanced

at Matt.

"Bad news?"

"They want Mallory back at the sheriff's department." Wade sighed. "Just when I was making headway. This will have her running scared again."

"Maybe they just want to let her know they found out who the murderer is."

Wade appreciated Matt's support, but Detective Shimkus wouldn't call her in for good news. Worry gnawed in his gut as he headed out the front door.

Close to an hour had passed since the call. The buildings blurred as they drove past. Mallory hadn't uttered a word since Wade coerced her into his truck. Conscious of the oppressive sinking sensation in the pit of his stomach left him imagining how Mallory must feel. He glanced at the clover tattoo on her ankle, watching her foot vibrate so fast she probably could have kept a helicopter airborne. She already completed the ritual of wringing her hands, chewing on her cuticles, and corner of her lip, twirling her hair, and scratching red marks onto her arms.

Now she'd cycled back to the hair. Wade snatched her hand and held tight. "Stop, or you'll have a bald spot." She tugged against his grip, but he held firm.

"Don't you need that for driving? I believe ten and two is the proper hand position when you're driving."

"If I do that, then I can't hold the attractive blonde's hand next to me. Twelve will have to suffice." Wade gave her a squeeze.

She chewed on her lip again.

"I can do that for you."

She got it, but it took her a minute. Mallory yanked her hand free and swatted his shoulder. Her chuckle relieved some of the tension in the air. "You're terrible." She paused. "But you seem to always make me smile."

"You okay?"

"What do you think he wants now?" She shook her head. "Oh, God. You don't think somebody else is dead?" The cuticle gnawing began.

He grasped her hand again. "I don't think anyone else is dead, but I don't have any idea what the guy wants this time."

"Me in a cell. Peeing while Big Bertha watches."

"Everything will be fine."

"Then you pee in front of Big Bertha."

"No one is peeing in front of anybody…let's just go find out what he wants. Then you can stop worrying while you still have some hair and skin left."

The tan-colored brick building loomed. It was built on an incline, and had seen better days. One side gave the appearance of a one-story structure, but two stories were visible on the opposing side.

Two deputies walked a tall balding man toward the department. His hands were cuffed behind his back. The larger deputy released him to open the door, and he yanked free, bolting down the hill. Not bad for a guy who looked like a gust of wind would take him away.

Wade cringed as one of the deputies tackled him and due to gravity, they tumbled hard to the ground and rolled. They both cussed a blue streak. The second deputy, who appeared to be about seventy-five pounds overweight, caught up, gasping for air. Wade waited to see if he might stroke out, but he managed to yank the perp to his feet.

His partner stood and fingered his baton. Had they

not been standing out front chances are he would've pummeled the perp. He still groused as he followed his partner into the department. Wade wondered if he should mention he had a tear in the seat of his pants, but he decided against it.

"He ripped his pants." Mallory snickered.

"Yep."

"Wish it was Ralph."

Wade nodded. "You read my mind."

The nerves radiating from Mallory put him on edge. "You ready."

She exhaled hard. "Nope."

****

"He's doing this on purpose. Making us wait like this." Mallory drummed her fingers on the table. Her stomach had become a spongy conduit for acid.

"Probably, but hang in there."

Why did this guy make her feel so much better? He calmed her down, and not many people possessed that ability. Zehn was the only male in her life that had a soothing effect…until now.

The door clicked, and Mallory vaulted out of her chair.

Ralph and Detective Alvarez strolled in and sat across from them.

She'd smack the sneer right off of Ralph's face if it wouldn't land her in the slammer, but she refused to give him that satisfaction. Wade placed a hand on her back, and she sat.

Ralph took his sweet time before he spoke. Making a production of flipping through papers and jotting notes. He threw in a couple of big circles around some obviously unimportant information.

Man, she wanted to knock this guy off his high horse. Even Detective Alvarez appeared tired with his antics. Mallory swore her eye twitched as Ralph flipped through the pages one last time. The smirk on Wade's face confirmed he did too.

"Are you planning on telling me why I'm here, or are we suppose to sit here and watch you play dot to dot?" So, patience wasn't Mallory's virtue.

Ralph squinted his right eye. He glanced up, an evil expression enveloped his face.

A cold chill racked her as he peered at her with hate in his eyes. An intimidation tactic…maybe, but she wouldn't give him the pleasure of knowing he unnerved her. Instead she winked and struck a nerve. Even his moustache twitched.

Ralph returned to drawing marks on the papers.

Detective Alvarez blew out her breath. "Ms. Larsen, can you tell us about Mr. Malloney's—"

Ralph's open palm slammed on the desk. They all snapped their heads in his direction. He appeared to glow becoming the center of attention.

Detective Alvarez bit the side of her reddened cheek.

Must suck being the junior detective—especially when stuck with Ralph as a partner. A wave of pity coursed through Mallory.

"Anything else you remember about Mr. Malloney's death?" Ralph asked.

"No. If that's all, I have a pedicure in twenty." She flinched when Wade kicked her ankle and scowled. Ralph must have concluded the look of displeasure was meant for him, because he smiled. Or, what she guessed resembled a smile. His expression looked more like a rabid wolf who smoked and drank a lot of coffee.

Ralph leaned back in his chair, fingers interlaced on the table. "Have you decided to come clean about Kyle Malloney's death?"

Mallory gave a sharp shake of her head. "Nothing more to tell. I've told you verbatim multiple times what happened. What else do you want?"

"The truth." Ralph said.

"Terrific, then we're done here." Mallory slumped.

He ground his teeth together.

Mallory cringed at the shrill squeaking sound.

"Aren't you tired of all this, Mallory?" Ralph flapped his right arm.

Exhausted...weary...beaten down...take your pick. "Very much so." Mallory nodded.

Ralph locked his gaze on Mallory. "Tell me about Kyle's life insurance policy?"

An alarm sounded in Mallory. She skipped her next breath, as confusion engulfed her. "Life insurance policy?"

"Yes. His life insurance policy." Ralph thumbed through the papers again.

"We never talked about a policy. I mean I guess he had one through his employer. A lot of people do." This line of questioning put her senses on high alert.

"He had one through work, but he also purchased one for himself. Who do you think the beneficiary of that policy is?"

Mallory's gut rolled. "I don't know. He was very close to his sister." She swallowed something resembling a fur ball.

"All right. If that's your story." Ralph sat forward. "I had to ask myself who had something to gain by the death of Mr. Malloney. Guess what? You're the only person I could come up with."

"Good Lord. What could I possibly gain by his death?"

"How about one hundred thousand dollars." He narrowed his eyes. "That's a pretty big something to gain."

She sensed Wade stiffen beside her. Her brain stopped functioning at normal speed, and ice replaced the blood in her veins. Ralph wanted motive, and he'd discovered it. "I-I don't understand?"

"What part? Why someone would murder for money, or why he made you the beneficiary?" Ralph tapped his pen on the metal table.

"Enough." Wade spoke up. "This interview is over. All you have is a bunch of circumstantial evidence. You're spending so much time blaming my client for these murders that you're letting the real murderer walk free." He wrapped his hand around Mallory's forearm, nearly lifting her to her feet. He thrust her toward the door.

She feared it was because he believed they'd arrest her if he didn't get her out of here.

"I didn't say you could leave." Ralph surged to his feet.

"We don't need your permission. Ms. Larsen graciously agreed to answer your questions, which she's done. She didn't know about his policy. Fact is, he probably just hadn't had time to change his beneficiary since their relationship ended. Simple as that. So, if she isn't being charged, we're leaving."

Those options stunk, and she wished Wade would've skipped the part about being charged. But she relaxed when neither detective approached, or yelled for her to put her hands against the wall and spread 'em.

Wade opened the door, death grip on her arm intact.

She stopped and turned toward Ralph, hoping she wouldn't regret this hesitation. "If what you say is true, I don't want his money. It should go to his family. His sister is starting medical school this fall, and I know it would help her."

Ralph made a growling noise as the door closed. *Wham.*

She lurched forward. Something slammed against the door. Mallory glanced up at Wade.

"Keep walking, and don't stop for anything."

A pin drop would've sounded like a sonic boom on the drive home. She remained in his truck, parked in his driveway. She exhaled all her breath. "This is bad."

"Yep." Both looked straight ahead, gazes boring into the dark green garage door.

"What will I do?" She tilted her head back, stopping when it impacted the headrest. Somehow, she found the strength to rotate it until she peered into Wade's eyes. They stared at each other but no words found their way into the space between them.

Wade's cell phone chirped and ended the eternal silence. He grabbed it from his cup holder. "This is Wade.

"Uh huh.

Uh huh.

There were? Of a personal nature?

Read me a couple."

His eyes widened, and red splotches popped out on his neck.

Must have been good.

"Enough. I've heard all I need to. Can you trace it back?

Uh-huh.

You're kidding." He pinched the bridge of his nose.

Mallory beat down the urge to ask what?

"All right. There's nothing else we can do with that. You'll keep working on the other and let me know. Thanks for everything, Stan. I appreciate it." He ended the call, but he still clutched his phone.

The seconds ticked by. She blurted out, "Bad news?"

Wade startled. "In a matter of speaking."

"Want to talk about it?"

"Not really, but you have the right to know."

A small lump took up residence in the center of her chest. "About me?"

"About Skylar's cell phone." He shifted to face her. "There are texts of an—intimate nature from the same time-frame of the emails."

"I'd get excited, but by the look on your face, it's not good news.

"From a prepaid disposable cell phone. Untraceable."

She ran her hands through her hair. "When it rains, it pours." She sighed. "But truth be told, Skylar having a boyfriend she cheated on doesn't make him anymore a murderer than it does me."

Wade took her hand in his and gave a reassuring squeeze. "Give me some time. He's still working on tracing back the emails. And all we need is something proving there's someone else the police should investigate. Get their tunnel vision off of you."

His smile warmed her heart. "You're a pretty good guy, Wade Porter."

He released her hand and brushed her cheek with the back of his fingers. "Took you long enough to figure it out."

She leaned into his touch "Actually I've known all along. I just didn't want you getting a big head."

He laughed. "Thanks for keeping me humble." He leaned over and brushed his lips against hers. "I meant it when I said everything will be fine."

"I believe you." She smiled, their mouths still touching. She squeezed her lips together. "I better get home. Zehn is probably desperate for a walk."

"Wade...oh, Wade." Ms. Emery made a beeline right for them, yielding a basket of some delicacy. "I'm so glad I caught you."

Her loathsome gaze slithered over Mallory, which she interpreted for get away from my future son-in-law. *She really used to like me. I don't know what happened.* Mallory should've gone ahead home, but no way she'd give Ms. Emery the satisfaction. She stayed rooted to the place next to Wade on the sidewalk.

"I'm having lunch at my house on Sunday again. I would love if you'd come. Candy will be there." She managed to give him a wink and Mallory a snarl all at the same time.

Real talent.

"That's so nice of you, but I don't think I can make it Sunday." Wade eyed the basket.

The jerk wanted whatever goodies she carried in there. Mallory had to admit they smelled delicious.

"Oh, please try. Candy will be so disappointed."

She held out the basket. "My famous blueberry muffins. There will be more of these on Sunday."

Wade paused, and Mallory considered socking him.

"I need to go, lover boy." Mallory's voice would've made a sixty-year old smoker impressed.

"Love—"

Mallory thrust her first two fingers to his lips. "Shhh. I know. I had a great time too this afternoon. You were astounding." She pursed her lips and gave him her sex kitten eyes. Not that she even had those. They probably looked more like a zebra got it on with a lizard eyes.

"I'll miss you bunches and bunches." Insert side-to-side hair flip. "And next time, I promise you get to be on top." She removed her fingers from his lips, blew a kiss, spun on her heel, and sashayed across the street. Pretty sure she left both with their mouths agape. She swayed her hips with a little extra pop on each stride. Trump that, blueberry muffins.

A spasm attacked her hip as her foot landed on the bottom step of her parents' porch. She lunged for the railing, stopping her humiliating descent to the ground. Hauling her lifeless leg along behind her, she dragged up each step. By the time she made it to the porch sweat broke out on her forehead. She couldn't force herself to peek and see if Ms. Emery caught her swagger falter. *I'd never make a good prostitute.* As she limped inside, she thrust a fist into her gluteal muscle.

Chapter Twenty-One

When you're sitting in cut-off jean shorts and a tank top, it's hard to get into winter fashion trends. But Mallory made good choices for her client. She always did. She had a discerning eye for what's trending. That's why they hired her. A few last clicks on the keyboard, and she'd completed work for the day.

"Come on, Zehn...pee-yew." She fanned under her desk with a magazine.

Zehn groaned, rolled onto his back, and splayed his legs wide. "What did Dad feed you now?" She glanced at the time on her computer. The satellite people were scheduled between twelve and three today to install a dish at her new home. For whatever reason, they always gave a range.

She clicked onto a website for dogs. "I'm ordering some probiotics and changing you to a freeze-dried dog food. You are not stinking up my new home." Zehn's soft snores drew her attention under her desk. She shook her head. Ten minutes later, Zehn's new food and digestive support had been ordered, and she headed down the steps.

She grabbed her purse and flung open the front door.

The delivery man let out a high-pitched squeal.

Mallory slammed the door shut. She leaned her back against the door and used her hand to smoosh her heart back into her chest. "Geez, Mallory, it was only the delivery guy." She opened the door again.

"I'm so sorry. I didn't mean to startle you." A hand-held computer was pressed to the delivery man's chest.

"Likewise," she said.

"Good reflexes."

"Thanks. I have a strong self-preservation instinct."

The man dressed in all one color headed back to his truck.

The box blocked her way out. What in the world had her mom bought now? She considered about running after the delivery fellow and making him take it back, but decided what her mom bought while watching infomercials wasn't her business. "Ride Your Way to Fitness. I'm afraid to find out what that means." She grabbed the box and it didn't budge. She walked to the other side and gave a shove. Nothing. "Hmm." She sat on her butt and thrust it inside with her feet. "Look out, Warrior Princess, you're being replaced."

"Wonderful. It's here." Charlotte clapped her hands together.

Great, she shows up after I get this monstrosity inside. Mallory wiped her brow. "So what did you buy now?"

Charlotte squeezed her lips together. "Just a little something for my health."

"I moved that box inside. There's nothing little about it." Mallory scrutinized her mother.

"Don't let me keep you. You look to be on your way out."

She put her hands on her hips. "I got time. I'll go grab a knife to open this with—"

"No! I mean, no, sweetheart, I couldn't ask you to do that."

"No worries, Mom." Mallory disappeared into the kitchen returning a minute later with a pair of scissors.

Charlotte had a phone cord wrapped around the box and attempted to haul the unmoving item into the den.

For a moment, Mallory leaned against the doorframe watching her struggle. "Trying to hide it?"

Charlotte staggered backward, dropping the cord. "Oh my. You startled me."

"Yeah, well, there's a lot of that going around today." She pushed off the doorframe. "Let's open the box, and I'll help you move it."

Charlotte pursed her lips. "Fine."

Mallory cut open the box. Overturned it to rest on its side and slid the mystery contents out. She removed the packing material and uprighted something that resembled a flying saucer with handles. She looked up at her mother, question in her eyes.

"What?" Charlotte asked.

"You know what." Mallory pointed at the conundrum. "What is this thing?"

"It's called Ride To Fitness."

Mallory splayed open her arms. "A little more information, Mom."

"It's supposed to be like riding a horse. It firms all of your core muscles. Tones your butt and thighs. It's also good for your back, balance, and will help my posture."

Mallory's eyes grew large. "You've got to be kidding me?"

"Don't be such a naysayer. Just because I'm your

mother doesn't mean I don't want to stay in shape."

"Go for a walk or take a yoga class." She folded her hands into a prayer pose. Held for a silent beat, before her hands burst wide apart. "Don't stay up all night watching infomercials and impulse buying."

"This was not an impulse. I researched the product thoroughly."

"Where?"

"There was a program on cable—"

"Ha!" Mallory threw back her head.

"If you don't want to know, why did you ask?"

"I don't know, Mom." She shook her head. "Get a hold of your new horse's head, and I'll take the tail." They carried it into the den next to her mom's Thigh Trainer, Ab roller and Powerglide Board. "Whoa. Easy there, little fellow."

Charlotte narrowed her eyes. "Not funny."

"I can't believe you wouldn't let me have a pony when I was growing up."

"Weren't you leaving?" She shooed her in the direction of the door.

"Yeah…yeah. Oh, and Mom."

"What?"

"Don't get bucked off."

A couch pillow hit Mallory in the head, and a hearty laugh escaped. She blew her mom a kiss.

You've Lost That Lovin' Feelin' silenced Mallory's giggles. She closed the front door and fished her phone out of her purse. Maybe it's time to change her ring tone. Possibly something like Gene Autry's *Back in the Saddle Again*. She chuckled at her own joke.

She glanced at the number. "Hey there, neighbor for a few more days."

"Hi. I'm sorry I haven't called this past week. Work has been crazy."

"No worries. I didn't call either, and I call your crazy work week and raise you one working on a new house." She'd had Internet and a business line installed. Put up the pictures she bought and placed area rugs. Also painted the bathrooms, and hung most of her clothes in her walk-in closet, yippee. It's starting to look like home…albeit one without any furniture.

"Would you like to have dinner with me tonight?"

"Like a real date?" She stopped next to her vehicle.

"Well—yeah. I thought it was time."

Nerves tickled her belly. "That sounds nice. I'm heading over to the house to wait on the satellite person. They are supposed to show by three at the latest. What time did you have in mind?"

"How about sevenish?"

"Perfect. I have enough stuff over there I can get cleaned up while I'm waiting and be all ready to go."

"Just give me a call if you're running late."

"Will do." Hurray! She did a happy dance, shaking her butt and spinning in a circle.

"You do realize I'm looking out the front window?"

She thrust her shoulders ramrod straight and smoothed her hair with her hand. "Spiders. Covering the street. Everywhere. Eww, I hate spiders." She stomped her foot and ground her toe into the pavement.

"Uh-huh. I'll see you at seven, and I plan to hold you to your promise from last time we talked."

"Huh? What promise?" she asked to the disconnected line. Last time we talked he gave me a ride to the sheriff's department. Then he gave me a ride home. Wait. Ms. Emery wandered out and—oh no. A flush ignited in her core and migrated outward. "Me and my big mouth." She climbed into her car and whipped a U-turn. *I hope the satellite person is running early.*

Chapter Twenty-Two

"You'll need to top those trees if I put the satellite on the house." The satellite guy, or Leroy according to the embroidery on the pocket of his shirt, pointed over the top of her house. "See, you're not getting a good signal." He held up some device and pointed to meaningless numbers.

"I can't get television then?" Mallory bit her lip. *I need my reality television.*

"Sure you can, but you'll either have to have someone come out and cut off those limbs." He pointed again.

Again, she had no idea which ones he meant.

"Or you won't have a clear view of the sky, and your service will be interrupted every time a leaf wiggles."

"So I have to have a tree topper come out?"

"Not necessarily."

Mallory pinched the bridge of her nose. Why won't some people get to the point? "Please tell me what my options are."

"What we could do is put it over here." Leroy waved her to follow him. "See right here, we can aim it over the tops of those trees." He stopped about fifteen feet from her house, in front of one of her retaining walls.

Why didn't he lead with that? "So do that."

"To do that, installation won't be free. It's only free if we can attach the dish to your house."

"Why?"

"Because you have to dig the hole, put the dish on a metal pole, run the cable through a plastic pipe, bury it in the ground, and pour concrete into the hole. There's a lot more time consuming work involved."

And of course, he gets a bigger piece of the pie. She'd never make her date at this rate. She shook her head. "Please just do what you need to do. I would like to have the television to watch. Even if the leaves are wiggling."

He let out a belly laugh. "I'll get right on it and have you fixed up in a jiffy."

Exactly how long a jiffy entitled wasn't specified, but ended up being almost three hours. Mallory had borrowed her mom's fifteen-inch kitchen television and made sure everything worked okay. The guy showed her how to hook up her big screen once she moved it in.

She closed the door behind him and glanced at her watch, five o'clock. She could still make it. Mallory grabbed her purse off the floor and locked up. She dashed to her car, jumped in, and tossed her purse on the backseat. A chime sounded before she made it to the end of her driveway. She twisted, snagged her purse, and shook the contents until her cell phone worked its way to the top of the pile. Maybe Wade is cancelling?

She scrolled through until she got to the message screen. Bile rose in her throat. The tremble in her hand sent the phone plummeting to the floorboard. She stared out the windshield unable to move, think, or speak. Dizziness overwhelmed her, and she gasped, forcing air into her lungs. The spinning subsided, and she retrieved the phone from the floor. Mallory glided her finger across the screen and the phone surged to life. Certain she'd misread.

Kyle Malloney still in bold letters across the screen.

She swallowed what must have been dust, because no moisture existed in her mouth. This is a joke...a cruel joke. Fingers trembling as she tapped the screen to open the message, instead she opened an old message from Ella. Backing out, she tried again.

Kyle: *"Meet me at the cabin."*

What does this mean? After three tries and a battle with autocorrect.

Mallory: *"Who is this?"*

She waited, idling in her car at the end of her driveway. Two minutes. Five minutes. Eight minutes...no response. Kyle's alive? How is this possible? She drummed her fingers on her steering wheel as she battled a moment of indecision. She exhaled and struggled to muster her courage. She shifted into first and wheeled out onto the road, heading the opposite direction she had planned to go. But, she needed to know. Why had the authorities confirmed the body as Kyle if he wasn't in the trunk?

Her thoughts ran wild and for a moment, she'd forgotten about her date. She whipped her gaze to the clock. Five-twenty. She'd never make it back for her date. After stopping on the side of the road, she called Wade, voicemail. *Dang it.* "Um...Wade...um. Geez, why couldn't you have picked up? I needed the voice of reason. Um...well...where do I—"

"If you are satisfied with your message, press one."

"What? If I'm satisfied? I'm not done yet. I haven't even started…wait what did you say to push to continue? Come on, tell me again."

"Thank you for your call."

"Crap." She hit the call button again. "Wade. I'm not crazy, your phone cut me off. I wanted to tell you—"

"Thank you for your call."

"Come on!" She squeezed the phone tight enough the glass should've popped out. Again, she called. "I might be late. Got message from Kyle to meet at cabin—"

"If you are satisfied with your message, press one."

"Dang it. Dang it. Dang it." She alternated each dang it with smacking the phone on the steering wheel. She dialed again.

"Mailbox full."

"Oh, come on." *Hopefully, he can make out I'm running late.* She can't turn back. Kyle might need her help, or she required the opportunity to beat him to death for letting people think he was dead. *Class-A-Jerk.* She tossed her phone over on the passenger seat, and it slid across and down into the seat abyss. *I'll rescue it later.* She retrieved the address in her car's GPS history to locate the quickest way back to the cabin, or what had once been a cabin.

****

The phone's shrill ring drew Wade's attention away from the report he was typing. "Wade Porter."

"It's Stan."

"Hey, Stan. I've been waiting for your call."

"I've tried twice, but it kept sending me straight to voicemail or cutting me off."

Wade shook his head. "I don't know what's wrong with this thing. I think it's time to switch carriers and bury this phone."

"I know what you mean. Mine drops calls like crazy, and it's in the middle of town without a cloud in the sky. Anyway, I traced the email address back to the owner, and I thought you'd want to know right away."

"Let me have it." Wade listened as Stan reviewed the information. His muscles tensed more as each word Stan spoke sank in. A jackhammer pummeled the inside of his head, forcing out all reasonable thoughts.

He wasn't sure if he hung up on Stan or if the call dropped, but he heard the information he required. What did this mean? He needed to talk to Mallory. Three voice mails showed on his cell phone screen. Miserable piece-of-crap technology. Listening to Mallory's messages, he confirmed his piece-of-crap assessment of the phone. "Wait. What?"

He pressed four to replay her last message. The connection crackled, but after the third play, he caught Kyle's name, and that Mallory was on her way to the cabin. Did she mean her house? Surely, she'd have the sense not to drive back out to the crime scene. Wade tensed. This was Mallory. Heaven only knows what she'd do. His thumb scrolled down his contacts list, located her name, and tapped the screen. Listening to the beeps dialing her number, he held his breath.

****

You've Lost That Lovin' Feelin' echoed from deep under her seat. She shoved her hand into the seatbelt hole, but her fingers didn't touch the phone. She stretched farther, and gravel popped and crackled as it skidded under her tires. She bolted up right, steering her car back onto the road. "Okay, I get the picture. No talking on the cell phone while driving," she said to any higher power that might be listening.

The soothing and yet annoying GPS voice informed her in one mile she needed to turn right and arrive at her destination. The eerie atmosphere hadn't changed since the last two times she'd been here. The crime-scene tape still surrounded the cabin, but sections had broken free and hung loose, flapping in the breeze, while other pieces stretched out lifeless on the ground.

"Kyle?" Mallory yelled and then paused to listen…no response. She walked toward the side of the structure where two partial walls stood. They were scorched, but she could still make out the bottom edge of the previous window.

A hawk screeched overhead.

Mallory's entire body stiffened. She blew out her breath and forged ahead to the back wall of the house. "Kyle?" She hollered again. "Are you here? It's Mallory." She stood silent, waiting for his response.

The tree frogs gave her one. Squirrels rustled the leaves as they shot across the ground and back up into the trees. The hawk screeched again as it circled overhead.

I hope he doesn't think I'm dinner. She glanced up as it glided out of sight again. Her body temperature seemed to rise fifty degrees and Mallory's palms sweated. She wiped them on the slim-fitting white capris she changed into for her date. Thinking about it now, white wasn't such a great idea. And she could lump coming here into the bad idea category. The backless three-inch wedge heeled shoes she'd crammed her feet into were rooted to the ground. They didn't want to proceed, they wanted to turn and run for her car.

"Kyle?" Her voice cracked, but she managed to convince her feet to carry her behind the cabin. She pivoted and peered into the thick woods surrounding it. She scratched her arm, leaving red marks behind. Her weight shifted from foot-to-foot. Sweat trickled down her chest. It had to be a hundred degrees outside, instead of the eighty-one her car registered. "Kyle. Answer me. You're not scaring me." Terrific, lie in the face of terror. *I'll never make it through those pearly gates. Yes St. Peter, I lied but…*

"This isn't funny." Mallory forgot how thick the woods were last time she'd been here. The massive trees and dense understory obscured any view, an overwhelming sense of being alone made her skin crawl. The wind swirled through the leaves in the trees, warning her she didn't belong here. Fear spiraled in her stomach. She strove to stay rational, but when she swore something touched her neck, she threw in the towel. "Suit yourself, Kyle," she yelled. "You made your bed, now go lie in it. I'm out of here." All fake bravado, but a necessary evil to keep her anxiety in check.

She walk-jogged toward her car. The paver sidewalk had been destroyed by all the emergency vehicles, and her wedge heels proved to be a poor choice for this expedition. She stepped on a stick and folded her ankle to the side, which wasn't designed to bend that way. Then the shock subsided, and pain sent her crashing to the ground, landing on her hip with a forceful thud. "Ouch." She drew up her foot and rubbed her ankle. "Stupid shoes." Her ankle throbbed and burned. "If Kyle isn't dead, then I'll kill him." It already started swelling, but she could flex it, so she was pretty sure it wasn't broken.

Mallory crawled to her knees and used her good right foot to propel her upright. She touched down the toe of her left foot and flinched. She gazed at the brown-and-green stains coating her knees and hips. She swiped at the debris and brushed off what she could, but no way she'd wear these on her date now.

A deep breath in and she put weight on her left foot. She clenched her fists and launched her right forward again to get relief. *Okay, I made it a step. Only about two hundred more of these, and I'll be back in my car.* Five steps later, her forehead beaded with perspiration. *Great, not only am I dirty for the date. I stink too.* Prickly tingles ran rampant through her consciousness, and she scanned the area. *Just my imagination.* She shook off the heebie-jeebies, and turned her attention back to the task at hand. The ankle throbbed, but held up…so far.

A stick cracked behind her and she whirled. She stumbled but channeled her inner flamingo, and steadied her one good leg before she'd crashed to the ground. She visually searched her surroundings. "Kyle?" Her voice a broken whisper. The sensation of thousands of baby spiders raced up her back. Her pulse pounded in her ears, and she shook her head to clear the white noise and listen. *Silent.* Her spidey-senses vibrated to the point a seismic reading would register.

She kicked off her shoes, grabbed them, and if speed limping was an Olympic sport, she had a real chance of taking the gold. Leaves rustled, and a loud thump stopped her. Slowly, she pivoted, and a shrill scream lodged in her throat.

Mallory's heart hammered into her ribcage, and she wondered if a rib might crack. She took a couple of slow deep breaths as the figure cleared the shadows. "You scared me to death." She hobbled a step closer. "You're not planning on having me arrested for trespassing, are you?" A nervous laugh escaped her throat.

He didn't say a word. Just stared without expression.

He doesn't like me…that's a given, but usually, he's not at a loss for words. She considered his black jeans, black polo, and black military hiking boots. A menacing handgun holstered on his right hip, a knife in a sheath, and a tactical baton on his left. The word mercenary popped into her mind. The contradiction of Yosemite Sam and a mercenary fascinated and unsettled her. Maybe an idea for the new winter fashion line. "What are you doing here, Ralph?"

The left side of his lip curled up.

The silence droned on for what seemed like forever.

"Shouldn't I be asking you the same thing?"

Mallory studied his weapons and weighed her options. They were without witnesses in the middle of nowhere, maybe best not to antagonize a well-armed man. "I thought I'd get some closure if I returned to the scene." Not a total lie, but 'I arrived to meet the ex-fiancé you believed to be dead in the trunk' didn't sound like a good direction to take this conversation.

"Closure, huh? How's that working for you?"

She shrugged. "Not as well as I'd hoped. Might as well abort and head home."

Ralph stood stock-still, and his pupils expanded and darkened by the second.

She shivered. "Um…okay…well bye then." She swiveled on her good foot.

"Mallory."

He said her name like a curse word. She wanted to be in the safety of her car and ambled onward without responding.

"Mallory." His voice a threatening whisper.

She inhaled deep and held the breath, slowly releasing it. "Yes."

"You're not leaving."

She swallowed the dust bowl in her mouth and gathered her courage to face him, speaking as she turned, "Actually, I am." Her stomach swayed, but she held his gaze. Suddenly wondering where he parked his vehicle.

"Actually, you're not." He closed the gap between them until he stood about ten feet away.

"This has been fun." Mallory gave a clipped wave and turned for her car.

"Why are you really here?"

She halted again. Stupid feet. She needed to have a discussion with them about when to keep moving. "I told you already."

"Yeah. Closure. Sure. Didn't get a text or anything?"

Ice water rushed through her veins. She rotated on her good foot. "What did you say?"

Ralph shrugged.

She locked her gaze on the cell phone twitching in his hand. "You sent it." It wasn't said as a question, but more an accusation.

A malevolent grin did a slow spread across his face.

Mallory struggled to swallow the fear crawling up the back of her throat. "Why? Why would you send that message and drag me out here?"

His grin disappeared, and his posture relaxed a bit. "You were a real bitch in high school."

Wait…what? "First off, no I wasn't, and second, you didn't drag me out here to rehash high school. For Pete's sakes, that's been over eight years ago. Get over it already."

"You made me the laughing stock of the school." He stroked the tactical baton fastened to his waistband.

Okay, maybe he wouldn't get over it. "You did that to yourself."

"We were an item, and you dumped me in front of the entire school." His hand opened and closed into a fist.

Disgust momentarily replaced Mallory's fear. "We were never an item. You stalked me. You waited for me outside my classes. You followed me home. You broke into my locker and put roses in there."

"Sounds awful. That's what couples do."

Mallory forced her words through gritted teeth. "They were black, and we weren't a couple. Tell me you know that. Surely you remember. I never led you on. I did my best to be nice at first, but then…well, you just got scary, and I had to let you know to back off."

"Bull. We were supposed to get married."

She gasped. "Where did you ever get that in your head?"

"We were in love."

"No, we weren't. You were obsessed. You showed

305

up at my softball games and track practice. Anywhere I went you showed up and I never told you where I was going. You even showed up at prom and nearly put my date in the hospital."

"You were my date, and he attacked you. You should have thanked me."

"No! You weren't my date. My date was dancing with me...until you jumped him."

"You got me suspended. Just another way you made me the joke of the school."

Mallory sighed. He wouldn't listen to reason, and the matter-of-fact way he spoke made her wonder if he truly believed the things he said. The behavior of an amoral man, she'd read about it in a psychology class in college. "You got yourself suspended. And you want to be this poor victim. It's bull, and you know it. I had to be escorted to each class because I was so afraid of you. I had to make arrangements to get picked up every day, because I was no longer safe to walk alone. Then you told the freakin' world I was pregnant with your kid and I"—she jammed her finger into her chest and sucked in a breath—"had to be grilled by the school advisor, principal, psychologist, nurse, not to mention my parents. I was only a kid, and you humiliated me." This wasn't working, and she questioned his mental stability. Arguing about the past was pointless, and it didn't really matter all these years later.

His eyes turned even darker. His jaw muscle flexed and released. "You're a bitch, and I can't believe I wasted my time on you in high school."

Pointless. "Welp. I agree. Bye."

"Not yet."

Her shoulders sagged. "What! What do you want?

Tell me why you wanted me out here. What does high school have to do with any of this?" She made a sweeping motion with her arm.

His eyes narrowed. "Skylar was pregnant."

Something kicked in Mallory's gut. "What?"

"You heard me."

She struggled to clear her head and process. "How do you know that?"

"Autopsy, of course, and truth be told, I found out…before." He took another step forward. "Sky was three months pregnant."

"Sky? No one called her Sky. She hated that."

"I called her Sky."

The wistful sound in his voice stopped her cold. As the realization hit, she blinked. "You were involved with Skylar?"

"We were in love. We were to be married." Ralph's posture was unyielding. "I had picked up the pieces of my life, made something of myself, and you ruined it."

She snapped up her head. "How did I ruin it?" She tilted her head to the side. "You blame me for your baby dying?"

His laugh should have been bottled and used in the next big psychological thriller.

An unsettled feeling welled inside of Mallory. How does someone laugh about the death of a baby, even one not of this world yet? The sinister atmosphere weighed on her. Did Ralph intend to hold her responsible for his baby dying? She placed her hand over her lower abdomen, maybe subconsciously grieving the loss of a life.

"Not…my…baby."

She shook off her fog and hurdled back into a horrid present. "What?"

"It wasn't my baby."

She might puke. "Kyle?" she asked in a hoarse whisper.

"Now she's getting it." Ralph circled to the side, still keeping the same distance. "We were together for two years, and suddenly, seven or eight months ago she backed away and found excuses to not see me." He circled back to Mallory's other side. His stare distant. "We talked about getting married. Having a family. I found a pregnancy test in her trash, and thought…" He stopped and met Mallory's gaze. "Then you and your fiancé wrecked it."

"Kyle cheated with my maid of honor. How did I wreck it?" Mallory shook her head, hoping to rattle the nonsensical puzzle pieces into a rational image.

"Why couldn't you just stay away? Sky was happy here with me. Then you invited her to visit you in the big city and introduced her to Kyle."

She could hear his teeth mashing together.

He raked his hands through his hair. "You did that. You introduced them." Squinting, he jammed his finger in her direction.

"I didn't even know you two were dating." The emails Wade read flashed in her brain, and acid rolled up her esophagus. "She never mentioned you." He circled again reminding Mallory of the hawk.

"She didn't want anyone to know. She especially didn't want you to know. Probably because of the way you treated me in high school."

Mallory was at a total loss. Warnings rang louder than the church bells on Sunday morning. "I didn't kill

her, Ralph. I'm sorry you lost her, but I didn't kill her."
She scanned her surroundings.

His eyes took on a malicious slant.

The air seemed to stop moving. Not even a bird chirped. A sense of darkness formed in her being and drove everything out, but the lub-dub sound vibrating through her body. "But you already know I didn't kill her." She took a step back, watching his face contort with vengeance.

Logic long gone, her body and brain conspired toward a united goal…survival. She bolted. Adrenaline numbed the stabbing pain radiating from her heel and into her calf. Her car, at least one hundred feet away. She hurried, but her ankle wasn't supporting her. Seventy-five feet. *Come on. Please*. She'd dropped the wedge heels somewhere around the ninety-foot mark.

The pounding of his boots hit the ground close behind.

But she didn't look back. Fifty feet. Tears stung her eyes, the pain too much to ignore, but she pushed. Twenty-five feet. His shoulder plowed into her ribcage, and her ankle folded. She crashed to the ground, all the air forced from her lungs on impact. The weight on top of her added to her distress. Some air returned into her lungs, giving her a surge, and she flailed her arms, contorting her body, landing strikes, desperate to break free.

He didn't budge.

She reached to scratch him. If she was to die, she planned to leave his skin cells and DNA under her nails. A scream ripped from her core, and her right hand made contact with his arm, drawing blood. She twisted her body and lunged for his eyes the second before the rock hoisted over her plunged for her head. A piercing shriek ripped into the air right before she faded into darkness.

Chapter Twenty-Three

"Six unanswered calls." Wade slammed his phone onto his truck's console. "Where is she?" He parked in front of the sheriff's department and snagged the file from the passenger seat. The smell of urine greeted him as he crossed the department threshold. *At least I know I'm in the correct place.* He tapped on the window to divert the deputy's attention from the huge hamburger wedged in his mouth.

The man grimaced through the safety glass.

Wade guessed him around five-foot-two inches, maybe one-hundred-thirty pounds, and a dead ringer for the all-American son of Mayberry. Not someone he visualized taking down a hardened criminal. "I need to speak with Detective Shimkus." The ketchup dripping from the corner of the man or boy's mouth distracted him.

The deputy studied him for a minute. "Not on shift today." He disregarded Wade and locked his jaw back onto his burger.

Again, Wade tapped the window.

The man stopped mid-chew and glared.

"How about Detective Alvarez?"

The deputy sighed his annoyance, but released his death grip on his burger. "What's this in regards to?" He wiped his mouth on his napkin.

"An investigation she's working on. Tell her Wade

Porter is here to see her regarding the Skylar Masterson murder."

He gave his burger one last wistful glance before walking away from the window, indiscernible grumbling floating in his wake.

The scent of bacon wafted in the air, and Wade stole a glance at the burger out of his reach. His stomach grumbled, reminding him he only ate a small lunch to save his appetite for his date tonight. The door buzzed and tore away his attention from the burger and subsequent theft of said food.

Detective Alvarez stood in the open door. "Mr. Porter. You asked to see me."

Wade wondered where the man-boy disappeared to and if he planned to come back for his food. "Yes, I have some things you need to see." He held up his folder.

"Been doing your own investigation?"

"Occupational habit." He gave her the most sincere grin in his arsenal.

She paused for a moment. Her posture relaxed, and she opened the door farther. "Come on back."

"Thank you." Wade followed her to her desk and took the seat across from her.

"The floor is yours, Mr. Porter."

"Wade. Please."

She nodded.

"You already know about Skylar and Kyle's extra curricular activities together. But, she was involved with someone before Kyle." He slid the emails in front of her and waited as she flipped through.

She met his gaze. "I don't see how this is important? So, she was in to kinky stuff with some other guy. So what?" She drummed her fingers on the desk.

Wade extracted the paper Stan emailed him with the IP owner's address. He slid it across the desk.

Her eyes flitted back-and-forth. The color drained from her face as she read. Then she sat speechless. She gave him a deliberate look and scrutinized Wade. "Is this for real?"

"Put one of my best guys on it. You can double-check all the information yourself, but right now, there isn't time." Urgency pulsed into every nerve ending, making it hard to sit still. He had questioned the wisdom in coming to Detective Alverez with this, but doing what needed to be done alone would be foolish. For this situation to come to an end it had to be done by the book. "There's more."

She curved down her lips. "Let me have it."

"I got a voicemail from Mallory that she'd received a text from Kyle asking her to meet him at the cabin. I don't think she meant her new place. Kyle wouldn't have known about that." Wade hesitated. "Is there any chance Kyle wasn't the person in the trunk of his car?" A strange thing to hope for, yet that's what Wade did.

"No. Dentals have confirmed the victim as Kyle Malloney."

"I haven't been able to contact Mallory since that message." He leaned forward resting his forearms on his knees and opened and closed his fists.

They both stared at each other, processing the meaning of this information. Mallory got herself in a heap of trouble.

Detective Alvarez stood, picking up her keys from her desk. "I'll drive."

Relief washed over him. She believed him. He fell into step beside her and she matched his long stride as they vanished out the back of the station.

****

Where in the world? Mallory's eyelids stuck together like glue, but after a struggle, they fluttered open. A breeze wafted across her face. Her head throbbed and she could feel the sticky residue of blood. She reached for her face, a sharp pain ripped through her shoulders. She fought through the fog in her mind. Unable to understand why her arms weren't working, she yanked again, and a small cry escaped her throat.

Mallory glanced around, and everything flooded back. "Ralph," she said. She sat on the ground, her hands bound behind her and around a tree. She wiggled her fingers and touched the cool metal of the cuffs. Her raw fingertips burned, and she could smell bleach. *How will I get out of this?* She tugged against the cuffs, but the struggle was pointless. *Why did I come out here? When will I ever learn?* Ralph's correct about one thing, trouble seems to find me.

The footsteps got her attention before Ralph strolled into her line of vision. She locked gazes with him. The urge to scratch out his eyes surprised her. She'd always been a passive person. Hey, let's talk about what's upsetting you, I'm sure we can work out something. Screw that philosophy. Pain, that's her new plan.

"Look who woke up." Ralph squatted in front of her. "Nasty bump you took on your head." He reached for her.

But she jerked her head away from his touch. "Don't touch me." Her eyes burned.

"A fitting end to all this. Don't you think?"

She glared. "Let me go."

Ralph shook his head. "Can't do it. This is too perfect how all this worked out."

A twitch in her stomach sent off a domino effect throughout her body. "How what worked out?" Her voice vibrated. She struggled to swallow the paralyzing fear.

"That you found out about your cheating fiancé having a love child with your maid of honor and the news sent you off the deep end. Finally, your conscience got the better of you, and you decided you had no other choice but to repent and bring your own life to an ever-so-tragic end."

Ralph's sardonic laugh pierced into her gut. Mallory's lips trembled, and she fought for courage. "Pretty sure I'm not committing suicide. How will you explain that away?"

He withdrew a bottle from his pocket. "This is a combination of acetaminophen, narcotic pain killers, benzodiazepines, and sleeping pills. You'll chase that with some vodka, and the result will be like throwing a Molotov Cocktail in your body."

"I'm not taking that."

"I'm sorry. Did you think I was giving you a choice?"

Dread clawed at her spine. "How will you explain the wound on my head? Did you think about that? A struggle will be evident." His sneer unnerved her even more.

He picked up the rock he had used and tossed it in the air with his gloved hand. "This here rock? Well, when you passed out from the drugs, you took a tumble sideways and your head landed on this." He placed the rock beside her.

Blood pounding in her ears, she stared at the scratches on his arm.

"Oh, I know what you're thinking. My DNA is under your nails." He took a small brush from a duffle bag and sniffed the air. "Yep, that's bleach you smell. Fingers a bit sore, are they?" He shrugged. "But, they're clean as a whistle."

I won't cry. I won't cry. A tear slid down her cheek despite her protest. She struggled against the cuffs. "I'm handcuffed. How will people think I did this to myself?"

"Once you're unconscious. I'll take back my cuffs and lay you over on the rock. Brilliant. Isn't it?"

"Not really. Your plan stinks, and you'll make a mistake and get caught."

"I don't think so. Worked out well for me so far."

Keep him talking. "How did you know Skylar would be at the club? Or me, for that matter?"

He rocked back on his heels, still squatting. "Guess it doesn't matter now anyway." He spread his hands wide. "Genius, actually. The idea occurred to me after I ran into you at the Chinese restaurant. You said you were going to Grayson's Club that night, and a plan formed." Ralph stood. "I contacted Sky, who for once wasn't with your fiancé in Chicago, and convinced her I accepted her decision and needed to return her apartment key." He paced as he wrung his hands. "She'd already asked me multiple times for it back, and eagerly agreed to meet me. I told her I was doing surveillance on the place next to the club and that as soon as I could slip away for a minute, I'd give her a call." He stopped in front of Mallory.

The massive pressure in her chest made it difficult to breathe. "How did you know when I would be there?"

"Everyone knows Grayson's gets hopping between eight and eleven. Not a problem for Sky...she loved to dance. I just had to wait for you to arrive. Then I gave it some time for you both to have some drinks and told her to meet me in the alley."

His menacing laughter bordered on hysteria.

"She didn't even know what hit her, and you should've seen her face when I mentioned I knew about the baby."

Mallory's throat tightened. "I walked out into the alley on my own accord. I don't understand." She squeezed her eyes closed, failing to beat back the images of Skylar.

"That was dumb luck. I couldn't have planned something any more sublime. Can't you see? Fate stepped in. I only needed you to be there and ensure you were alone at some point. Then direct suspicion your way." He knelt down and leaned in.

She convulsed as his breath impacted her skin. "You were watching me." His sneer confirmed her fears.

"Enough of this. The rest is history, and we have new business to attend to."

"Why me? Skylar cheated on you. Kyle cheated on me. Why am I being punished?"

"You know why." Ralph towered above her. "You brought them together. Skylar was happy with me until you introduced her to your fiancé. You caused all of this. You ruined my life." He paused, his hands on his hips. "You moving back here gave me a foolproof plan. The woman scorned."

Mallory shook her head. "It won't work. They'll find out you were involved with Skylar at some point."

"Don't think so. Once they find you, at the scene of the crime, with your note lying under you no questions will be asked. Case closed. Oh, did I forget to mention your suicide note?" He removed a typed letter sealed in a baggy from the duffle and placed it on the ground in front of her. "Here, enjoy some light reading while I get everything ready to go."

She wanted rip the handlebar mustache off his face. Mallory didn't want to give him the satisfaction of reading it, but curiosity overruled.

"By now you know the accusations made against me are true. I never intended to hurt anyone, but when I confronted Skylar about cheating with Kyle I learned about her baby. Hers and Kyle's baby. Rage filled me, and I lost all rational thought. I acted on impulse and out of grief and anger. I'm sorry for all those I've hurt. Mom and Dad, please know I love you and you raised me right. This mistake was mine alone, and I'm paying for it in the only way I know how. To all my friends, thank you for believing in me and standing by me no matter what. I didn't deserve your loyalty and support, but you gave it anyway. Please don't grieve for me. I can no longer live with my guilt over my actions. Just know I am finally at peace. I love you all. Mallory"

A violent stomach contraction sent bile up her esophagus. The survival part of her brain wouldn't allow her to believe this was happening. But, watching Ralph extract the vodka from his bag made it real. Her breathing turned shallow, fast, and ragged. A hum resonated in her ears, and the sensation of floating outside her body took over. This wasn't happening. She closed her eyes. *Please let me wake up.*

A hand clamped down on her nose, and her eyes flew open. She stared at Ralph in horror.

"Open up."

His shrill laugh rang in her ears. She jerked her head side-to-side and fought with every ounce of strength she had. She sucked her lips inward.

He held a rubber bite block over her mouth.

Her lungs seized and burned like fire. She kicked out.

Ralph dropped his knee down across her upper thighs, pinning her in.

Instinct took over, and her mouth opened for air.

He shoved the rubber wedge between her upper and lower teeth, and then released her nose. He lifted her chin with one hand and held the bottle of pills over her mouth.

Mallory thrashed her head, but his grip was strong. Pills filled her mouth, slipping into the back of her throat. She gagged and tried to force out the pills with her tongue.

"Don't make this harder than it has to be." Ralph tossed the pill bottle and picked up the open bottle of vodka.

A rush of liquid surged into her throat, burning, and forced her to swallow some pills. Animalistic sounds filled the air, and Mallory realized they came from her. Vodka ran down her face and onto her clothes. She choked, spewing liquid from her mouth.

Ralph dropped the bottle and yanked the wedge from between her teeth. His palm slammed into her lower jaw, and her teeth crashed together, forcing closed her mouth.

Mallory shook her head no. Pleading with her eyes as he pinched her nose once again. She needed to swallow. Needed air. *Please. Please help me.* Tears spilled from the corner of her eyes. Still flailing her body in its limited capacity. *Oh, God.* The biting liquid seeped down her throat. The pills tasted bitter in her mouth as they dissolved. White foam squished out between the tight line of her lips. She was going to die.

"Let her go!"

The voice must have startled Ralph as much as it did Mallory, because he jumped, and his grip slipped.

Part of the liquid flew out of her mouth and onto Ralph's hand and her shirt.

He shoved her mouth closed again. Ralph glanced over his shoulder at Wade, and Detective Alvarez, whose weapon was aimed at the side of his head.

"I'm not asking again." Detective Alvarez's command, steady and even.

Mallory flashed a wild-eyed gaze around. Panic still pulsed through her. How much had she ingested…was ingesting.

Ralph scanned his gaze between Detective Alvarez and Mallory. He made an abrupt roll to his right and grabbed his side arm in one fluid motion.

Numbness rushed through Mallory, maybe a self-preservation reflex when you know harm is coming.

Instead, Ralph aimed at Detective Alvarez, who fired a shot before he could. His body lurched backward. The momentum propelled him to the ground.

Detective Alvarez advanced, weapon zeroed in on Ralph.

Wade rushed to Mallory.

She spit the remnants onto the ground, her throat burned, and savage coughs racked her body until her back ached. Tears of relief streamed down her cheeks. Mallory's chest rose and fell, fast and shallow.

"She's cuffed," Wade yelled to Detective Alvarez.

Ralph lay on his stomach as she locked the final cuff around his wrist. Detective Alvarez tossed her keys to Wade.

He released one cuff.

The pain of forcing her arms forward made her whimper. She crawled away, dragging the still-attached cuffs and shoved two fingers down her throat. She heaved until nothing was left, and her diaphragm ached.

Wade ran to the car and grabbed a bottle of water. Returning, he handed it to Mallory.

With a few sips, she rinsed out her mouth, pouring the remainder on her face. The liquid rushing across her head wound stung, which reassured her because pain meant she was alive.

He cupped her cheek, and she leaned into his hand. "You okay?" He tilted her head to get a better look at her injury. "There's so much blood." Wade's hand trembled against her skin.

"I've never been so glad to see anyone in my life." Her voice rasped from the rawness her throat sustained after all her screaming, not to mention the vodka, drugs, and bile. Mallory's body was weak with relief, and the realization she would be all right.

Wade undid the other handcuff.

Mallory rubbed her wrists and absently brushed at the crusty chunks of dark crimson hair.

"It's clotted off." He lowered her hand. "Don't rub

it."

She nodded.

"Let's get you off the ground." Wade helped her to her feet.

She tumbled into him.

Lips pressed tight, he glanced down. "You have other injuries?"

She shook her head, nodded, and then shrugged.

He raised his eyebrows.

"Sprained ankle, I think, but it happened before." She glanced at Alvarez putting Ralph into her squad car. Apparently, not taking any chances until the paramedics arrived. The bullet struck him in the shoulder. Unfortunately, he would live. "I had on a pair of cute wedges for our date. No idea where they are now, but they're not great for a stroll in the woods." She faced him. "I'm sorry about our date."

He slipped his arm under her armpits, and drew her close, taking on most of her weight. "Life is never boring with you."

"I could do with a little boring."

"Yeah. Me, too."

The next couple of hours were filled with statements, police coming and going, paramedics, and the hospital. The paramedics applied a pressure bandage to her head, and she promised to go straight to the hospital. Since her vitals were normal they agreed not to call a second ambulance, but she still needed a thorough examination, blood work, and something about the possibility of activated charcoal…yuck. The wound didn't match the amount of blood she wore, but they told her head injuries bleed profusely. She would need a few stiches, but being in her hairline the scar would be easy to hide.

Instead, they loaded Ralph and police escorted him to the hospital.

Wade got into her subcompact vehicle and knocked his knees on her steering wheel. "What is it you ladies have against normal size cars?"

Mallory rolled her head toward him, too tired for any more substantial movement. "My car is normal. You're just over-sized."

He laughed, took her hand, and gave a squeeze. "Don't ever do that again."

The depth of caring in his eyes made her choke up. She sniffed and crushed her fingertips to her eyes. The scent of bleach still lingered.

"Don't cry." He gathered her alongside him and stroked her cheek with the back of his hand. He slid it behind her neck, tugged her closer, and their lips met.

His lips were like satin, and warmth reverberated through her frigid core.

He delicately placed his forehead against hers and brushed his thumb over her bottom lip. "I'm not letting you out of my sight."

Even though mentally and physically exhausted, at this moment she also felt safe and peaceful. "Wade Porter, I'm so glad I met you."

Epilogue

Music resonated through the outdoor speakers. The backyard reverberated with laughter and small talk. Mallory observed from the porch as Zehn leapt off the end of the dock, dousing Matt with water. She couldn't hear what he said as he reeled in his empty fishing line, but believed by his body language, he'd failed to enrich the English language.

Her fingers brushed the scar in her hairline. A couple weeks had passed since her ordeal and her wounds, both emotional and physical were healing. The yellowish discolorations still an outward reminder.

Ralph had officially been charged with both murders and awaited trial. Last time she spoke to Detective Alvarez, she had a sparkle to her eyes. Although she never said a cross word about him, it appeared Ralph's absence didn't break her heart.

Everyone joined in and made Mallory's official move a fairly painless event. After they finished unloading, Hazel, Wade, and Matt stayed and got cleaned up there so they could help Mallory set up for the barbeque. Poppy, on the other hand, sustained a traumatic nail chip and ran off to her manicurist to have her nails repaired.

Ella parked her car, returning after picking up her date. Poppy waylaid her before she closed her door. She snagged the hand Poppy thrust in her face and studied the engagement ring now highlighted by the perfect manicure. The light refracted off the diamond as Ella tilted Poppy's hand side-to-side, all while making the appropriate oohing and aahing noises.

Ella's date abandoned the show-and-tell moment and approached Mallory, she smiled as he joined her on the porch. She buried her nose in the beautiful bouquet he handed her. "Dr. Rodriguez, these are amazing. Thank you so much."

"Thank you for including me, and please call me Marcus." He leaned on the rail next to her and reached up to touch her forehead.

Mallory jerked back. "Keep those thumbs where I can see them, buddy, and we'll get along just fine."

A belly laugh erupted. "The hospital hasn't been the same without your comic relief, but I'm glad to see you're staying away."

"Not a place I want to hang out at...food's terrible."

"Your head is healing well." He lifted his hand again but lowered it when she pointed her finger. "Occupational hazard, I'm afraid."

"Well, you're not working today, so grab a drink and enjoy."

"How's the ankle doing?"

Mallory ended up having a tear in the peroneal tendon and sported a short leg walking boot. "Got a couple more weeks before I get checked again." She lifted her boot off the ground. "But it's feeling much better and gives me a reason to stay out of heels."

Ella tucked in under Marcus's arm and glanced up with an adoring gaze. "I'm so glad you got blown up Mallory." She winked.

"It's my sworn duty to ensure my friends are happy...at any cost." They all chuckled, and Ella and Marcus wandered off to grab a beverage.

Flames surged skyward when Jim Larsen flipped a burger on the grill. Mallory cringed, still somewhat sensitive to fire, but relaxed as he sprayed the flames with a water bottle. A hand snaked around her waist. She tensed and immediately calmed, inhaling the delicious citrus and sandalwood scent that was all Wade.

"Hope he doesn't burn down your house." He nipped her neck.

"I was thinking the same thing."

Jim sprayed at the dancing flames again, and they retreated like a lion being tamed.

Mallory turned and melted into Wade's dark-eyed gaze. The level of contentment she experienced when he drew near was unlike anything she'd ever known. She glanced at the wine glass in his hand and her heart surged. "Is that—"

"Cabernet Sauvignon." He finished and held out the glass to Mallory.

Pleasure rushed through her, and she bounced on one foot, clapped, and grabbed for it. She swirled the deep purple liquid and inhaled the scent of black currants along with bell pepper and underlying earthiness. She took a sip and let the rich liquid rest in her mouth for a moment. "Mmm." Mallory fluttered her eyes closed.

"You have any idea why people do that?"

"Hmm?" She opened her eyes. "Oh. Heavens no. I'm not a wine connoisseur, but I've seen it done on television. Something that tastes this good deserves the appropriate treatment, even if I have no clue why." She took another sip. "Does this mean this is considered our first date?" She tucked her chin and fluttered her eyelashes. Mallory clutched her glass.

"Dinner, drinks, great company, loads of fun, an amazing day, and a beautiful woman." The back of his fingers stroked her cheek. "Perfect first date if you ask me." He eyed her flowers. "Unless I'm too late."

"They're beautiful, aren't they?"

The right side of her mouth quirked up, and she leaned in to breathe in their scent again.

Wade cocked a single brow.

"Jealous?" She held the wine with one hand and her flowers in the other.

"Maybe…and maybe I should take back my wine."

"Don't you dare." She turned away her shoulder. "I think Marcus was making amends for poking me repeatedly in the eye when I was his patient." She placed the bouquet on the porch railing.

"Good thing. I didn't want to have to humiliate him during the volleyball game." They both redirected their gaze to where the game was taking form.

"You remembering about the wine means more than you know." At no time did Kyle do special things. He never remembered her birthday, no clue on what her favorite color was, or even favorite food. His self-absorbed nature became an accepted part of their relationship. Having someone do something just to see her smile surprised and warmed her heart. She inched up on her toes and met an abrupt halt. She scowled at her unforgiving boot.

"Let me help me you with that."

Mallory tilted her head and flashed him her best

"please kiss me" smile.

Wade leaned down and brushed his lips across hers. "You're welcome."

"I never knew you could read minds."

"Only yours." He shrugged. "And I didn't care if I misread as long as I got to steal a kiss."

"For you they're free anytime and anyplace. No stealing necessary."

He stepped behind her and encircled her in his arms. They both watched Matt, who Zehn convinced to give up on fishing, serve the first ball. "You should go play. They seem to be having a great time."

"I'd rather hang with you."

"Don't let my foot keep you from stripping off your shirt and joining in."

"I feel so violated."

Mallory shrugged. "No, seriously, go play. I can keep Poppy and her manicure company."

Wade squeezed her and kissed her cheek. "Save me a seat when the food's ready."

"You bet." She liked the way his body moved as he jogged off and joined the game.

Mallory carried her flowers inside to where her mom replenished the cheese and cracker tray. "Mom, go on and enjoy yourself. I can get that." She stretched up, opened the cabinet above the fridge, and removed a vase.

"I am enjoying myself. I'm your mother. I want to help." She glanced at Mallory's foot. "And I think you need to give that foot a rest."

Mallory filled the vase with water and put the flowers in. She shuffled them, trying to make them look nice. Out of her peripheral vision, she caught her mom watching. A smirk crossed her face as she yanked out a clump of baby's breath and wedged it awkwardly down in the middle of the arrangement. Her mom's sharp intake of breath had her struggling to control a chuckle. "I'll put these on the serving table."

"You take the food tray. I'll bring the flowers," Charlotte said in a rushed tone.

Mallory swallowed one more taste of her wine before setting it on the counter to carry out the platter. "I'll be back," she said to her delicious wine.

By the time her mom got outside, the flowers were arranged in a way that would make the head of the botanical gardens proud. Mallory couldn't hold her snicker when her mom placed them in the center of the table.

"I know you did that on purpose." Charlotte shifted a daffodil a millimeter to the right.

"And I knew you wouldn't be able to stand it."

Charlotte jutted out her chin. "Go help your father with the meat and that thing you're eating."

"It's a veggie burger, Mom," she said to her retreating backside.

Her mom gave a clipped wave. "I know where some exquisite-smelling wine is."

Grinning, Mallory shuffled after her. "You stay out of my wine."

"Catch me if you can." Charlotte jogged into the house.

"Mean. Just plain mean," Mallory said, coming up behind her dad.

"Who's mean?" Jim asked, flipping a burger.

"Your wife. That's who."

"Yep." He laughed. "Sounds like your mother.

Hand me that plate over there."

Mallory grabbed it and held the platter while he loaded the burgers and brats onto it. "Thanks for doing all this."

"My baby girl is back where she belongs. That calls for a celebration." Mallory gave him a one-arm squeeze as she precariously balanced the platter on one hand and stretched up to kiss his cheek.

Jim put the last brat on top of the tilted platter, and it rolled off plunging to the ground.

Zehn, the dog you would swear was deaf when you called him a hundred time to come for his bath, heard the sound of renegade food hitting the ground, and appeared out of nowhere.

"No, wait, baby. That's—"

Zehn snatched the brat and swallowed it whole.

"Hot." Mallory shook her head. "You've done this to my dog, you know." She shot a glance out of the corner of her eye toward her dad.

"He needed someone to teach him what real meat is. Drop a piece of tofu and he'll probably bury it."

Mallory laughed because he'd done that exact thing once before. Granted he buried it under her couch cushions, which she found petrified two months later. Maybe should've cleaned under there more frequently.

Charlotte brushed by with the potato salad, and Mallory fell in shuffled step behind her with the meat platter. "Put that game on pause and come and get it," Charlotte yelled. No need to tell anyone twice.

Marcus's serve slammed into the net. "Do over," he yelled. "After I fuel myself."

Everyone worked their way through the serving line, and they sat together at a large square wooden picnic table. Mallory glanced around the table at her family, old and new friends, and a man who'd come to mean the world to her. Words couldn't describe the pure joy of having all these people together. She had to stop reflecting before the happy tears she sensed forming poured down her cheeks.

Wade sat to her left, and he interlaced his fingers with hers and squeezed. Their heated gazes connected, and the air sizzled. One side of his mouth quirked up, and Mallory bit down on her lower lip, however the stupid grin couldn't be removed from her face.

Wade's gaze drifted to the hand he still held, and he brushed his thumb over the base of Mallory's ring finger.

Her heart lurched at his unspoken meaning, and they looked deep into the other's eyes, saying things no words could. He grazed her hand with his lips, and then clutched it to his heart. If someone could explode from happiness, then the people sitting at this table were in peril.

All the reasons she'd escaped this small town years before were lost now. Moving back had been the best decision she'd ever made. Her new life offered the chance of a promising future. Peace enveloped her, and she basked in a warm glow of contentment she'd never known.

Mallory glanced at each and every person eating and laughing. These people loved and supported her, no matter what. This knowledge sent inexplicable jubilance bursting into every crevice of her being. All these things were what made a place home, and she knew she'd come *and* was home, and there's no place she'd rather be.

A word about the author…

M.J. Wilson has made a living in an eclectic group of professions taking her from Washington to Georgia, finally settling on Lookout Mountain. The natural beauty there fuels her love of the outdoors and provides the perfect setting for creating stories.

When she is not writing, she can be found hiking with her dog or at the barn working with her other passion, a know-it-all Trakehner who determines how hard she works by how many peppermints she is bribed with.

Growing up as a closet writer, the act of achieving adulthood is what helped her decide to start sharing her stories with others.

She also sits on the board of a local non-profit dedicated to reducing the overpopulation of dogs and cats by offering spay/neuter assistance and education.

http://www.mjwilsonwrites.wix.com/mjwilson